CONTEMPORARY AMERICAN FICTION

BARKING MAN AND OTHER STORIES

Born and brought up in Nashville, Tennessee, Madison Smartt Bell has written five novels and one previous story collection, *Zero db*, published in 1987 to great critical acclaim. His most recent novel, *Soldier's Joy*, received the Lillian Smith Award. He lives in Baltimore with his wife, the poet Elizabeth Spires.

BARKING MAN
AND OTHER STORIES

MADISON
SMARTT
BELL

PENGUIN BOOKS

PENGUIN BOOKS
Published by the Penguin Group
Viking Penguin, a division of Penguin Books USA Inc.,
375 Hudson Street, New York, New York 10014, U.S.A.
Penguin Books Ltd, 27 Wrights Lane,
London W8 5TZ, England
Penguin Books Australia Ltd, Ringwood,
Victoria, Australia
Penguin Books Canada Ltd, 2801 John Street,
Markham, Ontario, Canada L3R 1B4
Penguin Books (N.Z.) Ltd, 182–190 Wairau Road,
Auckland 10, New Zealand

Penguin Books Ltd, Registered Offices:
Harmondsworth, Middlesex, England

First published in the United States of America by
Ticknor & Fields, 1990
Reprinted by special arrangement with
Ticknor & Fields/Houghton Mifflin Company
Published in Penguin Books 1991

1   3   5   7   9   10   8   6   4   2

The following stories in this collection have previously appeared elsewhere:
"Holding Together" and "Dragon's Seed," *Boulevard;* "Black and Tan" (for-
merly "Going to the Dogs"), *The Atlantic Monthly;* "Customs of the Country"
(revised for this volume), *Harper's Magazine, The Best American Short Stories 1989*
(Houghton Mifflin), and *New Stories from the South 1989* (Algonquin Books);
"Finding Natasha," *Antaeus* and *Louder Than Words* (Atlantic Monthly Press);
"Barking Man," *The Northwest Review;* "Witness," *Harper's Magazine;* "Mr.
Potatohead in Love," broadcast on National Public Radio (PEN Syndicated
Fiction Project).

LIBRARY OF CONGRESS CATALOGING IN PUBLICATION DATA
Bell, Madison Smartt.
Barking man and other stories/Madison Smartt Bell.
p.   cm. — (Contemporary American fiction)
ISBN 0 14 01.4903 1
I. Title.   II. Series.
[PS3552.E517B37   1991]
813'.54 — dc20   90–21294

Printed in the United States of America

For Beth,
body & soul

CONTENTS

I

II

I

/ / / / /

☷

HOLDING TOGETHER

☵

WE WERE NEVER meant to come so near the face of humanity. The feet, certainly. Ankles, perhaps. Knees, or even the waist, under certain circumstances: crossing a kitchen counter, for instance, with all due circumspection. But when that aspect, the whole human visage, is bent so directly upon us — well, that can never be a good sign.

The face is so enormous its features cannot be read. It appears, at first, as a mountain of flesh, blocking off the entire east wall of our new cell. Only upon close study does it surrender its details, and disjointedly even then. The tremendous pores: a field of craters whose monotony is at times interrupted by a varicolored, volcanic rising, one of the large number of pustules to which the "Adolescent Boy" is subject. Above all that, what seems the entrance to a cavern, but those stalactites, in fact, are only hairs in the great slimy nostril. Still higher, and yet more disconcerting, the bulbous, jellied trembling of the eye. An eye which seems to be barely sentient, reminding me more of those descriptions of Portuguese men-of-war preserved from the Legend of the Voyage than a window onto any sort of Soul. Yet just the same that eye responds, contracts and dilates with changes in the light, devours information and seems always to be turned on me.

A monumental blink, a stately, whalelike roll of the eye wallowing in its socket, and the gargantuan stew of features is withdrawn. It fades away across the room to merge with other human forms in a blurry, distant landscape almost beyond our focal range. I turn back to the contemplation of the stalks. Though of course they are *not* the proper yarrow stalks; I have had to gnaw them slowly out of the chips of wood that line our cell, all fifty of them, yes . . . And with no pen or ink or paper, I must hold the hexagrams in memory too, but then I have my skill for that.

> Thunder within the earth:
> The image of *The Turning Point*.
> Thus the kings of antiquity closed the passes
> At the time of solstice.
> Merchants and strangers did not go about.
> And the ruler
> Did not travel through the provinces.

The Turning Point: I review the tradition, the commentaries. To be sure, some movement will begin, but whether for good or ill is indistinct as yet. I refer to the sixth, the moving line:

> Six at the top means:
> Missing the return. Misfortune.
> Misfortune within and without.

This augury chills me through and through, but I strive to give no outward sign. That in the light and under observation I remain on all fours helps to mask my inward feelings. It would not do to discourage Li or Wu, now when morale is so important to maintain, at this *turning point*. Besides, as I remind myself, *Misfortune* in this case must be conceived as relative. The trouble coming from without, in fact, is summoned by some disorder within. With inner change and regulation the foretold catastrophe may be averted.

The Turning Point . . . Till now we had all three of us been inclined to think it a turn for the better. At the slave market it had seemed for some months that whatever came would more likely be a turn for the worse—indeed, probably the last turn of all. For some months there had been only one purchaser coming to the big common cell into which we'd been tumbled willy-nilly amongst some thirty others. I understood, from overhearing the auctioneers' conversation, that hamsters, or as often gerbils, are nowadays preferred by the clientele. What then could explain the repeated visits of this single customer, a white-haired man with crumpled mouth distended over his false teeth, who came so regularly every week or so? What use could he have had for such a steady trickle of white mice?

Of course, it was not long before we knew. Though the others, uncivilized Occidental mice, resembling us only in their color, had no idea and never would. No sooner had I noticed that he always chose the fattest than I warned Li and Wu that we must all begin to refuse our food. The uncouth Western mice gladly gobbled all we left, so there was no suspicion. And certainly no possibility of explaining it to them. They are completely out of reach. I'm sure they could never read or write, even given the materials. They speak a clumsy, squeaking argot, barely comprehensible to us, scarcely verging upon abstract ideas, and they have proved ineducable. They have no history, no trove of legend, no systematic memory. They are useful only as a camouflage, a screen. And they screened us well, as they grew plump, and week by week their numbers were depleted. One by one they were netted out, slipped into a cardboard carrier and borne away in that man's wrinkled, slightly quavering hand. At the end of the journey each would surely meet the stabbing claws and rending beak of a hawk or owl, or the cold tightening coils of a snake. *Horrible. Horrible.* And none of them suspected . . .

Yes, we have every reason to consider ourselves fortunate now. Our new cell suggests we are meant to be kept for some little time, at least. A bedding of fresh wood chips (from which I fashioned that new set of sticks to read the oracle). The steel elbow of the water tank, dipping through the bars, and below it a dish of supercharged food tablets, enough for several days, or longer considering that drastic diminution of our appetites. And more than that, a sort of Ferris wheel, on which Li is now vigorously running, though in his half-starved state he can scarcely need the exercise. Perhaps it's a distraction, something for the nerves . . .

I think we're pets. Someone about to be fed to a snake need not be offered such a diversion. Yes, I believe we are safe, at least for the nonce. Wu is crouching, staring at the food dish—unlike Li he has no talent for taking his mind off hunger, though, on the credit side, he is also less light-minded. In any case, there is no longer any need for such severe restraint.

"Eat," I whisper to him. "Go on, indulge yourself a little. I'm sure it's all right now."

I see from the twitch and turn of his pinkish ears that Li has also heard, but he keeps on running on the wheel, as if indifferent to the chance of food, keeping up a perpetual metallic squeak I'm sure I'll come to find annoying in time. Wu waits a moment more, not to seem too eager, and then moves forward to the tray, delicately lifts a chalky cylinder of food and starts to chew the edge of it. When he is halfway finished the wheel stops spinning and Li springs down beside him at the tray. I wait just a little longer, savoring my self-control, before I go to join them.

The unaccustomed plenitude of food has made us all extremely thirsty, and we all may have sucked too much of that rather bitter-tasting water from the steel lip issuing from the tank. I wonder if that bloated feeling might be what is keeping me awake long after the humans have switched off their lights and gone off to their beds. For a time I lie wide-eyed, reproaching myself for my intemperance, but that is a useless enterprise which I abandon, turning instead to a rehearsal of the Voyage, something which almost never fails to soothe me.

Precision in each image is the key to this exercise, so I compel myself really to look at all details, to picture even the different patterns of the stiff kimonos of those first Voyager Mice who walked boldly down to the harbor one ancient night and marched in single file up a mooring rope into the bilges of some great barbarian ship. Next, I re-create their consternation at the first wild rollings of the boat on the open sea, and how the Samurai, though sick themselves, restored order among those who panicked, while the Scriveners (to which class I belong) essayed to calm the fearful with the oracle, or with contemplative passages from other, actual books, which had not then been lost.

Next, and always most seductive to my own imagination, are the wonders of the sea, challenging for me to see vividly in the mind's eye, as I have never seen them in fact, and know these marvels only from our centuries of tradition. Through the eyes of some forefather mouse, rocking high in the rigging, I imagine the spectacle of that infinite plain of water full of flying fish, dolphin, great jellyfish, whales, kraken, mermaids, sea serpents — *I can't breathe, I can't breathe* — *Those icy loops of sinuous muscle have smashed all the air out of me, and try as I will I cannot drag the least puff back. Worse, I feel my bones begin to break, to pulverize, my very flesh being mashed to pulp. I always understood you died before that happened, that you suffocated first and never lived to witness yourself being squeezed into a skin bag full of soup that the snake will sip almost as a drink . . .*

When I tear myself out of that nightmare, at first I can't say where I am. I can only tell I'm no longer at the market, and for a single heart-stopping moment I wonder if the dream may have come true, for I once saw it, I once saw just such a horror, when a corn snake escaped and made its greedy way into the common cell next to ours . . . But no, the tinny squeak of that turning wheel brings me back to where I really am, tumbled among the chips I've scattered in my panic, my fur matted with sweat from the terrors of that dream.

It's Li, still running on that futile wheel, I can see his profile against a night light in the kitchen. Whatever is he doing that for? It must be after midnight, surely, and I should advise him to stop, as who knows what the morrow may bring? But I don't do it. Let him continue, if he finds it so amusing. In a way I'm almost grateful, for it may have been the racket of the wheel itself that helped to break my dream.

I comb my fur, and the panic drains away from me, but sleep will not return. From a rustle in the chips nearby I know that Wu is restless too, but I do not speak to him. It comes to me that I forgot to read the second hexagram from the day's oracle, the one to which that moving line of the first was leading:

$$\equiv\!\equiv$$

Well, the truth is, I have never seen the actual Book of Changes, nor yet did any of my preceptors that I ever knew. In slavery we are not permitted books, nor can we well contrive to make them or conceal them. But it's no matter. The hexagrams are measured in my mind in sixteen squares within one another, through which I turn as I'd imagine turning pages. The bars of the one I'm seeking seem to glow before my eyes the while. On the third wall of the seventh square, I find it and its text:

> *The Corners of the Mouth.*
> Perseverance brings good fortune.
> Pay heed to the providing of nourishment
> And to what a mouse seeks
> To fill his mouth with.

I must say, that hardly seems relevant to our position at the moment. I review the commentaries, but find none es-

pecially helpful. Oh, for the real Book now . . . But maybe
it's only that incessant squeaking that makes my thought
unclear. I hiss at Li to stop at once, but he affects not to hear
me. Out past the wheel, past the cell bars, the whole house
roars with the sounds of its barbarously inexplicable machin-
ery, but after a careful study of all I can hear, I'm certain that
no actual human beings are stirring. It's safe enough, then,
to sit up in full lotus position, placing my palms together, a
movement which I hope will clear my head. But no reasonable
interpretation of that hexagram will come, and the squeaking
of that wheel is as distracting. Ah well, perhaps it is only
insomnia.

Peace. The small departs.
The great approaches.
Good fortune. Success.

Auspicious sign. Why is it, though, that none of us can
sleep? A pretty irony: there is no peace in us, it would seem.
We have scarcely slept an hour amongst the three of us all
week. Anxiety? The stress of change? I am so stupid with
exhaustion that I can scarcely manage this whole business of
the sticks; I miscount in threes instead of fours, or they fall
from the spaces between my claws where I must balance
them. All exacerbated by that "Boy," the monstrous oaf,
who keeps pushing his great cliff of a face against our cell.
He carries a notebook with him now, in which he makes
some blotted smudgy marks with his log of a pen, to what
purpose I cannot imagine. We had more privacy at the market.

I've taken to reading the oracle at night, safe from this
interruption. Now, in the half dark, I can sit up in full lotus
position, demonstrating the proper respect for the whole en-

terprise. The light leaking in from the kitchen suffices me. Of course, I'm always a little distracted by the maddening grate of that wheel, for Li runs on it all through the night now, stopping only for food or water two or three times a day. Wu has dug himself into a cave of chips, in the midst of which I can hear him miserably thrashing. His simple mind has small defense against this sort of suffering. I worry for his and all our mental health, and as I cannot sleep I may as well improve the hours.

Six in the fifth place calls up lines involving the imperial princesses, of which I can make no sense whatever. Though my memory is still perfect (I could not even bear the thought of losing that) this failure of interpretation may be the fault of my disordered mind. But:

Six at the top means:
The wall falls back into the moat.
Use no army now.
Make your commands known within your own town.
Perseverance brings misfortune.

Oh yes. That's rather more pertinent. *The wall falls back into the moat.* Truly, our condition is controlled by fate alone. There is no use in struggling; all we may do is submit. That's a reading that might bring peace of sorts, albeit rather dreary sorts. I unfold my legs and stretch out, composing myself not for sleep (alas) but for that thoughtless pale hiatus which is the closest to it I've attained these last few days. Soon that squeaking bumping wheel will drive me mad. My arms and legs are all unpleasantly atingle, and there's a sensation in the bottom of my stomach which feels very much like sudden fear, though it has been there at the same constant level for as long as seventy-two hours. And now, out of that pulsing white nothing my mind seems to be turning into, comes the answer:

Pay heed to the providing of nourishment . . .

We're being drugged, it's obvious. How could I ever have

failed—I picture again the "Boy's" pen point scoring his coarse papers with deep blue grooves. Why, we're not pets at all. We're . . . *experimental*. The very word makes that cold spot in my belly clench still tighter. I've been misled, since we arrived, by the fact that this place seems to conform more to my image of "House" than of "Laboratory." After all, it is inhabited by a "Family," is it not? Well, unpleasant as it is to contemplate, it might be better to know. I clutch my oracle stalks into the soft fur of my belly, as comfort of a kind. Perhaps there still is a way for us to regain some degree of control.

After three more wretched days and nights I've made a discovery. The poison isn't in the food. It's in the water. Which brings our case very near to being hopeless. I managed to get Wu and Li to join me in a day-long experimental fast. But when that had no effect, they both of them refused to do without water. Not outright, but simply as if the advice I gave them did not penetrate. We're all more than a little blurry now, of course. Still, they did not drink one whit less of the water than before.

That's deliberate insubordination, certainly, yet I can't absolutely blame either one of them. This sleeplessness has made us all a little wild. Has it been ten days? I can't remember. And I am here to testify that going entirely without water is very, very difficult. I managed it, at first, for twenty-four hours, enough to prove my point, for last night my nervous system calmed enough for me to steal a few snatches of sleep, though my swollen, cracking tongue kept me almost as wakeful as before. Another day of total abstinence would be death, so today I let myself drink a little. A very little, yet already I can feel that chemical agitation running through me. It may be possible to strike some sort of balance. Maybe, but the hope is faint. Soon we must all go mad.

Wu, who keeps up his seismic trembling under the chips so constantly I've almost ceased to notice it, bursts out of the bedding so suddenly now I can hardly focus my eyes on him. Dazedly I stare as he charges at the turning wheel where Li goes on mindlessly rushing, scrambling on and on without progress. Wu rips at the underside of the wheel with his claws, and I see that he must be trying to stop it, stop it at whatever price. Nor do I blame him, for the endless motion, along with its equally endless squealing, has begun to make me almost physically nauseous too. Li keeps on running as if desperate for an important destination, the narrow wedge of his head stretched out flat before him like a racer pressing toward his goal. And for whatever reason, Wu seems entirely unable to stop the wheel. He clings to it and falls, rises to get a fresh grip, is even carried up a little way on the backspin — and falls once more.

Strange, for Wu is the most powerful of the three of us, without question. *Fool*, I think, *you have only to jump up there with him, knock him out of there, that's the way to manage it*. But what can have come over me, to promote strife among my companions? Even in a thought? Wu has given up, collapsed in the chips below that fretfully spinning wheel, his back disconsolately humped up. Oh, for some word that might cheer him, but I have none. He makes a quarter turn and I just see a red flash in his eyes before with another spring he is on *me*. Tumbling me over backward and, inexplicably, without the least provocation, sinking his teeth into the thickest meat at the bare base of *my tail*.

An involuntary squeak breaks out of me, surprise and pain in equal mixture, and without thinking I whip around and rake at Wu's broad face with both my forepaws. A mistake, for Wu outweighs me at least an ounce, and moreover he is of the Samurai class and so has martial training, whereas I have none. I'm winded by a rear paw buried in my belly, stunned by a forepaw hammered behind my ear, flung bodily up and out in a giddy arc that stops with a slam into the bars. Even unarmed, Wu is formidable. As I slide down I feel the hot needles of his teeth pierce into my tail again, a little closer to the tip this time. *God! God! Buddha! How it hurts me!* Tears flood my eyes, and I grip the bars with my forepaws, for I dare not venture any further resistance.

Perhaps I can reason with him somehow? But this is all so senseless! It's insanity, of course, I knew it would come, though I never suspected it would take such a form. Cautiously I peer back over my left shoulder. Wu's eyes, hot rabid red, rise to meet mine for an instant, and he gives my tail an agonizing shake, as if to emphasize some point. He doesn't want me to look at him? All right, I won't. As I turn back, fixing my trembling muzzle between two bars to hold it firm and keep from crying, Wu shifts his bite again. I tremble to the core, for this time I think I felt one tooth cut through to bone.

I must set my mind to something else, some distraction, anything. But I can summon no bright work of images to dance for me now; the pain drives everything before it. The interlocking squares, where the Changes are recorded, twirl before my eyes as crazily as Li's wheel, as I struggle to fix on one of them, it hardly matters which. What was it that ironic draw of *Peace* was turning into? Wu bites through on a new and narrower section of my tail, and the fresh burst of pain seems to underline it:

$$\equiv$$

The wind drives across heaven:
The image of *The Taming Power of the Small.*
Thus the superior mouse
Refines the outward aspect of his nature.

Ohyesohyesohyes . . . That would seem to be my only choice for the moment. Clearly there is not the least thing I can do to change this circumstance. But oh, let me bear it with patience, with fortitude. I will let nothing forth from me but the gentlest acceptance, check Wu only with my meekness. Such is *The Taming Power of the Small*. And already, far out beyond the razor edges of this pain, I can envision the gently lapping borders of a great placid sea of calm.

≡

It's been five days, or is it six, since last I was able to consult the oracle. The torment so steadily administered by Wu has kept my attention fully occupied. So painfully that at times I've been tempted to wonder what offense I could possibly have committed to bring such a punishment down on me. Though that question is itself inspired by decadent, almost barbaric thinking.

Surely, it must be karma.

But for most of last night, and all of today, Wu has left me in relative peace. *Peace*, if you like to call it that. He's tunneled back into the chips again, and now rarely emerges even to eat or drink. While Li still rattles and scrapes interminably along the infinite curve of his wheel. How he keeps it up I can't conceive . . . As for me, I have remained wedged here in this corner of the cell for the most part, reluctant to move because movement hurts my poor tail terribly. My tail, so recently a fine and flexible whip of flesh, is swollen to several times its normal size, and covered from base to tip with red-ringed puncture wounds, some still bleeding a little, most already beginning to fester. These last few hours the pain has dimmed to a dull ache—small comfort, since all it means is that amputation will doubtless soon be necessary. I cannot even flex it, though I can't be sure if the relevant tendons have been completely severed, for any attempt in that direction makes me half faint from pain. To drag it limply behind me as far as the food dish or water spout is excruciating enough.

In default of all else, I gather my sticks and laboriously calculate the Changes. Never mind that it's broad daylight.

Never mind that the "Boy" has come and that he's watching me, has opened his notebook and is boring furiously into it with his pen. He'll never comprehend the significance of my action anyway, so why should I trouble to conceal it?

> On the mountain, a tree:
> The image of *Development*.
> Thus the superior mouse abides in dignity and virtue
> In order to improve the mores.

Dignity and virtue, what droppings, what owl pellets, indeed. This superior mouse is abiding in agony and idiocy, like it or not. Of course, it is true that the mores around here could bear a little improvement. *Screek screek* goes that demented wheel, so that I can barely string a thought together, and for one delirious instant I'm overwhelmed by the thought of how delicious it would be to fling Li down from it and gnaw some intimate part of him clear to the bone. But I must calm myself—

> Six in the second place means:
> The wild goose gradually draws near the cliff . . .

Blah blah blah, six in the second place means nothing of much interest to me. On with it—

> Nine in the fifth place means:
> The wild goose draws gradually near the summit.
> For three years the woman has no child . . .

Incomprehension. Sterility. Isolation. All perfectly appropriate to our condition now. And the second hexagram?

≡≡
≡≡

Decay. I have no energy to examine the commentary on that; the one word says it all. And tumbles me, finally, into complete despair. *Decay.* Yes, decay.

Throughout my life, ever since I first uncurled from my

original bald, blind mouseling being and opened my eyes to the great world around me, I have had, it seems, only one truly serious fear. Put aside those dreams of owls and snakes, for death must come to all mice finally, in one form or another. No, what I fear far more deeply is chaos. A suitable *bête noire*, I suppose, for a mouse of my education, a Scrivener and expert in the Changes. Suppose that (as the barbarian mice who barely have a spoken language are sometimes heard to whisper) all our lore is only a meaningless hodgepodge of misunderstood gleanings and poachings from any number of other traditions. Suppose our Legend of the Voyage is nothing but a lie. What if we never had that former home or any of its appurtenances, no swords, kimonos, prayer wheels, not even any books? Then every geometric figure of my so carefully constructed memory would mean no more than an idiot's unintended scrawl.

During my years of study and apprenticeship, a picture was once described to me. Of course, I've never seen it. We've had no pictures now for centuries. (And if we never had them? Never mind.) Two mice dressed in the finest silk kimonos gathered with the broadest brocade sashes, impeccably groomed in every respect, of noble bearing and aristocratic mien, are kneeling opposite each other at a writing desk. They are busy with painting and calligraphy, playing long-handled brushes in smooth elegant swoops, seemingly so fluid, so effortless, but in fact most precisely controlled by subtle movements of the arm and wrist. The tidy scrolls of their finished work pile up on either side of them.

Above them, seen as if through a cutaway section of the wall, are two more mice, this pair on all fours, naked, their dark fur bristling like the pelt of bears, eyes glazed with an unquestioning stupidity. They too face each other, and they too have their occupation. And what they are doing is *eating books*.

As a student I learned and believed that this picture represented Past and Present—that's to say, our evolution. But it has just occurred to me that it could just as well portray our Present and our *Future*, thus: degeneration. Oh fearful thought. But do I find anything around me to disprove it? It's obvious that Wu's mind has crumbled, and Li's equally, though perhaps in a slightly less malign direction. Why, neither of them has spoken so much as an intelligible word for a week or more, nor have they given any evidence of understanding anything *I* might say. They are dumb now, brutal, they are animals. And soon enough, I'm sure, I'll follow them. If death does not release me first.

Three long scraping strokes of the pen distract me from these alternative despairs, and I glance up to see the last one tear across the bottom of a page—quite as if to underscore the finality of our predicament. The "Boy" lets the pen fall from his hand, crashing down heavily like a tree and rolling on the table. He knits his fingers together and lowers his long ski slope of a nose till it almost touches the bars over my head.

"Well, Mr. Mouse," I hear him say, almost as though he realized I understand his speech. "That's all I'm going to be needing from *you*."

It's a lucky thing I've never been prone to motion sickness, for the "Boy," whether in some infelicitous fit of playfulness or for some other reason, is swinging our cell in wild arcs by the handle as he walks, so that I have to cling to the bars to keep from bouncing from wall to wall. It's increasingly hard for me to believe that last remark of his portended any good for us. Wu must have found some kind of purchase on the floor. Even Li can no longer run, is fastened tight to the rungs of his wheel, swaying from side to side a little. I can't see where we're going, only a swoop of blue, a swoop of green, over and over and over. The legendary storms of the Voyage could not have been so much worse than this.

An eternity of this maniacal yawing and pitching and then, abruptly, stillness. Through my considerable dizziness I see the "Boy's" rubber heels receding, seeming to reel away, then gone. The landscape all around us tosses on a diminishing pendulous swing, then after a short age it comes completely to rest. I notice how the air is crowded with the song of birds; never before have I heard so many. As the motion stops, I begin to see something I've only heard described before: the yellowing stubble of an autumnal field. And not far past, a thicket of fruit trees of some kind. From among them I can hear the ripple of water—clean, uncontaminated water. I can taste the scent of barely overripe windfall fruit, tumbled into the maze of grass which we must soon be entering.

For the door to our cell is open.

Li hops down from the wheel and rocks back on his haunches, forepaws bunched before him, gazing at that amazing barless square. Wu, risen from the chips that still cling here and there to his unkempt fur, is similarly transfixed. Surely their hearts must be pounding as desperately as mine. But now is the moment when I must govern myself. And try to govern them as well.

"Li."

He hears me now; he's shuffling round my way.

"Wu."

And Wu's responding. He sits up, at attention. As they both turn toward me, I see that their eyes are clear and comprehending, though certainly very tired. Already the influence of the drug must be beginning to dissolve, we can all feel it now. One good sleep would restore us. I want to weep with gratitude, though I know I must be firm.

"I have taken the oracle for the day, as follows:

"The wind blows low over the mountain:
The image of *Decay*.
Thus the superior mouse stirs up the people
And strengthens their spirit."

A brief pause, for effect. Li's eyes are locked on mine. Wu's lower a little. Guiltily?

"I need hardly remind you that we have just passed through

what I heartily hope will prove to be the most terribly degrading experience of any of our lives. We have been close, perilously close, to the Void."

With a certain satisfaction, I notice Wu's head drooping a little more.

"But never mind that now. What we have done is simply to provide ourselves with an example to avoid. We shall rise again, recivilize ourselves, surpass even what we were formerly, before this late catastrophe. We shall regain our self-esteem, and our regard for one another too. For we shall urgently require both as we strive to meet the challenges that lie ahead.

"Perhaps I don't need to recall for you that the second meaning of *Decay* is *Work on What Has Been Spoiled*. And—

"Work on what has been spoiled
has supreme success.

"Are you ready now to undertake that work? Both of you?"

Li's eyes slide over for a glance at Wu, whose gaze remains lowered to my knees. After a breathless moment, Wu answers with a barely perceptible bow, and I relax as I see Li follow suit.

"Good. Very good. *It furthers one to cross the great water.* But one more thing before we begin. A matter concerning Wu. There is just one thing you have to do. You must complete what you've begun. I must ask you"—here I find I have to clear a lump out of my throat—"*to bite off my tail.*"

His shock and distress are quite unmistakable, the emotion rocks him back on his haunches. It's hard to rattle a Samurai mouse, though of course our ordeal has affected him.

"Yes. No further questions, please." I raise my paw. "It's absolutely necessary . . . for health reasons. You *must* do it."

This time Wu's bow is low, profound, ceremonious. He takes a step or so toward me, and for a moment I see his whole body framed in that intoxicating open doorway. Even as he bares his teeth, I see sincere repentance in his eyes.

"As near the base as possible, of course."

Wu answers with a nod and a widening of his jaws. Yes, I can repose my faith in him, he'll do what's necessary. And Li will not attempt to interfere, though I can see the anguish on his face. And I, I will not cry out. So each of us will take our proper part, though little enough in our recent past has prepared us for this freedom.

BLACK AND TAN

Up until his family died out from under him, Peter Jackson used to grow tobacco. His place was a long ways out from town, up on the hillside above Keyhole Lake — you had a nice view of the lake from up there. It was forty or fifty acres that he owned, and an easement down to the lake shore. Maybe a third of that land was too rocky to farm and another third was grown up in cedars, fine old trees he never cared to cut down. There was the place his house was set and what was left you could grow tobacco on. He did just about all the work himself, hiring a couple of hands only once in a while, at cutting and drying time, for instance.

"Tobacco," he was known to say, and then he'd pause and spit a splash of it to one side of the courthouse steps. "Tobacco, now, that's eight days a week . . ." Like most farmers he'd come to town on Saturday, visit the Co-op or the Standard Farm Store, maybe get a few things at the supermarket. When he got done his errands he might wander through the courthouse square and talk a while with this one and that one. One Sunday a month, more or less, he'd drive in with his wife and they'd both go to church, and two, three times a year he'd come in by himself and get falling-down drunk. At the end of his evening he'd just go to sleep in the cab of his truck, then in the morning hitch himself straight and drive on out home. Never caused anybody any more trouble than that. Later on, after he'd got the dogs, he cut out the drinking and the church along with it, right about at the same time.

A steady fellow, then, and mostly known as a hard worker. Quiet, never had a whole lot to say, but what he said was reasonable. Whatever he told you he would do would get done if nothing serious kept him from it. That was the kind of thing any of us might have said of him, supposing we'd been asked.

Amy was the name of his wife, who'd been a Puckett before she married. Never raised any objection to living so far out from town. She was fond of the woods and fond of the lake, so maybe that made up for whatever loneliness there may have been to it. They didn't have any neighbors near, though a couple of Nashville people had built summer houses on the far side of the lake. Like Peter Jackson, Amy was a worker; she grew a garden, put up food for the winter. They were both in the garden picking tomatoes on the late September evening when she all of a sudden fell over dead. Heart attack was what did her in, faster than a bullet. Jackson said he spent a minute twirling around to see where the shot might have come from, before he went to her. They had been working opposite ends of the row, and she was already getting cold by the time he got to her, he said. And she not more than fifty, fifty-five.

Jackson wasn't as broke up about it as you could have thought a man might be, losing his wife in her prime that way. Or if he was, he didn't show it much. There was a good turnout at the funeral, for Amy was well liked around the town. The old hens were forever coming up to him and saying how *terrible* they thought it was, and every time he told them, *No. No, it ain't so terrible, not really. If her time had come to go, then better she went quickly, with no pain.* So everybody said how well he was bearing it. And then his children started to die.

They had two children, son and daughter: June and Richard were their names. Both of them looked fair to rise above their raising, both going on past high school, which neither of their parents had. The boy was putting himself through UT Knoxville on an ROTC scholarship, and then one summer he got himself killed in a training accident, some kind of a foolish, avoidable thing. Well, he went quick too, did Richard. It put Peter Jackson back at the graveside just under a year after they buried Amy. He was dry-eyed again, but tight around the mouth, and whatever people spoke to him he didn't have much to say back. June stood with him the whole time through, hanging on to his elbow and sort of fending people off. It might have been she was already sick herself by that time, though nobody knew anything of it yet.

June was the older of the two. She'd gone to nursing school in Nashville and kept living there once she was done, had herself a job at the Baptist Hospital. After she got that cancer she stayed on as a patient a while but there wasn't anything they could do for her, and in the end she came home to Keyhole Lake to die. Peter Jackson nursed her right on through it, never had any other help at all. It wasn't quick or anything like it; it kept on for five or six months and you didn't have to hear a whole lot about it to know there must have been pain and to spare.

It was mid-March or so when they buried her; there'd been a hard winter and there was still some thin snow on the ground. Peter Jackson stood alone this time, grim and silent for the most part. Nobody had a lot to say to him either. He had gone lean under his hardship, but he was still a fine-looking man, and people said he looked well in his funeral suit. Of course, he'd had his share of opportunity to get the hang of wearing it. As a young man he'd had deep red hair, and now it was rust-colored, patched with gray. His eyebrows were thick and bushy, turning out in devilish points at the sides, and underneath, his deep-set eyes surprised you with the brightness of their green. This time he wouldn't turn back from the grave once they had filled it, and after a minute the priest walked over to stand with him. Shoulder to shoulder, they looked like a matched pair, Mr. Chalk in his black cassock and Jackson in the suit.

Mr. Chalk was fairly new to the town; he'd done a lot of work in the prisons and he wasn't known for wasting his words. A few people crept up near to listen for what he'd find to tell a man like Jackson, which was this:

"Well, you're still here," Mr. Chalk was heard to say.

Jackson spat on the snow and said, "What of it?"

"You're surviving," Mr. Chalk said. "Today's today and then there'll be tomorrow."

"That's right, and it's a curse," Peter Jackson said, and turned on the priest with the tunnels of his eyes. "I been cursed with survival," he said then, speaking in a different tone than before, as if, after all, it were a new discovery.

That spring he didn't plant tobacco. Round about the time he should have been, he was driving all around the county looking at dogs, and going clear to Nashville too. He looked at all the good-sized breeds: collies, Great Danes, German shepherds. There was a story that went along with it, which got out and made the rounds. Funny how many people got to hear of it, because it was a personal kind of a thing for a man like Peter Jackson to go telling.

It appeared that when Peter Jackson was born, his parents had a big old dog that they let live in the house and all. Jackson didn't recall himself what breed of a dog it might have been and there wasn't anybody for him to ask, because his parents were long dead and he never had any brothers or sisters. Anyway, they had worried the dog might eat the baby when they brought him home but it turned out the opposite: the dog loved the child. So much so that in the long run they trusted the dog to watch the baby. They might go out and work their land or even leave the place altogether for a short spell, knowing the dog would see everything was all right. This all happened at that same place at Keyhole Lake, and one time, so the story went, little Peter Jackson, only two or three years old, let himself out of the house somehow and went wandering all the way down to the shore. This old dog went right along with him, saw he didn't drown himself or get hurt any other way, and in the end when the child was tired, the dog brought him on back home.

So Peter Jackson spent that spring driving practically all over creation, looking at different kinds of dogs, and when people wondered how he could be so choosy when he didn't even appear to know what it was he wanted, that was the tale he would tell them. Finally he ended up at the place of this woman way out the Lebanon Road who bred Dobermans. He went out and looked at her dogs a while and went home and came back another day and told her, "Let me have two of them."

"What do you mean, two?" she said. "Do you even know if you want one? Which two did you have in mind, anyway?"

"Pick me out two likely ones," Peter Jackson said. "A male and a female. Ones that ain't too close related." And the next thing anybody knew, he was breeding Dobermans himself. Rebuilt his old drying barn into kennels and fenced in some pens out in front of it. Told anybody who cared to know that Dobermans weren't naturally mean like they had the name for, but that they were smart and naturally loyal and would be inclined to protect you and your house and land without any special training. Although he could supply the training too, if that was what you wanted. He started selling a good many as pets and maybe an equal number as guard dogs. That was about the time the K-9 patrols came into style, so he drew business from the police, and in a year or so people were coming good long distances, even from out of state at times, to buy their dogs from Peter Jackson. He was thought to be so good at it that eventually people began to bring him dogs that other trainers couldn't handle. Which may have been what first gave him the notion of taking in those boys.

Marvin Ferguson, the county judge, was the man Jackson had to go see about this idea. In Franklin, the county judge doubles up as juvenile judge too, so Ferguson had the management of whatsoever people under seventeen or eighteen couldn't seem to keep themselves out of trouble. Of which there were always a few that he couldn't quite figure out what to do with. It was kind of left-handed work for him to be doing anyway. Still, he was leery of Jackson's idea at first. Because Jackson wasn't getting any younger, was he? and his place was clear the hell and gone from anywhere else to speak of, and who knew just how bone-mean some of those boys might turn out to be? But after they had talked a while they arrived at an understanding. When Peter Jackson had gone on home, Judge Ferguson pulled his file on a boy named Willard Clement, and pretty soon he was on the phone arranging for a deputy to drive the boy out to Jackson's place.

The highway runs on the near side of the ridge from the lake, and you got to Peter Jackson's by turning off on a little old dirt driveway that came up over the crest of the hill and dipped down on the other side to stop in front of Jackson's house, an old log house that had been clapboarded over and added on to a couple or three times. A ways below the house were the dog pens, and any time a car turned in, all those dogs would start in barking. Past the kennels a trail went winding down the hill and twisted in amongst the cedars; you couldn't see quite how it got there from above, but way on down it came out near the little dock where Jackson kept a pirogue tied, for when he wanted to paddle out on the lake and fish.

But the first thing a stranger would be apt to notice, coming over that rise, would be the lake itself. It always looked sort of surprising from the ridgetop. It isn't really keyhole-shaped, just narrow at one end and wide at the other. How come they give it that name is that the middle of the wide part is so deep nobody ever found the bottom, and somebody had the idea it was like that part of a keyhole that just goes clear on through the door. From up by Peter Jackson's house you could always see how the color of the water would change as it neared the middle, homing in on that deep dark circle of blue.

Jackson's dogs stayed in the pens, all but two that were his pets; them he let live in the house and have the run of the whole place. Bronwen he called one of them and the other was Caesar. All his dogs had peculiar names like that, which he looked up in books. When the deputy pulled in to deliver Willard Clement, he found Jackson waiting out in the yard, the two dogs on either side of him. The deputy unlocked Willard out of that caged-up back seat and brought him on down to get introduced. Jackson said hello and then made both of the dogs put up their paws to shake — they were that well trained, almost like folks. Then he turned around all of a sudden and pointed back up the hill and called out, "Hit it, Bronwen," and snapped his fingers twice. The dog went bounding up the hill and jumped up in the air and locked her jaws on a piece of two-by-four Jackson had nailed between two cedar trunks about five feet off of the ground, and she just kept right on hanging there, her whole weight on her teeth so to speak, until Jackson said. "All right, leggo, Bronwen," and then she dropped down. Willard Clement was staring googly-eyed, and you could just practically see it, the deputy said, how any thought he might have had of causing Peter Jackson some type of trouble was evaporating clean out of his mind.

Jackson put Willard Clement up in what had been Richard's room, and that's where he put all the others that came along after him. He kept them busy working with the dogs, first just putting the food out and cleaning the pens, and later on taking them for exercise and helping with the training some. The boys mostly stayed out there six weeks to two months, which was long enough to learn a little something about how to train a dog. And the work told on them, gentled them down some. A number kept on working with animals, one way or another, after they were done their stay at Jackson's. Willard Clement, I believe, finally became a vet.

You couldn't miss the difference in those boys, between

the time they got dropped off out there and the time they got picked up again. You'd drive one of them out there locked into the back like something that had rabies, maybe, but when you went back to go get him, likely he'd look like somebody you could trust to ride in the front seat alongside of you. He would be saying *Yes sir* and *No sir* and standing up straight and looking you in the eye. Nobody quite knew what Jackson practiced on those boys, but whatever it was it seemed to work. And a good few of them seemed to really be grateful for it too. There were some that tried going back out to visit him, a lot later on once they were grown, but the funny thing was that Jackson himself never seemed to care too much about seeing any of them again.

There must have been eight or ten of those boys between Clement and Don Bantry. Anyway, he'd been having them for near about two years. There hadn't been a one of them he'd failed to turn around, either, else they probably never would have thought of sending Bantry out there, because that boy was a tough nut to crack. He was about sixteen at that time, but already big as a man. What he was most recently in trouble for was beating up a teacher at the high school and breaking his arm, but there was a long string of things leading up to that: liquor and pot, some car stealing, a burglary, suspicion of a rape he never got tried on. They wouldn't have him at the reform school again, just flat-out wouldn't. Ferguson was in a toss-up whether to try and figure some way to get him tried as an adult or send him out to Jackson's a while, and what he decided shows you how he'd come to think that Peter Jackson was magic.

Bantry had sort of short bowlegs, but big shoulders and longish arms. He had a pelt of heavy black hair all over him, and even his eyebrows met in the middle. He looked a good deal like an ape, and he wasn't above acting like one too. Well, the deputy turned him out of the car, and Jackson had Bronwen and Caesar put up their paws, but Bantry wasn't having any of that. "Ain't shaking hands with no goddamn dog," he said. But it wasn't the first time one of them had said it.

Jackson had Caesar run hit that two-by-four and hang by his jaws a half minute or so. You couldn't have told what Bantry thought, his face never showed a thing, but that trick had always worked before, so the deputy left on out of there. And right from the start, it was war.

Jackson went and got a shovel and handed it to Bantry. Explained to him how to go about cleaning out those dog pens, where he'd find the wheelbarrow at, where to go dump all he shoveled up. Bantry didn't reach to take hold of the shovel, so Jackson finally just let it drop and lean against his shoulder.

"Better get a move on," Jackson said, or something about like it, and then he started walking back down toward the house. He was halfway there when he heard some kind of a noise or shout and turned around in time to see Bantry flinging the shovel like a spear, not quite at him but close enough in his general direction that Bronwen and Caesar started growling. Jackson told the dogs to stay. Bantry had turned and started walking up the drive, where the dust of the deputy's car had not yet even settled, like he didn't know it was at least twenty miles to anywhere else, or didn't care, either one.

"Come on back here before I have the dogs bring you," Peter Jackson called after him.

Bantry kept walking, didn't even glance back. He was near the top of the hill when the dogs got to him, and he swung around and tried to get off a kick, but before he could land one, Bronwen had him by the one arm and Caesar by the other. They clamped on to him just short of breaking his skin and started dragging him on back down the drive to where the shovel had landed, just like Jackson had said they would. Bantry came along with them, had no choice, as long as he didn't want his arms torn off. His face was fish white, but Peter Jackson thought it was anger more than fear. Bantry was not the kind that scared easy, though he was sharp enough to know a fight he couldn't win. This time when Jackson offered him the shovel he took it, and he went on and cleaned out the dog runs. For the next week, ten days or so, whatever Jackson told him to do he did it, but did it like a slave, not looking at him or speaking either. He never said anything at all unless he was asked a question, not even at the supper table.

Jackson had a dog named Olwen, with seven pups near ready to wean. He had Bantry feeding the puppies their oatmeal and all. One day when Bantry was coming out of Olwen's run, Jackson snapped his fingers to Caesar. The dog hit Bantry square in the chest, knocked him over flat on his back and stood over him with that whole mouthful of teeth showing white and needle sharp. With all that, Bantry kept most of his cool. He turned his head to one side, slowly, and called out to Peter Jackson.

"What I do now?"

"You been doing something to Olwen's puppies," Jackson told him, walking up closer.

"You never seen me," Bantry said.

"But I still know it," Jackson said. "And if you don't stop, I'll know that too." And he let Bantry lay and think on that a minute before he called Caesar to leave him get back up.

Another week or so went by, Bantry doing his work with his head bowed down, not speaking until he was spoken to and then answering short as he could. Till one evening when Jackson was starting to cook supper and felt like he had a headache coming on. Bantry had just fed Bronwen and Caesar on the kitchen floor, so they were busy over their pans. Jackson stepped into his bedroom to get himself an aspirin, and then Bantry was in there right behind him, already shutting and bolting the door.

"You been waiting your chance quite a while, hadn't you, boy?" Jackson said. And straightaway he hit Bantry over the eye, twisting his fist so it would cut. He thought if he surprised him he might win, or anyway get a chance to open the door back up. But Bantry didn't have his reputation for nothing. Jackson got in a couple more shots and thought maybe he was doing all right, when next thing he knew he was lying on the floor not able to get up again. Then it was quiet for a minute or two except for the dogs scrabbling at the outside of the door. Every so often one or the other would back off and get a running start and throw himself up against it.

"You fight okay for an old man," Bantry said, panting. It was about his first volunteer word since he got there. "But you still lost." Jackson didn't answer him. It was hurting him too much to breathe right then. Bantry reached a handkerchief off the dresser and dabbed at the cut above his eye. Then he picked up the keys of Jackson's truck and twirled the ring around his finger.

"You won't never make it," Jackson said. They were both still again for a minute, listening to the dogs trying to come through the door.

"I could always kill you," Bantry said.

"You'll still come out behind," Jackson said. "I already lived a lot longer than you."

Bantry sat down on the edge of Jackson's bed, looking down at the floor. He still had to hold the handkerchief over his cut to keep the blood from running in his eye.

"What say we just call it a draw?" Jackson said. "We could just go on in the kitchen and eat supper and forget the whole thing."

Bantry looked over at him. "How I know you're telling the truth?" he said.

"Hell, you don't," Peter Jackson said. "But there's always a chance of it. And some chance is better than no chance at all."

Bantry sat and thought a while longer. Then he reached over and unlatched the door. The dogs came in fast, spinning around, slipping a little on the slick board floor. They were in such a hurry to find Bantry and eat him alive they were just about falling over themselves.

"Let him alone," Jackson called out, and both dogs simmered down right away. Then to Bantry: "You come on here and help me up. And let me have that aspirin bottle. That's what I was after in here in the first place."

Another week or so went by. Bantry's cut was healing up; it was not so bad as it looked at first. Jackson had thought his ribs were cracked but it turned out they were only bruised and soon enough they started feeling better. Bantry went on about the same as before, doing what he was told and not saying much, yet Jackson didn't think he was quite so sullen and angry as he had been. Then one afternoon Bantry came up to him and said, "I'm done with the dog runs. All right I go down by the lake a while?"

"Go ahead on," Jackson said. He was right pleased because it was the first time Bantry had asked him for anything, and for that matter it was the first time he'd acted like he knew the lake was even there.

So Bantry went on down the trail and Jackson went and turned out a dog named Theodore he was training for K-9. He had on all the pads he wore whenever he was going to let a dog have at him. After twenty minutes or so he took a break and walked around the low side of the kennels where he could see out to the lake, and that was when he saw Bantry out paddling in the pirogue.

Later on, Jackson couldn't tell just why the sight of it hit him so hard. He hadn't told Bantry he could use the boat, but then he hadn't told him he couldn't either. He might have been trying to run off again; there were people in the houses on the far side of the lake and Bantry might have thought he could get over there and steal one of their cars. But even from that far distance Jackson could see that Bantry didn't know much at all about how to handle a boat: he couldn't keep it headed straight, and he kept heeling it way over to one side or the other.

Whatever his reason was, Jackson decided he wanted to get down there quick. He took out running down the trail, shedding his pads as he went along. Bronwen and Caesar came along with him, and Theodore, who was still out loose, was frisking along after all of them, not taking it too seriously, just having a good time. The trail takes a zig and a zag through the cedar grove, and for the last leg or two Jackson couldn't see the lake at all. When he finally came out at the foot of the path, he saw Bantry had turned the boat over somehow and was thrashing around a good way from it. You could tell by one quick look he didn't know how to swim a stroke. And what kind of a fool would overset a flat-bottomed boat, anyway? He wasn't over the deep part of the lake; if he had been, the way things fell out, he would probably be there yet.

Jackson took off his knee pads, which he hadn't been able to get rid of while he was running. He took off his shoes and some more of his clothes and waded out into the lake. The dogs ran up and down the shoreline barking like crazy, and now and then one of them would put a paw in the water, but they were not dogs that liked to swim. Without thinking, Jackson swam straight out to where Bantry was at and laid a hold to him, only Bantry got a better hold on him first, and dragged him right on under. It was not anything he meant to be doing, exactly, just how any drowning man behaves. He was trying to climb out of the lake over Jackson's back, but Jackson was going down underneath him, getting light-headed, for no matter what he tried he couldn't raise his head clear for a breath. Then it came to him he had better swim for the bottom. When he dove down he felt Bantry come loose from him and he kept going down till he was free, then out a ways, swimming as far as he could under water before he came back up.

He was tired then, and his banged ribs had started to hurt from that long time he'd been down and holding his breath. For a minute or two he had to lie in a dead-man's float to rest, and then he raised his head and started treading water, slow. It was a cloudy day, no sun at all, and he could feel the cold cutting through to his bones. The surface of the lake was black as oil. Bantry was still struggling about twenty feet from him, but he was near done in by that time. He stared at Jackson, his eyes rolling white. Jackson trod water and looked right back at him until Bantry gave it up and slid down under the lake.

Ripples were widening out from the place where Bantry's head went down, and Peter Jackson kept on treading water. He counted up to twenty-five before he dove. It was ten feet deep, maybe twelve, at the point where they were at, colder yet along the bottom and dark with silt. He didn't find Bantry the first dive he made, though he stayed down until his head was pounding. It took him a count of thirty to get the breath back for another try, and he was starting to think he might have miscalculated. But on the second time he found him and hauled him back up. Bantry was not putting up any fight now; he was not any more than a dead weight. Jackson got him in a cross-chest carry and swam him into the shore.

The dogs were going wild there on the bank, yapping and jumping up and down. Jackson dumped Bantry face down on the gravel and swatted the dogs away. He knelt down and started mashing Bantry's shoulders. There was plenty of water coming out of him, but he was cold and not moving a twitch, and Jackson was thinking he had miscalculated sure enough when Bantry shuddered and coughed and puked a little and then raised up on his elbows. Jackson got off of him and watched him start to breathe. After a little bit, Bantry's eyes came clear.

"You'da let me drown," Bantry said. "You'da just let me . . ."

"You never left me much of a choice," Jackson said.

"You was just setting there watching me drown," Bantry said. He sat up one joint at a time and then let his head drop down and hang over his folded knees. The cut above his eye had opened back up and was bleeding some. In a minute, he started to cry.

Peter Jackson never had seen anybody carrying on the way Bantry was, not some pretty near grown man, at least. He didn't feel any too sorry for Bantry, but it was unpleasant watching him cry like that. It was like watching a baby cry when it can't tell you what's the matter, and there ain't no way for you to tell it to quit. He thought of one thing or another he might say. That he'd had to take a gambler's chance. That a poor risk was better than no hope at all. But he was worn out from swimming and struggling, too tired to feel like talking much. Bantry kept on crying, not letting up, and Peter Jackson got himself on his feet and went limping up to the house with the dogs.

That was what did it for Bantry, though, or so it seemed. Anyway, he was a lot different after that. He acted nicer with the dogs, feeding them treats, stroking them and loving them up, when he never as much as touched one before, if he had a way around it. He began to volunteer to do extra things, helping more around the house and garden, when his chores in the kennel were done. He put on pads and learned to help Jackson train dogs for K-9. He followed Jackson around trying to strike up conversation, like, for a change, he was hungry for company. He was especially nice with Bronwen and Caesar, and Caesar seemed to take a shine to him right back. Bantry had turned the corner, what it looked like. In about two more weeks, Peter Jackson called the courthouse and said they could send somebody out to pick him up.

As it turned out, it was me they sent. I was still a part-time deputy then, and the call came on a Saturday when I was on duty. Bantry was packed and all ready to go when I got there. Soon as I had parked the car he came walking over, carrying his grip. Caesar was walking alongside of him, and every couple of steps they took, Bantry would reach down and give him a pat on the head.

"Hello, Mr. Trimble," he said. He put out his hand and we shook.

"You look bright-eyed and bushy-tailed," I said. "I'd scarce have known you, Bantry."

"You can call me Don," he said, and smiled.

I told him to go on and get in the front while I went down to take a message to Jackson. It surprised me just a touch he hadn't already come out himself. He was sitting on his back stoop when I found him, staring out across the lake. Bronwen was sitting there next to him. Every so often she'd slap her paw up on his knee, like she was begging him for something. Jackson didn't appear to be paying her much mind.

"Well sir, you're a miracle worker," I said. "I wouldn't have believed it if I'd just been told, but it looks like you done it again."

"Hello, Trimble," Jackson said, flicking his eyes over me and then back away. He'd known I was there right along, just hadn't shown it. Bronwen slapped her paw back up on his knee.

"Marvin said tell you he'll have another one ready to send out here shortly," I said. Jackson looked off across the lake.

"I ain't going to have no more of 'm," he said.

"Why not?" I said. Bronwen pawed at him another time, and Jackson reached over and started rubbing her ears.

"Well, I figured something out," Jackson said, still staring down there at the water. "It ain't any different than breaking an animal, what I been doing to them boys."

I stepped up beside him and looked where he was looking, curious to see what might be so interesting down there on the lake. There wasn't so much as a fish jumping. Nothing there but that blue, blue water, cold looking and still like it was ice.

"What if you're right?" I said. "More'n likely it's the very thing they need."

"Yes, but a man is not an animal," he said. He waited a minute, and clicked his tongue. "Anyhow, I'm getting too old," he said.

"You?" I said. "Ain't nobody would call *you* old." It was a true fact I never had thought of him that way myself, though he might have been near seventy by that time. He'd been a right smart older than his wife.

Jackson raised up his left hand and shook it under my nose. I could see how his fingers were getting skinny the way an old man's will, and how loose his wedding band was rattling. Then he laid his hand back down on Bronwen's head.

"I'm old," he said. "I can feel it now sure enough. The days run right by me and I can't get a hold on them. And you want to know what?"

"What?" I said. Walked right into it like the sharp edge of a door.

"It's a relief," Peter Jackson told me. "That's what."

CUSTOMS OF
THE COUNTRY

I DON'T KNOW how much I remember about that place any-more. It was nothing but somewhere I came to put in some pretty bad time, though that was not what I had planned on when I went there. I had it in mind to improve things, but I don't think you could fairly claim that's what I did. So that's one reason I might just as soon forget about it. And I didn't stay there all that long, not more than nine months or so, about the same time, come to think, that the child I'd come to try and get back had lived inside my body.

It was a cluster-housing thing called Spring Valley, I wouldn't know why, just over the Botetourt County line on the highway going north out of Roanoke. I suppose it must have been there ten or fifteen years, long enough to lose that raw look they have when they're new built, but not too run-down yet, so long as you didn't look close. There were five or six long two-story buildings running in rows back up the hillside. You got to the upstairs apartments by an outside balcony, like you would in a motel. The one I rented was in the lowest building down the hill, upstairs on the northwest corner. There was a patch of grass out front beyond the gravel of the parking lot, but the manager didn't take much trouble over it. He kept it cut, but it was weedy, and a few yards past the buildings it began to go to brush. By my corner there was a young apple tree that never made anything but small sour green apples, knotted up like little fists. Apart from that there was nothing nearby that the eye would care to dwell on. But upstairs, out my front windows, I could look way out beyond the interstate to where the mountains were.

You got there driving about two miles up a bumpy two-lane from the state road. It was mostly wooded land along the way, with a couple of pastures spotted in, and one little store. About halfway you crossed the railroad cut, and from the apartment I could hear the trains pulling north out of town, though it wasn't near enough I could see them. I listened to them often enough, though, nights I couldn't sleep, and bad times I might pull a chair out on the concrete slab of balcony so I could hear them better.

The apartment was nothing more than the least I needed, some place that would look all right and yet cost little enough to leave me something to give the lawyer. Two rooms and a bath and a fair-sized kitchen. It would have been better if there'd been one more room for Davey but I couldn't stretch my money far enough to cover that. It did have fresh paint on the walls and the trim in the kitchen and bathroom was in good enough shape. And it was real quiet mostly, except that the man next door would beat up his wife about two or three times a week. The place was close enough to soundproof I couldn't usually hear talk but I could hear yelling plain as day, and when he got going good he would slam her bang into our common wall. If she hit in just the right spot it would send all my pots and pans flying off the pegboard where I'd hung them there above the stove.

Not that it mattered to me that the pots fell down, except for the noise and the time it took to pick them up again. Living alone like I was I didn't have heart to do much cooking, and if I did fix myself something I mostly used a plain old iron skillet that hung there on the same wall. The rest was a set of Revereware my family give me when Patrick and I got married. They had copper bottoms, and when I first moved in that apartment I polished them to where it practically hurt to look at them head on, but it was all for show.

The whole apartment was done about the same way, made into something I kept spotless and didn't much care to use. A piece of dirt never got a fair chance to settle there, that much was for sure. I wore down the kitchen counters scrubbing out the old stains, I went at the grout between the bathroom tiles with a toothbrush, I did all that kind of thing. Spring Valley was the kind of place where people would sometimes leave too fast to take their furniture along, so I was able to get most everything I needed from the manager, who saved it up to try selling it to whatever new people moved in. Then I bought fabric and sewed covers to where everything matched, and I sewed curtains and got posters to put up on the walls, but I can't say I ever felt at home there. It was an act, and I wasn't putting it on for me or Davey, but for those other people who would come to see it and judge it. And however good I could get it looking, it never felt quite right.

I'd step into the place with the same cross feeling I had when I got in my car, an old Malibu I'd bought a body and paint job for, instead of the new clutch and brakes it really needed. But one way or another I could run the thing, and six days a week I would climb in it and go back down to the state road, turn north and drive up to the interstate crossing. There was a Truckstops of America up there, and that was where my job was at. I worked the three snake bends of the counter and it was enough to keep me run off my feet most days. Or nights, since I was on a swing shift that rolled over every ten days. I wouldn't have ate the food myself but the place was usually busy and the tips were fair. I'd have made a lot more money working in a bar somewhere, being a cocktail waitress or what have you, but that would have been another case of it not looking the way it was supposed to.

The supervisor out there was a man named Tim that used

to know Patrick a little, back from before we split. He was how I got the job, and he was good about letting me have time off when I needed it for the lawyer or something, and he let me take my calls there too. By and large he was an easy enough man to work for except that about once a week he would have a tantrum over something or other and try to scream the walls down for a while. Still, it never went anywhere beyond yelling, and he always acted sorry once he got through.

The other waitress on my shift was about old enough to be my mother, I would guess. Her name was Priscilla but she wanted you to call her Prissy, though it didn't suit her a bit. She was kind of dumpy and she had to wear support hose and she had the worst dye job on her hair I just about ever saw, some kind of home brew that turned her hair the color of French's mustard. But she was good-natured, really a kindly person, and we got along good and helped each other out whenever one of us looked like getting behind.

Well, I was tired all the time with the shifts changing the way they did. The six-to-two I hated the worst because it would have me getting back to my apartment building around three in the morning, which was not the time the place looked its best. It was a pretty sorry lot of people living there, I hadn't quite realized when I moved in, a lot of small-time criminals, dope dealers and thieves, and none of them too good at whatever crime they did. So when I came in off that graveyard shift there was a fair chance I'd find the sheriff's car out there looking for somebody. I suppose they felt like if they came at that time of night they would stand a better chance of catching whoever they were after asleep.

I didn't get to know the neighbors any too well, it didn't seem like a good idea. The man downstairs was a drunk and a check forger. Sometimes he would break into the other apartments looking for whiskey, but he never managed to get into mine. I didn't keep whiskey anyhow, maybe he had some sense for that. The manager liked to make passes at whatever women were home in the day. He even got around to trying me, though not but the one time.

The man next door, the one that beat up his wife, didn't do crimes or work either that I ever could tell. He just seemed to lay around the place, maybe drawing some kind of welfare. There wasn't a whole lot to him, he was just a stringy little fellow, hair and mustache a dishwater brown, cheap green tattoos running up his arms. Maybe he was stronger than he looked, but I did wonder how come his wife would take it from him, since she was about a head taller and must have outweighed him an easy ten pounds. I might have thought she was whipping on *him*—stranger things have been known to go on—but she was the one that seemed like she might break out crying if you looked at her crooked. She was a big fine-looking girl with a lovely shape, and long brown hair real smooth and straight and shiny. I guess she was too hammered down most of the time to pay much attention to the way she dressed, but she still had pretty brown eyes, big and long-lashed and soft, kind of like a cow's eyes are, except I never saw a cow that looked that miserable.

At first I thought maybe I might make a friend of her, she was about the only one around there I felt like I might want to. Our paths crossed pretty frequent, either around the apartment buildings or in the Quik-Sak back toward town, where I'd find her running the register some days. But she was shy of me—shy of anybody, I suppose. She would flinch if you did so much as say hello. So after a while, I quit trying. She'd get hers about twice a week, maybe other times I wasn't around to hear it happen. It's a wonder all the things you can learn to ignore, and after a month or so I was so accustomed I barely noticed when they would start in. I would just wait till I thought they were good and through, and then get up and hang those pans back on the wall where they were supposed to go.

What with the way the shifts kept rolling over out there at the TOA, I had a lot of trouble sleeping. I never did learn to sleep in the daytime worth a damn. I would just lie down when I got back till some of the ache drained out of me, and then get up and try to think of some way to pass the time. There wasn't a whole lot to do around that apartment. I didn't have any TV, only a radio, and that didn't work too well itself. After the first few weeks I sent off to one of those places that say they'll pay you to stuff envelopes at your own house. My thought was it would be some extra money, but it never amounted to anything much of that. It just killed me some time and gave me something to do with my hands, in between smoking cigarettes. Something to do with myself while I was worrying, and I used to worry a good deal in those days.

The place where Davey had been fostered out was not all that far away, just about ten or twelve miles on up the road, out there in the farm country. The people were named Baker, I never got to first names with them, just called them Mr. and Mrs. They were some older than me, just into their forties, and they didn't have children of their own. The place was just a small farm but Mr. Baker grew tobacco on the most of it and I'm told he made it a paying thing. Mrs. Baker kept a milk cow or two and she grew a garden and canned. Thrifty people, in the old-time way. They were real sweet to Davey and he seemed to like being with them pretty well. It was a place a little boy would expect to enjoy, except there weren't any neighbors too near. And he had been staying there almost the whole two years, which was lucky too, since most children usually got moved around a whole lot more than that.

But that was the trouble, like the lawyer explained to me, it was just too good. Davey was doing too well out there. He'd made out better in the first grade too than anybody would have thought. So nobody really felt like he needed to be moved. The worst of it was the Bakers had got to like him well enough they were saying they wanted to adopt him if they could, and that was what plagued my mind the most. If I thought about that while I was doing those envelopes, it would start me giving myself paper cuts.

Even though he was so close, I didn't go out to see Davey

near as much as I would have liked to. The lawyer kept on telling me it wasn't a good idea to look like I was pressing too hard. Better take it easy till all the evaluations came in and we had our court date and all. Still, I would call and go on out there maybe a little more than once a month, most usually on the weekends since that seemed to suit the Bakers better. They never acted like it was any trouble, and they were always pleasant to me, or polite might be the better word. They wanted what I wanted, so I never expected us to turn out good friends. The way it sometimes seemed they didn't trust me, that bothered me a little more. I would have liked to take him out to the movies a time or two, but I could see plain enough the Bakers wouldn't have been easy about me having him off their place.

Still, I can't remember us having a bad time, not any of those times I went. He was always happy to see me, though he'd be quiet when we were in the house, with Mrs. Baker hovering. So I would get us outside quick as ever I could, and once we were out, we would just play like both of us were children. There was an open pasture, a creek with a patch of woods, and a hay barn where we would play hide-and-go-seek. I don't know what all else we did — silly things, mostly. That was how I could get near him the easiest, he didn't get a whole lot of playing in way out there. The Bakers weren't what you would call playful and there weren't any other children living near. So that was the thing I could give him that was all mine to give. When the weather was good we would stay outside together most all the day and he would just wear me out. After it turned cold we couldn't stay outside so long, though one of our best days of all was when I showed him how to make a snowman. But over the winter those visits seemed to get shorter and shorter, like the days.

Davey called me Momma still, but I suppose he had come to think your mother was something more like a big sister or just some kind of a friend. Mrs. Baker was the one doing for him all the time. I don't know just what he remembered from before, or if he remembered any of the bad part. He would always mind me but he never acted scared around me, and if anybody says he did, they lie. But I never really did get to know what he had going on in the back of his mind about the past. At first I worried the Bakers might have been talking against me, but after I had seen a little more of them I knew they wouldn't have done anything like that, wouldn't have thought it right. So I expect whatever Davey knew about that other time he remembered all on his own. He never mentioned Patrick hardly and I think he really had forgotten about him. Thinking back, I guess he never really saw that much of Patrick even where we all were living together. But Davey had Patrick's mark all over him, the same eyes and the same red hair.

Patrick had thick wavy hair the shade of an Irish setter's and a big rolling mustache the same color. Maybe that was his best feature, but he was a good-looking man altogether —still is, I suppose, though the prison haircut don't suit him. If he ever had much of a thought in his head, I suspect he had knocked it clean out with dope, yet he was always fun to be around. I wasn't but seventeen when I married him and I didn't have any better sense myself. Right through to the end I never thought anything much was the matter, his vices looked so small to me. He was good-tempered almost all the time, and good with Davey when he did notice him. Never one time did he raise his hand to either one of us. In little ways he was unreliable—late, not showing up at all, gone out of the house for days together sometimes. Hindsight shows me he ran with other women, but I managed not to know anything about that at the time. He had not quite finished high school and the best job he could hold was being an orderly down at the hospital, but he made a good deal of extra money stealing pills out of there and selling them on the street.

That was something else I didn't allow myself to think on much back then. Patrick never told me a lot about it anyhow, always acted real mysterious about whatever he was up to in that line. He would disappear on one of his trips and come back with a whole mess of money, and I would spend up my share and be glad I had it too. Never thought much about where it was coming from, the money or the pills, either one. He used to keep all manner of pills around the house, Valium and ludes and a lot of different kinds of speed, and we both took what we felt like whenever we felt in the mood. But what Patrick made the most on was Dilaudid. I used to take that without ever knowing what it really was, but once everything fell in on us I found out it was a bad thing, bad as heroin they said, and not much different, and that was what they gave Patrick most of his time for.

I truly was surprised to find out that was the strongest dope we had, because I never really felt like it made me all that high. It sure didn't have anything like the punch the speed did. Yet you could fall into the habit of taking a good bit of it, never noticing how much. You would just take one and kick back on a long slow stroke and whatever trouble you might have, it would not be able to find you. It came on like nothing but it was the hardest habit to lose, and I was a long time shaking it. I might be thinking about it yet if I would let myself, and there were times, all through the winter I spent in that apartment, I'd catch myself remembering the feeling.

I had come just before the leaves started turning, and then I believed it was all going to happen quick. I thought to have Davey back with me inside of a month or six weeks. But pretty soon the lawyer was singing me a different tune, delaying it all for this reason or that. He had a whole lot of different schemes in his mind, having to do with which judge, which social worker, which doctor might help us out the most. I got excited over everything he told me, in the beginning I did at least, but then nothing ever seemed to come of it at all. It turned off cold, the leaves came down, that poor little apple tree underneath my window was bare as a stick, and still nothing had happened.

You couldn't call it a real bad winter, there wasn't much snow or anything, but I was cold just about all the time, except when I was at work. The TOA was hot as a steam bath, especially back around the kitchen, and when I was there I'd sweat until I smelled. In the apartment, though, all I had was some electric baseboard heaters, and they cost too much for me to leave them running very long at a stretch. I'd keep it just warm enough I couldn't see my breath, and spend my time in a hot bathtub or under a big pile of blankets on the bed. Or else I would just be cold.

Outside wasn't all that much colder than in, and I spent a lot of time sitting there on that balcony, looking way out yonder toward the mountains. I got a pair of those gloves with the fingers out so I could keep on stuffing my envelopes while I was sitting out there. Day or night, it didn't matter, I was so familiar with it I could do it in the dark. I'd sit there sometimes for hours on end, counting the time by the trains that went by. Sound seemed to carry better in the cold, and I felt like I could hear every clack of the rails when a train was coming, and when they let the horn off it rang that whole valley like a bell.

But inside the apartment it was mostly dead quiet. I might hear the pipes moaning now and again and that was all. If the phone rang it would make me jump. Didn't seem like there was any TV or radio next door. The only sound coming out of there was Susan getting beat up once in a while. That was her name—a sweet name, I think. I found it out from hearing him say it, which he used to do almost every time before he started in on her. "Susan," he'd call out, loud enough I could just hear him through the wall. He'd do it a time or two, he might have been calling her to him, I don't know. After that would come a bad silence that reminded you of a snake being somewhere around. Then a few minutes' worth of hitting sounds and then the big slam as she hit the wall and the clatter of my pots falling down on the floor. He'd throw her at the wall maybe once or twice, usually when he was about to get through. By the time the pots had quit spinning on the floor it would be real quiet over there again, and the next time I saw Susan she'd be walking in that ginger way people have when they're hiding a hurt, and if I said hello to her she'd give a little jump and look away.

After a while I quit paying it much mind, it didn't feel any different to me than hearing the news. All their carrying on was not any more than one wall of the rut I had worked myself into, going back and forth from the job, cleaning that apartment till it hurt, calling up the lawyer about once a week to find out about the next postponement. I made a lot of those calls from the TOA, and Tim and Prissy got pretty interested in the whole business. I would tell them all about it, too. Sometimes, when our shift was done, Prissy and I would pour coffee and sit in a booth for as much as a couple of hours, just chewing that subject over and over, with Tim passing by now and again to chip in his opinion of what was going to happen. But nothing much ever did happen, and after a while I got to where I didn't want to discuss it anymore. I kept ahead making those calls but every one of them just wore down my hope a little more, like a drip of water wearing down a stone. And little by little I got in the habit of thinking that nothing really was going to change.

It was spring already by the time things finally did begin to move. That sad little apple tree was beginning to try and put out some leaves, and the weather was getting warmer every day, and I was starting to feel it inside me too, the way you do. That was when the lawyer called *me,* for a change, and told me he had some people lined up to see me at last.

Well, I was all ready for them to come visit, come see how I'd fixed up my house and all the rest of my business to get set for having Davey back with me again. But as it turned out, nobody seemed to feel like they were called on to make that trip. "I don't think that will be necessary," was what one of them said, I don't recall which. They both talked about the same, in voices that sounded like filling out forms.

So all I had to do was drive downtown a couple of times and see them in their offices. The child psychologist was the first and I doubt he kept me more than half an hour. I couldn't even tell the point of most of the questions he asked. My second trip I saw the social worker, who turned out to be a black lady once I got down there, though I never could have told it over the phone. Her voice sounded like it was coming out of the TV. She looked me in the eye while she was asking her questions, but I couldn't make out a thing about what she thought. It wasn't till afterward, when I was back in the apartment, that I understood she must have already had her mind made up.

That came to me in a sort of flash, while I was standing in the kitchen washing out a cup. Soon as I walked back in the door I'd seen my coffee mug left over from breakfast, and kicked myself for letting it sit out. I was giving it a hard scrub with a scouring pad when I realized it didn't matter anymore. I might just as well have dropped it on the floor and got what kick I could out of watching it smash, because it wasn't going to make any difference to anybody now. But all the same I rinsed it and set in the drainer, careful as if it might have been an eggshell. Then I stepped backward out of the kitchen and took a long look around that cold shabby place and thought it might be for the best that nobody was coming. How could I have expected it to fool anybody else when it wasn't even good enough to fool me? A lonesomeness came over me, I felt like I was floating all alone in the middle of the cold air, and then I began to remember some things I would just as soon have not.

No, I never did like to think about this part, but I have had to think about it time and again, with never a break for a long, long time, because I needed to get to understand it at least well enough to believe it never would ever happen anymore. And I had come to believe that, in the end. If I hadn't I never would have come back at all. I had found a way to trust myself again, though it took me a full two years to do it, and though of course it still didn't mean that anybody else would trust me.

What had happened was that Patrick went off on one of

his mystery trips and stayed gone a deal longer than usual. Two nights away, I was used to that, but on the third I did start to wonder. He normally would have called, at least, if he meant to be gone that long of a stretch. But I didn't hear a peep until about halfway through the fourth day. And it wasn't Patrick himself that called, but one of those public assistance lawyers from downtown.

Seemed like the night before Patrick had got himself stopped on the interstate loop down there. The troopers said he was driving like a blind man, and he was so messed up on whiskey and ludes I suppose he must have been pretty near blind. Well, maybe he would have just lost his license or something like that, only that the back seat of the car was loaded up with all he had lately stole out of the hospital.

So it was bad. It was so bad my mind just could not contain it, and every hour it seemed to get worse. I spent the next couple of days running back and forth between the jail and that lawyer, and I had to haul Davey along with me wherever I went. He was too little for school and I couldn't find any-body to take him right then, though all that running around made him awful cranky. Patrick was just grim, he would barely speak. He already knew for pretty well sure he'd be going to prison. The lawyer had told him there wasn't no use in getting a bondsman, he might just as well sit in there and start pulling his time. I don't know how much he really saved himself that way, though, since what they ended up giving him was twenty-five years.

That was when all my troubles found me, quick. The sec-ond day after Patrick got arrested, I came down real sick with something. I thought at first it was a bad cold or the flu. My nose kept running and I felt so wore out I couldn't hardly get up off the bed and yet at the same time I felt real restless, like all my nerves had been scraped raw. Well, I didn't really connect it up to the fact that I'd popped the last pill in the house about two days before. What was really the matter was me coming off that Dilaudid, but I didn't have any notion of that at the time.

I was laying there in the bed not able to get up, and about ready to jump right out of my skin at the same time, when Davey got the drawer underneath the stove open. Of course he was getting restless himself with everything that had been going on, and me not able to pay him much attention. All our pots and pans were down in that drawer then, and he began to take them out one at a time and throw them on the floor. It made a hell of a racket, and the shape I was in I started feeling like he must be doing it on purpose, to devil me. I called out to him and asked him to quit. Nice at first: "You stop that now, Davey. Momma don't feel good." But he kept right ahead. All he wanted was a little noticing, I know, but my mind wasn't working like it should. I knew I should get up and just go lead him away from there, but I couldn't seem to get myself to move. I had a picture of myself doing what I ought to do, but I just wasn't doing it. I was still laying there calling for him to quit and he was still banging those pots around, and before long I was screaming at him outright, and starting to cry at the same time. But he never stopped a minute. I guess I had scared him some already and he was just locked into doing it, or maybe he wanted to drown me out. Every time he flung a pot it felt like I was getting shot at. And the next thing I knew, I had got myself in the kitchen somehow and was snatching him up off the floor.

To this day I don't remember doing it, though I have tried and tried. I thought if I could call it back, then maybe I could root it out of myself and be rid of it for good. But all I ever knew was, one minute I was grabbing hold of him and the next he was laying on the far side of the room with his right leg folded up funny where it was broke, not even crying, just looking surprised. And I knew it had to be me that threw him over there because sure as hell is real, there was nobody else around that could have done it.

I drove him to the hospital myself. I laid him out straight on the front seat beside me and drove with one hand all the way so I could hold on to him with the other. He was real quiet and real brave the whole time, never cried the least bit, just kept a tight hold of my hand with his. I was crying a river myself, couldn't hardly see the road. It's a wonder we didn't crash, I suppose. Well, we got there and they ran him off somewhere to get his leg set and pretty soon this doctor came back out and asked me how it had happened.

It was the same hospital where Patrick had worked and I even knew that doctor a little bit. Not that being connected to Patrick would have done me a whole lot of good around there at that time. Still, I've often thought since that things might have come out better for me and Davey if I only could have lied to that man, but I was not up to telling a lie that anybody would be apt to believe. All I could do was start to scream and jabber like a crazy person, and it ended up I stayed in that hospital a good few days myself. They took me for a junkie and I guess I really was one too, though that was the first time I'd known it. And I never saw Davey again for a whole two years, not till the first time they let me go out to the Bakers'.

Sometimes you don't get but one mistake, if the one you pick is bad enough. Do as much as step in the road the wrong time without looking, and your life could be over with then and there. But during those two years I taught myself to believe that this mistake of mine could be wiped out, that if I struggled hard enough with myself and the world I could make it like it never had been.

Three weeks went by after I went to see that social worker, and I didn't have any idea what was happening, or if anything was. Didn't call anybody, I expect I was afraid to. Then one day the phone rang for me out there at the TOA. It was that lawyer and I could tell right off from the sound of his voice that I wasn't going to care for his news. Well, he told me all the evaluations had come in now, sure enough, and they weren't running in our favor. They weren't against *me* — he made sure to say that — it was more like they were *for* the Bakers. And his judgment was, it wouldn't pay me anything if we went on to court. It looked like the Bakers would get Davey for good, and they were likely to be easier about visitation if there wasn't any big tussle. But if I drug them into court, then we would have to start going back over that whole case history—

That was the word he used, *case history,* and it was around about there that I hung up. I went walking stiff-legged back across to the counter and just let myself sort of drop on a stool. Prissy had been covering the counter while I was on the phone and she came right over to me then.

"What is it?" she said. I guess she could tell it was something by the look on my face.

"I lost him," I said.

"Oh, hon, you know I'm so sorry," she said. She reached out for my hand but I snatched it back. I know she meant well but I was just not in the mood to be touched.

"There's no forgiveness," I said. I felt bitter about it. It had been a hard road for me to come as near forgiving myself as ever I could. And Davey forgave me, I really knew that, I could tell it in the way he behaved when we were together. And if us two could do it, I didn't feel like it ought to be anybody's business but ours. Tim walked up then and Prissy whispered something to him, and then he took a step nearer to me.

"I'm sorry," he told me.

"Not like I am," I said.

"Go ahead and take off the rest of your shift if you feel like it," he said. "I'll wait on these tables myself, need be."

"I don't know it would make any difference," I said.

"Better take it easy on yourself," he said. "No use in taking it so hard. You're just going to have to get used to it."

"Is that a fact," I said. And I lit myself a cigarette and turned my face away. We had been pretty busy, it was lunchtime, and the people were getting restless seeing us all bunched up there and not doing a whole lot about bringing them their food. Somebody called out something to Tim, I didn't hear too well what it was, but it set off one of his temper fits.

"Go on and get out of here if that's how you feel," he said. "You think you're the most important thing to us in here? Well, you're wrong." He was getting red in the face and waving his arms at the whole restaurant, including them all in what he was saying. "Go on and clear out of here, every last one of you, and we don't care if you never come back. We don't need your kind in here and never did. There's not a one of you couldn't stand to miss a meal anyhow. Take a look at yourselves, you're all fat as hogs . . ."

And he kept on, looked like he meant to go for the record. He had already said I could leave, so I hung up my apron and got my purse and I left. It was the first time he ever blew up at the customers that way, it had always been me or Prissy or one of the cooks. I never did find out what came of it all because I never went back to that place again.

I drove home in a poison mood. The brakes on the car were so bad by that time I had to pump like crazy to get the thing stopped, but I didn't really care all that much if I got killed or not. I kept thinking about what Tim had said about having to get used to it. It came to me that I was used to it already, I hadn't really been all that surprised. That's what I'd really been doing all those months, just gradually getting used to losing my child forever.

When I got back to the apartment I just fell in a chair and sat there staring across at the kitchen wall. It was in my mind to pack my traps and leave that place, but I hadn't yet figured out what place I would go to. I sat there a good while, I guess. The door was ajar from me not paying attention, it wasn't cold enough out to make any difference. If I turned my head that way I could see a slice of the parking lot. I saw Susan drive up and come limping toward the building with an armload of groceries. Because of the angle I couldn't see her go into their apartment but I heard the door open and shut, and after that it was quiet as the tomb. I kept on sitting there thinking about how used to everything I had got. There must have been God's plenty of other people too, I thought, who had got themselves accustomed to all kinds of things. Some were used to taking the pain and the rest were used to serving it up. About half the world was screaming in misery, and it wasn't anything but a habit.

When I started to hear the hitting sounds come through the wall, a smile came on my face like it was cut there with a knife. I'd been expecting it, you see, and the mood I was in I felt satisfied to see what I expected was going to happen. So I listened a little more carefully than I'd been inclined to do before. It was *hit hit hit* going along together with a groan and a hiss of the wind being knocked out of her. I had to strain pretty hard to hear that breathing part, and I could hear him grunt, too, when he got in a good one. There was about three minutes of that with some little breaks, and then a longer pause. When she hit that wall it was the hardest she had yet, I think. It brought all my pots down at one time, including that big iron skillet that was the only one I ever used.

It was the first time they'd ever managed to knock that skillet down, and I was so impressed I went over and stood looking down at it like I needed to make sure it was a real thing. I stared at that skillet so long it went out of focus and started looking more like a big black hole in the floor. That's when it dawned on me that this was one thing I didn't really have to keep on being used to.

It took three or four knocks before he came to the door, but that didn't worry me at all. I had faith, I knew he was going to come. I meant to stay right there until he did. When he came, he opened the door wide and stood there with his arms folded and his face all stiff with his secrets. It was fairly dark behind him, they had all the curtains drawn. I had that skillet held out in front of me in both my hands, like maybe I had come over to borrow a little hot grease or something. It was so heavy it kept wanting to dip down toward the floor like a water witch's rod. When I saw he wasn't expecting anything, I twisted the skillet back over my shoulder like baseball players do their bats, and I hit him bang across the face as hard as I knew how. He went down and out at the same time and fetched up on his back clear in the middle of the room.

Then I went in after him, with the skillet cocked and ready in case he made to get up. But he didn't look like there was a whole lot of fight left in him right then. He was awake, at least partly awake, but his nose was just spouting blood and it seemed like I'd knocked out a few of his teeth. I wish I could tell you I was sorry or glad, but I didn't feel much of anything, really, just that high lonesome whistle in the blood I used to get when I took that Dilaudid. Susan was sitting on the floor against the wall, leaning down on her knees and sniveling. Her eyes were red but she didn't have any bruises where they showed. He never did hit her on the face, that was the kind he was. There was a big crack coming down the wall behind her and I remember thinking it probably wouldn't be too much longer before it worked through to my side.

"I'm going to pack and drive over to Norfolk," I told her. I hadn't thought of it till I spoke but just then it came to me as the thing I would do. "You can ride along with me if you want to. With your looks you could make enough money serving drinks to the sailors to buy that Quik-Sak and blow it up."

She didn't say anything, just raised her head up and stared at me kind of bug-eyed. And after a minute I turned around and went out. It didn't take me any time at all to get ready. All I had was two boxes of kitchen stuff and a suitcase and another box of clothes. The sheets and blankets I just yanked off the bed and stuffed in the trunk in one big wad. I didn't care a damn about that furniture, I would have lit it on fire for a dare.

When I was done I stuck my head back into the other apartment. The door was still open like I had left it. What was she doing but kneeling down over that son of a bitch and trying to clean his face off with a washrag. I noticed he was making a funny sound when he breathed, and his nose was still bleeding pretty quick, so I thought maybe I had broke it. Well, I can't say that worried me much.

"Come on now if you're coming, girl," I said.

She looked up at me, not telling me one word, just giving me a stare out of those big cow eyes of hers like I was the one had been beating on her that whole winter through. And I saw then that they were both stuck in their groove and that she would not be the one to step out of it. So I pulled back out of the doorway and went on down the steps to my car.

I was speeding down the road to Norfolk, doing seventy, seventy-five. I'd have liked to go faster if the car had been up to it. It didn't matter to me that I didn't have any brakes. Anybody wanted to keep out of a wreck had better just keep the hell out of my way. I can't say I felt sorry for busting that guy, though I didn't enjoy the thought of it either. I just didn't know what difference it had made, and chances were it had made none at all. Kind of a funny thing, when you thought about it that way. It was the second time in my life I'd hurt somebody bad, and the other time I hadn't meant to do it at all. This time I'd known what I was doing for sure, but I still didn't know what I'd done.

FINDING NATASHA

"HEY, CAPTAIN," Stuart said. He'd seen the dog as soon as he turned the corner, stretched over the door sill of the bar in a wide amber beam of the afternoon sun. "Hey, babe, you still remember me?" He hesitated just outside the doorway in case the big German shepherd did not remember him after all. No doubt that Captain was a lot older now, shrunken into his bagging skin, the hair along the ridge of his back turning white. A yellow eye opened briefly on Stuart and then drowsed slowly back shut. Stuart took a long step over the dog and was inside the shadowy space of the bar.

He had expected Henry to be behind the counter and he felt a pulse of disappointment when he saw it was Arthur instead. On Saturday nights Arthur would often cover the bar while Henry and Isabel went out to dinner, but ordinarily they wouldn't have left so early, not at midafternoon. Stuart sat down at the outside corner of the bar. When Arthur got over to him Stuart could see he didn't remember who he was.

"Short beer," Stuart said, not especially wanting to get into it just yet. There were two people sitting at the far end of the counter, he couldn't quite make out their faces in the shadows, and nobody else in the place. He swiveled his stool back toward the door, and as his eyes adjusted to the dim he saw the new paint, new paneling. It had all been done over, the broken booths and tables all replaced, a new jukebox right where the pay phone used to be. The opposite wall was practically papered with portrait sketches of the Mets.

"Hey, what's going on?" Stuart said. Arthur had put down the glass of beer and picked up the dollar Stuart had laid on the bar. "Hey, you even got new glasses too? Henry and Isabel do all this work?"

"They retired," Arthur said, staring at Stuart like he knew he ought to recognize him now. "What, you haven't been around in a while, right? You move in Manhattan?"

"Farther than that," Stuart said. He pushed the beer glass a little away from him. A weird little bell-shaped thing, nothing like the straight tumblers Henry had used.

"Who would it be but Stuart?" said one of the men at the far end of the bar. Stuart peered back into the dim. "Give him a shot on me, Arthur."

"Clifton," Stuart said. Arthur was reaching behind him for a bottle of Jack. He'd remembered that much now, at least.

"Nah," Stuart said. "No thanks."

"What, you don't drink anymore either?" Clifton said.

"I drink," Stuart said. "It's a little early."

Clifton was on his feet, walking up into the light toward him now. He looked like he'd had little sleep and there was reddish stubble on his face. Stuart shifted to the edge of his stool and put one foot on the floor.

"You're back, hey?" Clifton said.

"Righto," Stuart said.

Clifton parted T-shirt from jeans to scratch at his shriveled belly.

"Miss your old friends?"

"Some of them," Stuart said. "Any of them still around?"

"Like the song goes," Clifton said. "They're all dead or in prison."

"Ah, but I see you're still here, though."

"Yeah. Partially."

"What about Ricky?"

"He's around, sometimes. Moved over to Greenpoint, though."

"And Rita?"

"I don't know, I heard she went to L.A."

"Thought I saw Tombo over around Tompkins Square . . ."

"Probably you did. He's still around there, as far as I know."

"What about Natasha, then?"

"Ah," Clifton said. "You know, I can't remember when I last saw Natasha."

"She still doing business with Uncle Bill, you think?"

"Uncle Bill got sick and died," Clifton said, and glanced up at the clock. "Speaking of which, I got to make a little run . . ."

"Yeah, well," Stuart said. "Great to see you and everything."

"Yeah," Clifton said. "What do you need?"

"Man," Stuart said, "you can't talk about that in Henry's place."

"You been away quite a while, babe," Clifton said. "It's not Henry's place anymore. So, you know. I can be back in a hour."

"Not to see me," Stuart said. "No more."

"Yeah? We'll see you," Clifton said. "Dig you later, babe." He stepped over the dog and went out through the bar of sunlight reddening in the doorway.

Stuart raised his hand and let it drop on the counter.

"They moved too?" he said. "They moved out of upstairs?"

"Yeah," Arthur said. "Out to Starrett City."

"Man," Stuart said. "Can't quite get used to it."

"The new guy opens the kitchen back up," Arthur said. "That should really make a difference."

"What now?" Stuart got up and went toward the back. A half partition had been raised in front of the area where Henry and Isabel used to have their own meals and now there were four small tables set up as for a restaurant.

Stuart turned back to Arthur. "Captain lets people go back in there now?" He walked back to his stool and sat. "Man, used to be if you just stepped over that line he was right there ready to take your leg off for you."

"I think he'll have to get over that," Arthur said. "He's old for all that anyhow." The dog heaved himself up from the door sill, walked back into the room and lay stiffly down again.

"Yeah, Captain, getting cold, you're right," Arthur said. Then to Stuart: "Want to shut that door?"

Stuart got up. It had been a mild fall day but now the air had a winter bite. He pushed the door shut and stayed for a minute, squinting through the window at the dropping sun, across the VFW decal on the pane.

"Can't believe they'd of left the dog here," he said, turning back toward the counter.

"Henry comes by to see him," Arthur said. "You couldn't take him out of this place, though. He would just die."

Upstate, the week before, it had turned cold early, and alongside the railroad track the river was choked with ice. Stuart had bought papers at the station, the *News*, the *Post*, but he couldn't seem to focus on the print. From the far shore of the Hudson, chilly brown bluffs frowned over at him, sliding back and back. The train ran so low on the east bank it seemed that one long step could carry him onto the surface of the river, though solid as the ice appeared it could hardly have held anybody's weight so early in the season. He stared through the smutty window of his car, the view infrequently broken up by a tree jolting by, or a building, or the long low sheds at the stations: New Hamburg, Beacon, Cold Spring. Opposite West Point the ice vanished and the river's surface turned steel smooth and gray.

If he'd been a fish, Stuart caught himself wondering, how

much farther down could he swim without dissolving? Chemicals warmed the water down here, as much and more than any freaks of weather. What fish would swim into that kind of trouble? He'd slept little the night before, his last night in Millbrook, so maybe that and too much coffee accounted for the jitters that worsened as Tarrytown and Yonkers fell back by, and rose toward actual nausea when the George Washington Bridge, almost a mirage downriver, floated into clearer view. If he'd been a fish he could breathe water, though the water here might kill or change him. He was headed into a hostile element, a diver for what pearl he couldn't say. The train dragged toward 125th Street like a weight pulling him under. The couple of years he'd been away were long enough he should have stayed forever. No point to come back now, so late, unless to recover something, what? The train dropped along the dark vector of the tunnel to Grand Central, and Stuart, like a hooded hawk, grew calm.

An hour or two and he'd remembered how to swim again, or glide. A thermal carried him up into a Times Square hotel, one of the kind where they did a take when he said he wanted the room all night, but by the week it turned out to be a bargain. Suspended in some other current, Stuart lazed back out onto the street and drifted, from a bar to a street-corner stand to one of the old needle parks to another bar, and so on. *Don't go where you used to go*, they'd told him at the center, *don't see those same old people or you'll fall*. No doubt that bigger, meaner fish still eyed him from their neighbor eddies, but he wasn't bleeding anymore, and a flick of tail or fin shot all of them away.

The weather was still bland down here, much milder than upstate, though it began to have its bitter aftertaste of cold. Stuart cruised up into the chill of the evening, watching whores and dealers check him over before they swirled away, always wondering if he might run into Natasha. He was not exactly looking yet, but developing a ghost of an intention. If he had asked himself *Why her?* he would have had no

answer. Just . . . Natasha. He had written her a time or two
from Millbrook, hadn't had anything back, not that he'd
expected it. Why Natasha? Others had been as close, or closer,
and he didn't want to look for them. He wasn't looking for
Natasha either. It had been spontaneous at first, this feeling
that she was about to appear.

Clifton had been wrong about Rita, Stuart eventually found
out. She wasn't in L.A. after all; she was in Bellevue getting
over hepatitis A. They made him take a shot of gamma glob-
ulin when he went in to see her, even though he tried to tell
them how long he'd been upstate. He also tried a joke about
needles, but the nurses didn't laugh. When Rita invited him
to sit down he had to tell her no.

"Funny, almost everybody seems to say that," Rita said.

Her smile was not particularly bright. She was on a big
ward, but curtains ran on tracks between the beds, and there
were a couple of chairs pulled up to her nightstand with
magazines piled on the seats. The whites of her eyes were
still a funny color and she was so thin that Stuart had trouble
telling what were the lines of her body and what were only
wrinkles in the sheet.

"Well, now," Stuart said. "You look good."

"Don't give me that," Rita said. "I look like I'm gonna
die."

"You're not," Stuart said.

"Not this time," Rita said.

Stuart groped for a commonplace.

"Clifton told me you went out west."

"No way," Rita said, patting the mattress with a bony
hand. "I been right here."

"When do you get out?" Stuart said.

"I don't know. Two weeks more, maybe. They don't want
to give me a date."

Rita's folding alarm clock ticked loudly across the next
patch of silence.

"You need anything?" Stuart said.

"Not that I can get."

"Well, let me know, okay?" Stuart pulled the curtain back and paused in the gap. "Hey. I been kind of trying to get hold of Natasha, you wouldn't know what she's been up to, would you?"

"I know she hasn't been up here," Rita said. "Not a whole lot else. Last I heard she was tricking for Uncle Bill."

"My God," Stuart said. "That sounds like a losing proposition."

"You know how it is," Rita said. "She's got a nice big nut to make every day."

"I guess," Stuart said. "Hey, but Clifton told me Uncle Bill was dead."

"Is that right," Rita said. "Clifton seems to be kind of full of bad information these days."

Bars and coffee shops, coffee shops and bars. Stuart circled the island from end to end of the old boundaries: the Marlin, McCarthy's, Three Roses, the Chinatown spots, anywhere she might have come in for any reason, rest her feet, get out of the weather, kill time waiting to score. Some places they remembered what he drank, but mostly not, and every now and then he'd meet somebody else who hadn't seen Natasha.

"Nah, man, she ain't been around *here*."

"Didn't I hear she went to Chicago? I can't think if it was her or somebody else. Memory slips a little on the fourth one . . ."

"Haven't seen her in about eight months. Maybe not since last summer . . ."

"Hey Stuart, what ever happened to that snippy little black-haired girl you used to hang around with?"

Wish I knew . . . On sleepless nights, he'd eat small-hour breakfasts at the Golden Corner or some place just about like it, hunched down behind a newspaper, eavesdropping on the booths around him full of hookers on break, waiting for the

voice or the name. By the time winter set hard in the city
he'd started on the false alarms, recognizing Natasha in just
about any middle-sized dark-haired white girl. It happened
more than once a night sometimes: he'd have to walk right
up to whoever he'd spotted and then at the last minute veer
away. He did that so many times that the hookers started
calling him Mr. No-Money Man.

Uncle Bill's place was up at 125th Street near the Chinese
restaurant, just past the train trestle. A black kid with his hair
done up in tight cornrows was waiting by the entry when
Stuart arrived, one leg cocked up on the railing, the loose
foot swinging to its limit like the pendulum of a clock. Stuart
stood sideways to keep one eye on him while he studied the
row of bells. The third one now said CHILDRESS instead of
B.B. like it should have, but he reached to ring it anyway.

"Man done gone," the black kid said.

Stuart turned all the way toward him. "What man is that?"

"Billbro, who else?"

"Know where he went?"

The kid spat over the railing. "You got a cigarette on you,
man?"

Stuart passed him a single Marlboro.

"He in the trench," the kid said. "There's a place just about
ten blocks up can fix what it is you need."

Stuart laughed briefly. "You think I'm the right color to
be going about ten blocks up from here?"

The kid grinned and blew some smoke. "Long's you go
with *me* you are."

"Thanks anyway," Stuart said. "It was a personal visit kind
of thing. What was this trench you were talking about?"

"Out on one of them islands, I forget." The kid's tennis
shoe, fat with thick lacing and white as new bones, beat
back and forth on the hinge of his knee. "You know, when
you die without no money, then they shove you in the
trench."

"Oh," Stuart said. "That trench. Do you get a box, at least?"

"I don't think so, bro," the kid said. "Maybe you might get a bag."

Up at Millbrook, Stuart's image of Natasha had been clear as a photograph tacked to the wall, but once he was back in the city it began to blur and fade and run together in a swamp of other faces: magazine covers, or actresses on posters outside the movies, and always and especially the dozens of near-misses that kept on slipping past him. Now her memory was less a face and figure than just a group of gestures, and these too began to dissipate and dissolve, until when he thought of Natasha he often thought of a painting he'd once seen by Manet: a full-length portrait of a woman in a gray dust coat down to her feet, one hand lightly extended toward . . . what? A bird cage? He couldn't even remember the painting all that well. The woman in the portrait was nothing like Natasha; she had a totally different face, was taller, heavier, had red hair. Yet the cool repose of her expression also managed to suggest that she was poised at the edge of something. Stuart began to doubt if he would recognize Natasha when he found her, and what if he'd already passed her by? He recognized people that *weren't* her frequently enough, that much was for sure.

Stuart was trying to outlast a drunk with a three A.M. break-fast at the Golden Corner when a hooker slid into the booth across from him.

"I been thinking about you, Mr. No-Money Man," she said. "I been thinking, if you ate a little bit less breakfast, you might have a little bit more money."

When she laughed, her eyes half disappeared into warm crinkles at their corners. Stuart saw she was a lot older than she wanted to appear, but not bad looking still, in a stringy kind of way. He sort of liked her face, under all the makeup.

She was wearing white lipstick and white eye shadow on skin the shade of tan kid leather. The wig she had on was a color no hair had ever been. "I bet you got fifty cent right now," she said. "Buy me a cup of coffee."

"Get the number ten breakfast if you want it," Stuart said. "Or anything else they got." He was in a slightly reckless condition and a lot of his concentration was being spent on keeping her from splitting into twos and fours.

"*Hell*, yes," she said, and shouted an order toward the counter. "I knew you had that money all along."

"Not that much," Stuart said, laying down his fork.

"Enough," she said, aiming a long fingernail at his nose. "Your trouble is, you think you can't find what you need. You know I seen you looking. Up and down and up and down—" She slapped the table. "You might not think it, but I can do it all myself, do it real well too."

"Breakfast only," Stuart said, and as if those were the magic words, an oblong plate of hash and eggs came skidding into the space between her elbows.

"I got it now," she said, biting into a triangle of damp toast. "You not looking for some*thing*. You looking for some*body*, right?"

"Yeah," Stuart said. "Right."

"Have to be a girlfriend."

"As a matter of fact, no," Stuart said. "Just somebody I used to know."

"What for, then?"

"I don't know," Stuart said. "I think I got survivor syndrome."

"Say what?"

"I feel responsible," Stuart said, hearing his words begin to slur. "For like . . . for everybody. Don't ask me why, but I always felt like she'd be the only one I could do anything about." He elbowed his plate out of the way and clasped his hands in front of him. "It's got to be like a long chain of people, see? I take hold of her and she takes hold of somebody else and finally somebody takes hold of you, maybe, and then if everybody holds on tight, we all get out of here."

The hooker shoveled in a large amount of hash and eggs with a few rapid movements and then looked back up. "Out of where?"

"Ah, I can't explain it," Stuart said, fumbling out a cigarette. "Whose idea was this, anyway?"

The hooker stared at him, not smiling so much now. "You be knee-walking drunk once you stand up, won't you?" she said after a while. "Man, where you coming from with this kind of talk?"

"Straight out of hell," Stuart said, trying to get his cigarette together with his match. "You familiar with the place?"

Over the winter he started going to the kung fu movies along Forty-second Street and around Times Square. It was a better time killer than drinking for him now; he'd tried getting drunk a few more times but he didn't much like where it took him. He went to the movies at night or sometimes in the afternoons, wearing a knit cap pulled down to his eye sockets so others couldn't tell much about him in the dark. It would take him a while, sometimes, to find a seat. Often whole sections had been ripped out, and also he liked to get one that put his back to a post or some other barrier. In the half light reflected back from the screen, the rest of the audience milled through clouds of dope smoke, dealing for sinsé or street ludes or dust, each cluster playing a different boom box, usually louder than the soundtrack. They only turned to the screen when there was fighting, but the fight scenes always got their whole attention, bringing screams of approval from every cranny of the huge decaying theaters.

Stuart, on the other hand, always watched all the way through, even the tedious love scenes. He was not very discriminating, could watch the same picture again and again, often staying so long he would have forgotten whether it was day or night by the time he returned to the street. The movies were all so similar that there was not much to choose between them, if you were going to bother to watch them at all. He observed that the theme of *return* was prevalent. What the returning person usually did was kill people, keeping it up until there was no one left or he was killed himself.

Twisted among the lumps and rickets of his moldy ricket of a bed, Stuart falls into a dream so deep and profoundly revealing that at every juncture of it he posts his waking self a message: you *must* remember this. The dream is room within room within room, each suppressing its breathless secret, and on every threshold, Stuart swears he will remember. Each revelation has sufficient power to make him almost weep. When he sits up suddenly awake, the message is still thinly wrapped around him, bound up in a single word, a name.

Clifton. Stuart stared at a gleaming crack in the gritty window pane, an arm's reach across the space between the bedstead and the wall. *Clifton*, that was nothing but nothing, and the dream was entirely gone. He flopped back over onto his side, eyes falling back shut, fingers begin to twitch and a shard of the dream returns to him. The self of his dream comes hurrying from a building and in passing glances at a peddler on the sidewalk, a concrete-colored man propping up a dismal scrap of a tree. Its branches are hung with little figurines carved in wood and stone, and Stuart, hastening on his way, takes in as a matter of course that each of them astonishingly lives, is animate, moving toward the others or away. In the dream he rushes past as though it were completely ordinary, but now he is transfixed by the gemlike movement of the tree, this nonsense miracle, a mere wonder outside the context of the dream, and uninterpretable. Stuart sat back up in the knot of his grimy blanket, muttering, *Clifton.* Surely, somewhere in all of this there must be something to extract.

Back in Brooklyn, Stuart checked in Henry's old bar to see if anyone knew where Clifton was living now and found that no one did. He tried the old place up on Broadway and the super sent him back around the corner to a half-renovated building between two shells on South Eighth Street. It was a sunny day, though cold, and even the well to the basement door was full of light. Stuart rolled his newspaper tighter in his right hand and rapped on the door with his left. It took five or ten minutes of off-and-on knocking before the door pulled back on the chain, then reclosed and opened all the way.

"You been a long time coming," Clifton said. Inside, the light that leaked down from the street level was thin and watery. Clifton shimmered vaguely as he yawned and stretched; it looked like he'd been caught asleep, though it was well past noon. There was something that smelled to Stuart a little like old blood. He followed Clifton into the room and kicked the door shut behind him with his heel.

"The worried man," Clifton said, bending away from Stuart to get a T-shirt from the bed. "Well, babe, you ready for me to make your troubles go away?"

"Can you?" Stuart said. "Clifton?"

When Clifton began to turn toward him, Stuart lashed at him with the rolled newspaper, and the heavy elbow of pipe he'd furled inside it knocked Clifton all the way over and sent him sliding into the rear wall.

"What in hell is the matter with you?" Clifton said. He sat up against the wall and stroked at the side of his mouth, his finger coming away red from a little cut. "Have you gone crazy or what?"

Stuart looked down at him, trying to feel something, anything, but could not. He thought for no reason of the trench, bags jumbled into it, barely covered with a damp film of dirt.

"Just curious," he said haltingly.

"Yeah, well, are you satisfied now?"

"Not really," Stuart said. The newspaper hung at the full length of his arm, pointed at the floor. "I was thinking I might beat your face out the back of your head, but I don't really feel like it now."

"That's real good, Stuart," Clifton said. "I'm glad you don't feel like it now. You don't maybe want to tell me why you felt like it a minute ago?"

"I don't know why," Stuart said. "What happened to Natasha?"

"Man, are you kidding me, man?" Clifton said. "I'm going to tell you the truth now, okay, *I don't freaking know.*"

Stuart took a step forward, hefting the newspaper. Clifton raised one hand more or less in front of his face and pushed up into a crouch with the other.

"Hey, I would tell you now if I knew, man," he said. "You got the edge on me, okay? Besides, what would I want to hide it for? I don't know any more than you do, man."

"Okay," Stuart said, and let the newspaper fall back to rest against his thigh. Clifton reached into the side of his mouth and took something out and looked at it.

"This is my tooth I got here, man," he said. "I cannot believe you did this over that dumb freaking chick."

"I had a dream," Stuart said, "but maybe this wasn't what it was supposed to be about."

Clifton pushed himself up off the floor and stood, pressing the T-shirt over the bleeding edge of his mouth. "Yeah, well, thanks for stopping by," he said, words a little slurred by the cloth. "Next time I see you I'm going to kill you, you do know that, I hope."

"No, you won't," Stuart said.

"Maybe, maybe not," Clifton said. "Don't turn your back."

Almost every day he bought a paper and almost every day he didn't read much of it. Sometimes he'd take a look at the want ads, but with barely focused attention, though the savings he'd been living on were about to empty out. Not long before he'd be Mr. No-Money Man for real, but mostly he'd just flip through the paper quickly and then roll it and carry it all day, till the front pages began to curl and tatter and the ink started to bleed off on his fingers. After a while the feel of the rolled newspapers stopped reminding him directly of Clifton and only made him uncomfortable in a dull way he couldn't identify.

There was always too much news about missing people, and too many of the ones that weren't missing were dead. Every time he heard about someone else missing he wondered how many just vanished without being missed. Every third person he passed on the street was probably missing from somewhere.

"Missing" was no more than a whitewash; a better word would be "gone." *Gone people*. Whenever Stuart looked at the faces on the milk cartons, he had a deep feeling the children were dead. He didn't own a picture of Natasha, but all the same he was convinced that if she'd died he would have known that too.

When it got warm enough to sit outside again Stuart sat in Tompkins Square with one more unread newspaper flattened on the bench beside him and watched Tombo coming across from the east side. He would have let him go on by, but Tombo saw him before he could get the paper up, came over and sat down.

"Long time," Tombo said. "I wasn't even sure you were still around."

"I'm here," Stuart said.

Tombo leaned back on the bench, shooting his long legs out before him. He had on a nice pair of gray pleated pants, expensive looking. None of it ever seemed to age or even touch him. He still had his dark and vaguely foreign prettiness, perfect skin, red pouty mouth, long eyelashes like a girl's. Stuart watched him blink his eyes and sniffle.

"Hey, you know Clifton's been talking you down a lot," Tombo said, shifting around in Stuart's direction. "He keeps on telling everybody he's gonna fix your business."

"Good," Stuart said. "If he's talking about it, then he won't do anything."

"You think?"

"Clifton's got a temper," Stuart said. "But he'll never let it take him all the way to jail."

"Maybe not," Tombo said. He snorted, pulled out a handkerchief and blew his nose. "Allergies, man," he said. "It always gets to me around this time of year."

"What are you giving me that line for?" Stuart said. "I'm not a cop."

"Right, I forgot," Tombo said, glancing over at him under his eyelashes. "You still clean?"

"Yeah," Stuart said.

"They do a pretty good job on you up at Millbrook, huh? It sticks?"

"So far," Stuart said. "One day at a time and all that kind of thing."

Tombo shifted around on the bench. "I'd been thinking maybe I might go up there sometime myself," he said.

"Well," Stuart said, "when you decide to go, then you'll go."

"People tell me you're looking for Natasha," Tombo said.

"Do they," Stuart said. "Everybody likes to talk to you about my business, seems. Why, you haven't seen her, have you?"

"Not in a year at least, nope. Sorry, bud . . . What are you looking for her for?"

"I quit looking for her," Stuart said. "You can't look for somebody around here, it's ridiculous. I'm just . . . I'm just waiting to find her, that's all."

"Interesting strategy," Tombo said, standing up. "Well, good luck."

With the improving weather, Stuart started making trips to Brooklyn, back to what had been Henry's place, though he didn't much like the feel of it, not after the remodeling. Why he kept going out there he didn't really know, maybe just for the inconvenience of it, for the journey. Clifton had stopped coming in, the new bartender was a stranger, there was seldom anyone he knew there except the dog. They still hadn't opened up the restaurant section. Sometimes Stuart's visit would coincide with Henry's, who tended to drop in most Thursday and Friday afternoons. He'd take Captain out around the block and then come back and sit at the bar, drinking white wine on ice from one of the old straight glasses they'd apparently saved just to serve him with. It pleased Stuart that this one little thing was still the same, and he felt happier in the place when Henry was in there too, though they didn't have much to say to each other past hello, and though the old man looked all wrong, sitting on the outside of the bar.

Whenever the weather was good enough he walked back across the bridge and caught the subway at Delancey Street on the Manhattan side. He was in a lot better shape than he'd been in the old days, but it was still enough of an effort that doing it fast set his heart slamming. That sense of an urge out in front of him was familiar, though now he wasn't going for a fix; the energy he set out ahead of him had become its own point. The walkway was a little more run-down than he remembered it. A lot of the tiles had come loose and blown away and now he could look through cracks in the steel plating and see all the way down to the place far below the roadway where the water slowly turned and moiled. But the rise of excitement was the same as it always had been as he pushed himself up to the crux of the span, where the howling of the traffic stopped being a scream and became a sigh. Arrived just there, with the afternoon barely past its daily crisis, he stopped and looked farther across at the tall buildings limned explosively with light, exultant, thinking, *This is what you always will forget, this is what you never can remember, this is what you have to be here for.*

It's not the first but the fifth or sixth day of spring when Stuart finally finds Natasha. All winter he's felt old and moribund, frozen half through, but now a new green shoot of youth begins to uncurl inside of him. It's a fresh and tingling day, the weather so very fine that it alone would be enough to make you fall in love. Everybody in Washington Square has bloomed into their summer clothes and they all look almost beautiful. Stuart walks around the rim of the fountain, hands in his pockets, a cigarette guttering at the corner of his mouth, smiling a little as the fair breeze ruffles his hair. he's headed straight for Natasha before he's even seen her, and then he does: she's tapped out there on one of the benches just at the bottom edge of the circle, head lolled back, mouth a little open, hands stretched palms up on her knees. When he gets a little closer, he can even see her eyes darting under the closed lids, looking at the things she's dreaming of. Man, she's way too thin, she's got bad-looking tracks, infected, and it's a fifty-fifty chance she's dying, but Stuart won't think about any of that right now, just keeps on walking, up into the moment he's believed in for so long.

For Wyn Cooper

DRAGON'S SEED

MACKIE LOUDON LIVED alone in a small house made of iron and stone on a short street west of Twenty-first Avenue. She had lived there, alone, for a long time. Old ivy grew in a carpet across her front steps and in her yard the grass was tall, with volunteer shoots of privet standing in it. The street was old enough to have a few big trees and the houses were raised on a high embankment above the sidewalk. It was quiet down the whole length of her block, almost always very, very quiet.

Indoors, it seemed that inertia ruled, though maybe that was just a first impression. The front room had once been a parlor, but now, scattered among the original furnishings were all of Mackie Loudon's sculpture tools. There were pole lamps, a rocker, a couple of armchairs, some fragile little end tables, also hammers and chisels and files and other devices, and a variety of sculptures in wood and stone. In former times people had come from the North to take the sculptures away and sell them, but it was a long time since their visits had stopped. She did not remember the reason or care about it, since she was not in want.

The things she didn't need to use stayed put exactly where they were. In the kitchen, on the gas stove, an iron skillet sat with browning shreds of egg still plastered to it, a relic of the very last time Mackie Loudon had bothered to make herself a hot meal. Asians had moved to a storefront within walking distance of her house, to open a store and cafeteria, and she went there to provender herself with things she never knew the names of. She bought salt plums, and packets of tiny dried fish whose eyes were bigger than their heads, and crocks of buried vegetables plugged with mud. She dumped the empty containers in the sink, and when it filled she bagged them up and carried the bag down a rickety outside staircase to a place in the alley from where it would eventually disappear. There was one pot that she used for coffee and that was all. On the window sill above the sink was an old teacup, its inside covered with a filigree of tiny tannin-colored cracks. Each morning, if the day was fair, a bar of sunlight would find a painted rose on its upper rim, warm it a moment, then pass on.

She wore flowered cotton dresses, knee length with no shape, and in winter a man's tweed overcoat. With the light behind her, her legs showed through the fabric. They were very slightly bowed, and her shoulders were rather big for a woman, her hands strong. She had a little trouble with arthritis, but not so much she couldn't work. Her features were flat, her skin strong and wrinkly like elephant hide. A few long white hairs flew away from her chin. The rest of her hair was thick and gray, and she hacked it off herself in a rough helmet shape and peered out from underneath its visor. Her right eye was green, her left pale blue and troubled by an unusual sort of tic. Over five or so minutes the eyelid would lower, imperceptibly and inexorably closing itself till it was fully shut, and then quite suddenly fly back open in a startled blue awakening. Because of this, some said that Mackie Loudon had the evil eye, and others thought she was a witch, which was not true, although she did hold colloquy with demons.

Before the fireplace in the parlor was a five-foot length of a big walnut log, out of which Mackie Loudon was carving a great head of Medusa. For a workstand she used a stone sculpture she'd forgotten, mostly a flat-topped limestone rock with an ill-defined head and arm of Sisyphus just visible underneath it. She stood on a rotting embroidered ottoman to reach the top of the section of wood, and took her chisels from the mantelpiece where they were lined. The front windows had not been washed in years and what light came through was weak and dingy, but she could see as much as she required to. Her chisels were ordered from New York and each was sharp enough to shave with. She didn't often need to use her mallets; wherever she touched her scoop to its surface the walnut curled away like butter. She carved, the strange eye opened and closed on its offbeat rhythm and the murmur and mutter of her demons soothed her like a song.

There were two of them, Eliel and Azazael. Each made occasional inconsistent protestations of being good, or evil. Often they quarreled, with each other or with her, and at other times they would cooperate in the interlocking way of opposites. Eliel reported himself to be the spirit of air and Azazael the spirit of darkness. Sometimes they would exchange these roles, or sometimes both would compete to occupy one or the other. They laid conflicting claims to powers of memory and magic, though Mackie Loudon could always point out that there was little enough in the real world they'd ever accomplished on their own.

Azazael was usually hostile to Medusa. *You don't know what you're getting into*, he said. *You're not sure yourself just what you're calling up, or why*.

"The one sure thing is you're a gloomy devil," Mackie Loudon said. But she said it with affection, being so much in control this morning that the demonic bickering was as pleasant to her as a choir. "You've always got the wrong idea," she said to Azazael. "You're my unnecessary demon." She moved the chisel and another pale peel of the outer wood came falling away from its dark core.

. . .

Mackie Loudon was headed home from a foraging expedition, her shoulders pulled down by the two plastic shopping bags that swung low from the end of her arms. Her head was lowered also and she scanned the pavement ahead of her for anything of interest that might be likely to appear. A couple of feet above the nape of her neck, Eliel and Azazael invisibly whirled around each other, swooping and darting like barn swallows at evening. They were having one of the witless arguments to which immaterial beings are prone, about whether or not it was really raining. It was plain enough to Mackie Loudon that it *was* raining, but not hard enough for her to bother stopping to take out the extra plastic bag she carried to tie around her head when it was raining hard. There were only a few fat raindrops splattering down, spaced far apart on the sidewalk.

She had almost come to the line of people shuffling into the matinee at the President Theater when she halted and sank to one knee to reach for a cloudy blue glass marble wedged in a triangular chip in the pavement. Just then there was some commotion in the movie crowd, and she looked up as a little black girl not more than five ran out into the street weeping and screaming, with a fat black woman chasing her and flogging her across the shoulders with a chain dog leash, or so Azazael began to maintain.

Did you see *that?* hissed Azazael, his voice turning sibilant as it lowered. On the street a car squealed to a sudden halt, blasted its horn once and then drove on. The line had re-formed itself and the tail of it dragged slowly into the theater's lobby.

See what? said Eliel. *None of* these *people look like they saw anything* . . .

They never see, said Azazael. *That's the way of the world, you know*.

Mackie Loudon grasped the marble with her thumb and forefinger and held it near her stable eye, but it had lost its luster. The cloud in it looked no longer like a whirlwind, but a cataract. She flipped the marble over the curb and watched it roll through a drain's grating.

Are you deaf and dumb and blind? Azazael was carping. *Don't you know what happens to children nowadays?*

"SHUT UP!!" Mackie Loudon cried as she arose and caught up her bags. "Both of you, now, you just *shut up*." On the other side of the street an ancient man who'd been dozing in a porch swing snapped his head up to stare at her.

In the bedroom was a low bed with a saggily soft mattress, and whenever Mackie Loudon retired she felt it pressing in on all the sides of her like clay. But if she woke in the middle of the night, she'd find herself sucked out through a rip in the sky, floating in an inky universal darkness, the stars immeasurably distant from herself and one another, and a long, long way below, the blue and green Earth reduced to the size of a teardrop. Somewhere down there her husband, son and a pair of grandchildren (that she knew of) continued to exist, and she felt wistful for them, or sometimes felt an even deeper pang.

You chose us, sang Eliel and Azazael. Out here, they always joined in a chorus. Out here, she sometimes thought she almost saw them, bright flickerings at the edges of her eyes. *And look, it's even more beautiful than you ever hoped it would be.*

"Yes, but it's lonely too," Mackie Loudon said.

You chose us, the demons droned, which was the truth, or near it.

Medusa wasn't going well; Azazael's objections were gaining ground, or somehow something else was wrong. Mackie Loudon couldn't quite make out what was the matter. She wandered away from the unfinished carving and her mind wandered with her, or sometimes strayed. As she passed along the dairy aisle at the A & P, small hands no bigger than insect limbs reached from the milk cartons to pluck at the hairs of her forearm. She wasn't sure just where or why but she suspected it had happened before, similar little tactile intimations grasping at her from brown paper sacks or withered posters stapled to the phone poles.

Oh, you remember, Azazael was teasing her. *You can remember any time you want.*

"No, I *can't*," Mackie Loudon said petulantly. Across the aisle, a matron gave her a curt look and pushed her cart along a little faster.

Never mind, Eliel said soothingly. *I'll remember for you. I'll keep it for you till you need it, that's all right.* And it was true that Eliel did remember everything and had forgiven Mackie Loudon for it long ago.

There was a boy standing in the alley when Mackie Loudon set her garbage down, just a little old boy with a brush of pale hair and slate-colored eyes and a small brown scab on his jaw line. He wore shorts and a T-shirt with holes and he stood still as a concrete jockey; only his eyes moved slightly, tracking her. Mackie Loudon straightened up and put her hands on her hips.

"Are you real?" she said to him.

The boy shifted his weight to his other leg. "Why wouldn't I be?" he said.

"Hmmph," Mackie Loudon said, and put her head to one side to change her angle on him.

"Lady, your yard sho is a mess," the boy said. "The front yard and the back yard both."

"You're too little to cut grass yet a while," she said. "Lawn-mower'd chew you up and spit you out."

"Who's that?" the boy said, and raised his arm to point at the house. Mackie Loudon's heart clutched up and she whipped around. It was a long time since anyone other than she had looked out of those windows. But all he was pointing at was a plaster bust she'd set on a sill and forgotten so well it was invisible to her now.

"Oh, that's just Paris," she said.

"Funny name," the boy said. "*Real* good-looking feller, though."

"He was a fool and don't you forget it," Mackie Loudon said in a sharper tone.

"Well, who was he, then?"

"Question is, who are *you*?"

"Gil mostly just calls me Monkey."

"That's not much name for a person," Mackie Loudon said. "What's your real name, boy?"

The child's face clouded over and he looked at the gravel between his feet.

"Won't tell, hey?" Mackie Loudon said. "All right, I'll just call you Preston. You answer to that?"

The boy raised his eyes back to her.

"All right, Preston, you drink milk?"

"Sometime, not all the time," Preston said.

"You eat cookies, I expect?"

"*All* the time," Preston said, and followed her up the steps into the house. She blew a small dried spider from a water-spotted glass and gave him milk and a lotus seed cake from a white waxed bag of them. Preston looked strangely at the cake's embossed and egg-white polished surface before he took a bite.

"What do you think?" Mackie Loudon said. She had poured an inch of cold coffee into her mug and was eating a lotus seed cake herself.

"I don't know, but it ain't a cookie," Preston said, and continued to eat.

"It's sweet, though, right? And just one will keep you on your feet all day. And do you know the secret?"

"Secret?"

"Got *thousand-year-old egg yolk* in it," Mackie Loudon said. "That's what puts the kick in it for you."

Preston bugged his eyes at her and slid down from his seat. He laid a trail of crumbs into the parlor, where she found him crouched on the desiccated carpet, lifting a corner of the sheet she used to veil Medusa.

"Oooooo, *snakes*," said Preston, delighted. Mackie Loudon pulled his hand away so that the sheet fell back.

"Let that alone, it's not done yet," she said. "It's got something wrong with it, I can't tell what."

Preston turned a circle in the middle of the room, pointing at heads on the mantel and the bookcases.

"Who's that?" he said. "And that? And that?"

"Just some folks I used to know," Mackie Loudon told him. "But didn't you want me to tell you about Paris?" When Preston nodded, she took a lump of plasticine from an end table drawer and gave it to him to occupy his hands, which otherwise seemed to wander. Half consciously, he kneaded the clay from one crude shape to another, and his eyes kept roving around the room, but she could tell that he was listening closely. She started with the judgment of Paris and went on and on and on. Preston came back the next morning, and within a couple of weeks she'd started them into the Trojan War. By first frost they were on their way with the *Odyssey*.

The demons kept silent while Preston was there, and were quieter than usual even after he'd left. Azazael did a little griping about how the boy was wasting her time, but he had nothing to say with any real bite to it. Eliel was rather withdrawn, since he was much occupied with the task of observing Gil through Mackie Loudon's eyes and storing up in memory all he saw.

Preston lived with Gil in a house right next to Mackie Loudon's. The paint was peeling off the clapboards in long curly strips, and on the front door was a red and blue decal of a skull cloven by a zigzag lightning bolt. The windows, painted shut for a decade, were blacked out day and night with dirty sheets, behind which strange bluish lights were sometimes seen to flash in one room or another. There was no woman living there, though every so often one would visit, and sometimes little gangs of other scroungy children would appear and remain for a day or several, though the only one there permanently was Preston.

Gil himself was tall and stooped, with thinning black hair and not much chin. He affected motorcycle garb, though it didn't suit him. He was thin as from some wasting disease, and the boots and black leather and studded arm bands hung slackly from him like the plumage of some mangy kind of buzzard. He drove a newly customized black van with its rear windows cut in the shape of card-deck spades. He never seemed to go out to work, but he dealt in prodigious quantities of mail, getting and sending rafts of big brown cartons. Mackie Loudon would have thought he trafficked in drugs or other, bulkier contraband if she cared to think about it at all, but all these notions had been assumed by Eliel ever since the first time Gil had come to her door to fetch Preston. "Come out, Monk," he'd said through the mail slot, his voice whiny and insinuating. "Time to come along with Gil . . ." And she and the demons had seen the thousand tiny gates behind Preston's lips and eyes slide shut.

Preston loved the *Iliad*, the *Odyssey*, he loved the story of Perseus and the Gorgon, though he flinched a little at Diana and Acteon, but he didn't want to hear one word of Jason and the Argonauts. Indeed, at the first mention of the name a wracking change came over him, as if he'd been . . . possessed. He paled, he shook, he formed a fist of sharp white knuckles and smashed the little plasticine figure Mackie Loudon had made to represent the hero. Then he was out the back door and running pell-mell down the alley..

Azazael was back in a flash. *What did I tell you?* he suggested. *There's something in this setup that is really, really queer.*

"Children take these fits sometimes," Mackie Loudon said, for Azazael's remark was only typical of the weak and cloudy innuendos he'd been uttering through that fall. She turned to

Eliel for confirmation, but for some reason Eliel didn't seem to be around.

Preston didn't come back for a week or more, but on the fifth day Gil came by to fetch him just the same. Mackie Loudon surprised herself by opening the door. Gil stood on the lower step, fidgeting with a dog's training collar, the links purling from hand to hand in a way that obscurely put her in mind of something disagreeable.

"The Monkey with you?" Gil said.

"That's no name for a human child," Mackie Loudon said. "And no, I hadn't seen him in a long time."

Gil nodded but didn't shift himself. He stretched the chain taut, its end rings strung on his middle fingers, then shut it between the palms of his hands.

"Didn't know you had a dog," Mackie Loudon said.

"Hee hee," said Gil. The front of his yellowing teeth was graven in black.

"Does that boy belong to you?"

Gil smiled again with his rotten teeth. "Yes, I believe you could say that," he said. "His skinny little butt is mine." He tossed the clump of chain and caught it with a jingle. "Old woman, I wouldn't suggest you meddle," he said, and turned to look back toward the street. "Nobody cares what goes on around here." He withdrew down the weedy walk, his feet slipping loosely in his outsize boots. Reluctantly, she followed him a little way, and when she stopped to look about her she saw that what he said was true. The houses on the block were held by knaves or madmen, or by no one. The lawns were dead, the trees were dying, a frigid wind blew garbage down the center of the street. From half the houses, broken windows overlooked her like sockets in a row of hollowed skulls.

On a cold blue morning Preston came to stand in the alley below the house again. For the first time Mackie Loudon noticed he didn't have a winter coat. She had to go and take his hand and lead him, to get him to come in. Though he seemed glad to see her, he wouldn't say a word. He sat in his usual wooden chair in the kitchen and stared at the pendulum swing of his feet.

"Cat got your tongue, has it?" Mackie Loudon said, and placed a yellow bean cake on the table near his hand. She went to the refrigerator for the milk she'd bought the day before, in some demonic premonition of his return, poured a glass and set it by him, took the carton back. In the light of the refrigerator's yellowed bulb she saw the faint blue photograph smeared on the carton's wall, and looked at it, and looked at Preston, and looked at the carton again. A line of blue letters crawled under the picture: *Jason Sturges of Birmingham, eight years old and missing since . . .* She shut the door and leaned on it and breathed before she turned to him.

"My God, boy," she said at last. "Do you know who you are?" And though the child didn't answer her, Eliel came back from wherever he'd been hiding and all at once returned to her the burden of her perception and her memory.

You blew it, Azazael snapped at her. *You bungled everything, like usual.*

Why couldn't you have just kept still a little longer? Eliel said. *God knows you stayed quiet long enough.* Mackie Loudon didn't answer them. She stalked from room to room, banging into the door jambs and the furniture. It was a long time since they'd been so angry with her, especially in concert, but she knew that they were justified. Preston, Jason, had bolted from the house the moment she'd asked that stupid question; she hadn't been quick enough to catch him. After that she'd called the police, called them once, called them twice —

That was pretty stupid too, Azazael said. *Everything considered, that might have been your worst move yet.* Mackie Loudon whirled on the parlor carpet and clawed one hand through the blank space where his voice came from. The Argonauts' little wooden ship crunched under her shoe; she booted its doomsaying figurehead into a corner. She went to her window and thumbed back a corner of the blind. Across the way, Gil's house hulked in the gathering twilight. It had taken the police all day and many calls to come — *All for nothing*, Eliel snapped. She had watched them come up to the porch and confer with Gil for a minute or two in the doorway and then leave.

"Goddamn," Mackie Loudon said, and let the blind fall back. She walked to the room's center and whipped the sheet off her Medusa. *What's the point?* said Azazael. She regarded the wooden expression of the broad blank face. The blunt heads of the snakes were blind because she'd never made their eyes. *No power there*, Eliel said sadly.

Mackie Loudon flung the chisel that had come into her hand; it stuck between Medusa's eyes and sagged. She was on Gil's board-sprung porch, pounding so heavily on the door that she almost fell forward when he snatched it from under her hand.

"The meddling old bat," Gil said contemplatively. "The *crazy* old bat, as the cops would say."

"Where's that boy?" Mackie Loudon said.

Gil raised one hand directly above the bald spot on his head and snapped his fingers once.

"Gone," he said. He made a plopping sound with his loose lips. "You understand, he just had to go."

"What did—"

"*Never you mind*," Gil said, and his face hardened. He stepped across the door sill and shoved her in the chest with the butt end of his palm. His arm was weak and reedy looking, but somehow it sent her staggering a long way back, down the porch steps into the littered yard. A slow fine drizzle sifted into her hair from the dark sky.

"I *told* you not to meddle," Gil said, and gave her another skinny little shove. "What good do you think it did anybody? The *police* say I should let them know if you *harass* me." He went on talking and pushing but Mackie Loudon wasn't really

listening anymore. She was wondering what had happened
to her strength. Her arms had always been powerful but now
she couldn't seem to lift them, she couldn't speak a single
word, and her legs seemed ready to give way and dump her
on the matted grass and mud.

"I'm telling you, old bat," Gil said. "You want to stop
messing in my business altogether." He gave her a two-
handed shove and she went over the edge of the embankment.
She tumbled down and cracked the back of her head on the
sidewalk, hard enough to jumble her vision briefly, though
it didn't knock her out. She lay with her left hand hanging
off the curbstone, knuckles down. The rain fell into the corners of her open eyes. The quarreling demonic voices spiraled
up and up away from her until they left her all alone in the
silence of a vacuum, empty even of a single thought. Two
or three people passed her by before anyone bothered to try
and pick her up.

"Oh Mackie, Mackie," Nurse Margaret said from the height
of her burnt-clay six foot two. Her hair was pinned back so
tight under the white cap that it seemed to pull her sorrowing
eyes even wider. "You last left here, you were talking so loud
and walking so proud, I hoped to never see you back." Under
Mackie Loudon's nose she shook two pills, one fire-engine
red, one robin's-egg blue, but Mackie Loudon would not
take her medication. She would not use her skills in craft
class. She would not go to therapy group, she would not
interact with anyone. She would not even speak a word. She
would not. She would not.

With the demons gone the interior silence was deep indeed
but Mackie Loudon was not aware of it. Human voices were
distant and as completely unintelligible as the noise of the
crickets in the grass. She let herself be herded from point to
point on the ward, moving like an exhumed corpse made to
simulate animation by a programmed sequence of electric

shocks. She sat on a sprung couch in the dayroom and moved no more than a ledge of rock. All on its own her left eye opened and shut its lizard lid. An orderly pushed a mop before her, up and down, up and down. Behind her was the slap of playing cards and a mumble of voices blended into the static that came from the untuned TV. The season's changes appeared on the shatter-proof glass of the front window as if projected on a screen.

"Mackie Lou! Mackie Lou!" She heard, but it had been a long time since she'd recognized her name or any variation on it. A bluish plume of flame flashed up toward the darkened ceiling and went out. She sat up suddenly and turned. Two beds away in the long row, Little Willa was springing up and down on her mattress. Normally they tied her in; how had she got loose? But everything that happened next was even more improbable.

"Mackie Lou! Watch me, watch me, Mackie Lou!" Little Willa stopped her simian bounce, squirted a stream of lighter fluid into her mouth and blew sharply across a match she'd struck. Another compact fireball rolled in midair toward the doorway, illuminating the trio of orderlies who came near to knocking one another down in their haste to pin Little Willa to the floor and stuff her arms into restraints and haul her kicking and shouting from the room.

"Watch me, Mackie Lou!" But the demonic voices drowned her out. Azazael and Eliel were back, furiously arguing over the implications of what they'd seen, yammering so fast she couldn't follow them. They jabbered at incomprehensible speed, but after an hour, when they'd come to some agreement, they slowed down and turned to her again.

We've got a notion for you, said Eliel. *We've thought of a way for you to solve your problem.*

Mackie Loudon gave her head a long sad shake against the pillow. "You're not even real," she said.

You know better, said Azazael.

"Well. But you can't *do* anything."

Maybe not, said Eliel. *But watch us show you how to do it.*

"All right," she said. "At least I'll hear you out." And she listened meekly and attentively until almost dawn. As usual she got up with the others, shuffled in a line of others to receive the breakfast tray. But once they'd been sent into the dayroom, she called for Nurse Margaret and asked for her pills and began one more of her miraculously swift recoveries.

It was spring when Mackie Loudon was released and the weeds were knee deep in her yard, but in the house nothing was much changed. She did a meager bit of dusting, then plucked the chisel from between Medusa's eyes, licked her thumb and moistened the wounded wood. After a long considering moment, she went to the bedroom and snatched a big mirror loose from the closet door and propped it on a parlor chair. The reflection reversed all her movements, making her tend to cut herself as she worked. It took her the rest of the day to get the hang of it, and she stayed up with it through the night, but by next morning it was done and she wasn't even tired yet.

She taped her cuts and made herself a breakfast of dried mushrooms and dried minnows, drank a pot of coffee, had a spoon or two of pickled vegetables. She found her bottle of linseed oil and gave the finished carving a light anointment, then covered it once more with the sheet. When she closed her eyes and concentrated she felt her strong pulse striking tiny hammer blows; she felt the Gorgon visage pushing out on her brow as if embossed upon a shield. With care, she brushed her hair down over her forehead and went out.

In the shed that faced the alley there was a lawnmower which, though rusted, looked as if it would probably run. She dragged it around to the front yard, then carried a gas can down to a filling station two blocks over and had it filled. At a neighboring hardware store she bought a three-foot crowbar, and came home with this awkwardly balanced load.

She was cutting the front lawn when Gil came out and did a double take.

"Well, if it ain't the old bat back," he said, shouting over the noise of the engine. Mackie Loudon gave him a cheerful wave and went on with her mowing. Cut ends of the tough privet stumps whirred around her head. Gil stared and shook his head and went down to his van. When its hind end had turned a corner, Mackie Loudon shut the mower off and went in her front door and out the back, collecting the crowbar on the way. One good jab and pry was good enough to break the flimsy lock on Gil's back door. She went in and softly shut the door behind her.

In Gil's front room a video camera watched her from the gloom, like an insect eye extended on a stalk. A light flick from the crowbar's tip shattered the lens into fine glass dust. She went through the whole house that way, smashing the cameras and enlargers, gouging out the works of the projectors and video decks with the hooked end of the crowbar. She didn't look at the tapes or the films, but she couldn't help seeing the big still prints, which showed children with children, children with grown-ups, children with assorted animals, a few children being tortured and killed.

They sowed bones, said Eliel, and Azazael answered, *They'll have their harvest*.

She didn't have long to wait for Gil, not much more than the time it took her to prepare. There was a two-gallon bucket under his sink, which she took empty to her house and brought back full. She dipped herself a ration in a mug and set it on a chair arm. Gil's key was turning in the lock; she stooped and hoisted the bucket. His eyes slid greasily around the wreck of his equipment, and he made a quick move toward her, but once she tossed the bucket on him he stopped, perplexed, and sniffed. She took the butane lighter from the patch pocket on her dress and with her other hand pulled back her hair to reveal the Gorgon. Gil's hands had just come up in supplication when he was turned to stone. She took a good swig from the mug and flicked the lighter's little wheel. A long bright tongue of fire stretched out and drew him wholly in.

It was a windless day and the house burned all alone, flames rising vertically into the cloudless blue sky. The firemen came, the police came, they blocked off either end of the street and soaked the roofs of the nearby houses, but there was nothing of the burning house to save. The people came out of the houses that were not yet abandoned and stood on the sidewalks with folded arms and grimly watched it burn. Mackie Loudon stood in her half-cut yard, leaning on the mower for support. Her other arm was tightly wrapped around herself, because in spite of the spring weather and the fire's harsh heat she was feeling very cold. She waited to be taken into custody, but no one seemed to notice her at all, and when the fire had fallen into its own embers, she went into her house and shut the door.

For Catherine Mims

II

/ / / / /

BARKING MAN

A GRACIOUS DAY of early spring began it. The weather was kind, soft, annealing, and the animals were powerfully aware of it. They felt it in their muscle and bone and it made them happy and active—the most cheerful animals Alf had ever seen inside a zoo. He moved from enclosure to enclosure, his books in a nylon backpack depending from a single strap that dragged down his left shoulder, and looked in. A pair of gorillas sat in lotus position on the lush green grass the winter rains had fed, combing each other's fur with their big rubbery fingers. A warm broad beam of sunshine lapped across them. Of a sudden they both heeled over to one side and rolled over and over, closed in an embrace at first, then separating. Then they sat up again and resumed the long luxurious strokes of their grooming.

Across a concrete moat the elephants were bathing, a baby elephant and an adult, perhaps the mother? The pool was generously large and deep, and when the elephants went in their hides turned from dusty brown to a slick slate gray. The baby elephant went under the roiled surface altogether and after a moment erected a few inches of his little trunk to breathe; he could have stayed submerged forever if he'd cared to. The mother elephant snorted and made a move to leave the pool, then turned and floundered in again, sinking to one side with a huffing sound, throwing up a gleaming sheet of water that curved and dropped to rejoin its own surface.

The lions were sluggish, having just eaten, and yet they seemed quite content, lacking the air of morose and silent desperation that most zoo lions exuded. They resembled the lions one saw in films of Africa, resting on the veldt after a kill and gorge. Adjacent, the tigers basked in the sun, fully stretched on their mappined terraces, each apparently content as a housecat on a window sill. Only one of the big males moved, with a kind of mechanical restlessness, loping back and forth on a track of his own devising, his yellow eyes hot and even a little crazed. He'd conceived some smaller circle inside his actual containment, and whenever he reached its limit he reversed his limber steps, conforming to a barrier which no one but himself could see.

The bottom of the zoo was bordered by an iron rail fence a little better than waist high, beyond which expanded the wide greensward of Regent's Park. On an impulse Alf climbed over this fence instead of going out by the South Gate. It was easily low enough for a vault, but his backpack dragged him slightly off balance, and a rail's tip caught his trousers on the inner thigh and made a neat right-angular tear. Alf stooped over to examine it and straightened up again. Big Brother would not be pleased, but possibly he wouldn't ever know about it. Possibly Hazel could mend it so it wouldn't show. He hitched up the pack and stepped out across the grass. A cool triangle lay on the inside of his leg where the cloth was torn. On to the south, farther than he could see or hear, well past the flowers of Queen Mary's Garden, he knew the traffic on Marylebone Road would be whisking back and forth like the multiple blades of some gigantic meat slicer. He stopped, turned in his traces and looked back.

Later, after a long time and much catastrophe, when Alf had passed into the care of others, he began to feel relaxed and calm. He looked at a dark spot on the wall, and his eyelids grew heavier and heavier; they grew so leaden that he could scarcely keep them open. His eyes were closed. His eyes were closed now, his breath was deep and slow. His limbs were warm and soft and tingling, his arms so heavy that he could not lift or move them. It was utterly beyond his power to open his eyes or move his arms or legs. His heartbeat slowed to requiem time. He descended a set of thirty steps into a dark place of warm and total relaxation. Asked to recollect the source of his affliction, he began to talk about the zoo, easily continuing the story of that afternoon up to the point where he had hesitated on the lawn.

"Yesssss . . ." The resonant voice of the hypnotist came from very far above, high in the mouth of the deep well into which Alf had lowered himself. "Yes. That is very good. You are a *good* subject. You are doing *very* well. What did you think about the animals?"

Responding to some foreign motive power, Alf's hands began to twist and gnarl, his fingers twining into tangles on his lap. His breath came fast, and he could feel his features screwing up like the face of a child about to cry. Real tears were pricking the backs of his locked eyelids, though he did not know why.

"I envied them," he said at last. "I wanted to go back."

Breakfast was transpiring in the flat's large airy kitchen. Big Brother was eating a soft-boiled egg with annihilating concentration. *Tap, tap, tap* went the edge of his spoon around the little end of his egg, creating a perfectly even fault line. He removed the eggshell dome and placed it on the left side of his plate, penetrated the egg white, lifted a portion and inserted it between his lips. His wrist revolved and the wristwatch on its sharkskin band presented itself briefly to his eye.

Alf choked on a bite of the scone he'd been consuming, coughed, belatedly covered his mouth with his hand and cleared his throat behind it. Big Brother lowered the spoon from his second bite of egg and raised his fishy eyes from the eggcup. The spoon's bowl connected to the plate with a minute click. For a suspended silent moment he faced Alf down the long checked range of the blue oilcloth.

"You eat like a yobbo off the street," he said at length. "Choice of diet and manners too. Inclusively."

Alf's gaze broke and fell to the crumbles of scone on his plate. Once more Big Brother began to ply his spoon. He had three bites remaining; it *invariably* took him five to eat an egg. Hazel, sitting half the table's length between them, turned and shot Alf a surreptitious wink, which he returned as he reached over for the butter. Big Brother finished his strong black coffee in two tidy sips and arose from his place.

"Goodbye, Love," he said. "I expect to be in by seven."

Hazel set her hands on her tight waist and arched back in her chair, lifting her face up toward him. The heavy blond braid of her hair hung down over the chair back like a plumb weight.

"Goodbye, Love," Hazel said. "There'll be fish for dinner. I'll see you in the evening."

Big Brother nodded to her and passed in the direction of the hallway.

"Big-big Bang," Alf said suddenly. "Pow, knock'm dead, Bee Bee."

Big Brother gave him an eerie look but continued his course without pause. There was a whetting sound as he lifted his sharkskin briefcase from the hall stand, then the tumbling of the door's many locks. Hazel stood up and curved her torso in Alf's direction. The morning sunshine rushed in through the kitchen's south windows to lighten the green of her eyes.

"More tea?" she said, and stroked the rounded belly of the teapot.

"No thanks, well yes, ah, I guess I will." Alf pushed his cup in the direction of the spout.

"Don't let me make you late for school," said Hazel. "What is it you have Tuesday mornings?"

"Supercalifragilisticmacroeconomics," Alf said.

Hazel threw back her head and laughed a laugh that reminded him of someone pouring a delicious drink.

In the usual London style the sunshine failed him as soon as he hit the street. Underneath the damp gray sky he walked a block across Fulham Road and turned. His shoulder sagged under the strap of the weighty bookbag. It had given him a seemingly permanent crick in his neck. He circumambulated the South Kensington tube stop, watching the rush of people in and out from the far side of the street. There was no reason for him to enter, nowhere he urgently had to go. He had actually succeeded in forgetting in which quarter of the city the London School of Economics was to be found, and indeed was rather proud of this feat.

A few raindrops patted up and down the sidewalk; Alf sniffed and squinted at the sky. A six-month sequence of dissembling had taxed his talent for killing time. His budget did not allow him long periods in cinemas or pubs, and he had dawdled through every museum in the city at least a dozen times. Spring should have opened up more outdoor distractions, but the difference in the weather appeared most days to be only a few degrees of temperature. Give him another good day at the zoo for choice, but it was a long way, and he doubted he'd enjoy it in the rain.

He took the umbrella from his pack and shot it up and turned south in the direction of the King's Road. He shambled from one shop to the next, standing before the various clothes racks, revolving his few blunt pound coins in his pocket. Alf's interest in clothes was nil, but clothes stores did have doors and roofs. Whenever he felt an attendant's eye upon him, he departed and moved on to the next shop. When the pubs opened he went into one and had a pork pie and a half of Courage. Yobbo's lunch. The other yobs, punks and skinheads that frequented the area jostled him up and down the counter, somehow always managing to show him only their backs.

By the time he left the pub the rain had stopped, though the sky remained dull. He walked to Saint Luke's and sat on a bench in the church garden, trying to remember his ostensible school schedule. As always, the flowers were immaculate in every elaborate bed. The gardeners had timed the bulbs so that every few weeks the color scheme underwent a magical change. Alf slouched lower on the bench, pushing his pack away from him. He would have preferred to return to the flat, but he wasn't sure if that would be plausible.

A woman in a beige suit came clipping down the walk, one of those London women who, though on close examination were clearly in their twenties, contrived to convey by their dress and demeanor the impression of being nearer forty-five. A small brown terrier was leading her along at the end of a white leash. Halfway down the walk she stooped and slipped the catch from the collar, then sat down on a bench and watched the little dog run free, sniffing along the line of displaced tombstones propped against the churchyard's western fence.

The woman took a compact from her bulky handbag and began to examine herself in its mirror, her lips pursed uncomfortably tight. She had a weak chin, but a powerful nose to compensate. The terrier turned from the fence and locked its nose to some trace of scent and began to execute geometric figures around the bench where Alf was slouched.

"The little dog laughed to see such sport," Alf suggested. "And the dish ran away with the spoon." The terrier stopped and looked skeptically up at him.

"Please do not permit your dog to foul the amenity area," Alf intoned, quoting loosely from the several green placards planted here and there on the lawn. The terrier sat back on its haunches and let out a little yip.

"—oof," Alf replied, falsetto.

"riffrirf," the terrier said, jumping up and smiling.

"aarffooorffurfurfiiiii!" said Alf, somewhat louder. Across the walk the woman snapped her compact shut with a cross click and stood up, shaking the leash.

At the head of the stairs of the maisonette flat, Hazel and Big Brother had their bedroom, and next to it Big Brother occupied what Hazel optimistically referred to as his study. In fact, it was a sort of electronic cockpit, packed with computers, printers, monitors, fax machines and modems hooked up to New York and Japan. Here, after nourishing himself from his exertions in the City, Big Brother would repair to continue trying to figure out every conceivable ramification of Big Bang for a good part of each night. From the windows of both of these rooms could be seen the Natural History Museum, the domes of the V & A, the Queen's Tower and other features of the skyline, though Alf doubted if Big Brother ever raised his eyes to them.

His own room was at the other end of a longish hall, right beside the bathroom, a location which admitted him to privacies of which he might have preferred to remain ignorant. As the spring continued, Alf spent much of his *out of class* time seated at the small desk before the windows, staring out across the binding of some textbook at the children playing in the trapezoidal courtyard of the council houses below. After the evening meal he'd most often retreat to this same position, staring inattentively at his own faint reflection in the darkened window panes.

"All's well, Love?" Hazel's voice came from down the hall; she must have opened the door to look in on Big Brother, for Alf could also hear that munching sound the computers liked to make as they gobbled information. He couldn't hear the Beeb's reply, if he made any, only a drop in the hum of the machines as the door closed. He propped his elbows on the pages of his book and shut his eyes to dream of Spain. For several weeks he'd been considering that he might claim a holiday after his *long year of study*, and though he didn't speak the language the excursion fares to Spain were cheap.

Hazel was coming down the hall, though he wasn't sure just how he knew it. Her bare feet made no sound on the carpet runner; it was more like a small breeze passing by. There came some groans and gurgles from the bathroom pipes, then her reflection appeared in Alf's window pane, framed by his open doorway.

"Still hitting the books this late at night?"

Alf flipped the pristine textbook shut and swiveled in his chair. The lights flickered and dimmed for an instant as the computers engorged some great mass of news. Hazel had let down her hair—it descended in a warm current parted by the oval of her face, rejoining on the rise of her bosom, where one hand smoothed it absently against her nightgown's cotton weave.

"The two of you," she said, smiling. "Seems like you never stop."

"Ah," Alf said, and stopped with his mouth open. Conscious of this, he shaped the opening into a sort of smile and began to scrape his fingers across his scalp.

"Hmm, well, *I'm* going to bed," Hazel said, and shook her head to toss her hair back onto her shoulder blades. "Sweet dreams, Alfie . . ." She pushed herself out of the doorway and swung his door half shut.

Alf turned back to face the window, pulled his hand loose from his head and looked down at it. His fingers were wrapped with stiff black hairs, indubitably his own. He lifted his forelock and leaned toward the window to examine his hairline. No doubt that it really was receding. A short harsh sound came out of him, something like a cough.

Hazel was leaning over the small gas stove top, rolling *kofta* meatballs and dropping them to sizzle in a pan of oil. She turned suddenly to reach for something and collided with Alf, who'd been peeping over her shoulder.

"Good Lord, you're always *right* behind me," Hazel said. Her face was pink and humid from the burners on the stove.

She made a shooing motion and Alf retreated, slinking along the edge of the table, which was laden with trays of tiny salmon and caviar sandwiches for the cocktail party that evening. He sniffed and cleared his throat with a rasping sound, then picked up a tray and started down the long hall with it toward the living room.

"Where do you think you're going with that?" Hazel called after him. "Just bring it back, it's way too soon, they won't be here for *hours*."

Alf reversed his steps and put the tray back where he'd found it. He began to turn an uneasy circle between the table and the stove.

"Well, I'm sorry," Hazel said. "Well, you're just under-foot, that's all. Haven't you got a class to go to? Then just go out and get some air, go on now, scat!" The kitchen steamed and she steamed with it; she had sweated nearly through her blouse. She smiled at him gaily through the vapors, and flapped her hands to send him away.

He walked up Exhibition Road to its end, went into Hyde Park and continued as far as the lower end of the Serpentine. Two men were fishing where he paused, their long poles leveled over the dank surface of the water. The concrete bank was littered with goose down and slimy green goose drop-pings. An unpleasant idea came to Alf completely of its own accord. Many years before when he was small and they still lived on the farm outside Cedar Rapids, he and his older brother had taken the BB gun to the little pond and whiled away an afternoon shooting toads. When he remembered the *phttt* sound the BBs made going through toad bellies, two voices separated in his mind.

It was Tom's idea, he was the oldest, claimed the first, and the second answered, *No no, Alfie, it was* you, *it was your idea from the beginning. If not for you it never would have happened* . . . The thing was that it didn't actually kill the toads, at least not right away, just left them drearily flopping around with drooling puncture wounds through their slack stomachs.

"RURRRRFFAAARRRH," Alf cried, and discovered the

subject had been instantly wiped from his mind. One of the fishermen looked up at him sharply, then away.

Alf couldn't get his bow tie right and finally decided to leave it with one end bigger than the other. Leaning into the mirror, he pulled the loose skin of his cheeks down into bloodhound jowls, then let it snap back with a wet smack. He passed a hand across his head, wiped the loose hairs on the edge of the sink and went downstairs to survey the situation.

An assortment of pinstriped Big Bangers and a smaller number of their fretful wives were circulating through the two front rooms. Big Brother, sharkskin Fileofax in hand, appeared to be rearranging his appointments. A somewhat scurvy-looking gent, Hazel's water-color teacher, stood alone, snapping salmon sandwiches into his mouth, glancing around after each gulp to see if anyone was observing him. Hazel stood with a gay hairdresser called Neddy who'd befriended her at the painting class. Alf ate a caviar and cracker and began to eddy up toward their conversation. She wore some sort of pseudo-Victorian velvet dress, fastened with a thousand tiny buttons down the back. Though it conformed to no current fashion it made the most of her bee shape; the swell of her rear and the arch of her back even suggested a bustle. Alf drifted in a little nearer. Hazel's hair was scooped up into a smooth blond orb, exposing the fine down on the back of her neck.

". . . then a body perm, and Bob's your uncle," he overheard Neddy saying. "Just whip a comb through it in the morning and you're off!"

Hazel plucked at her lower lip with a finger. "It does take a lot of time to look after . . . ," she said musingly.

Alf felt some rough obstruction rising in his throat.

"But after all," said Hazel, half turning to include him in the subject, "what else have I really got to do?"

A steely clasp shut on Alf's upper arm and he felt himself inexorably drawn away.

"Mr. Thracewell, my brother Alfred," Big Brother said. "Alf, fetch Mr. Thracewell a gin and French." He passed Alf an empty glass and leaned to whisper in his ear, "Jesus *Christ*, your tie's not straight."

As Alf receded into the hallway, he thought he heard the murmured invocation *London School of Economics,* and he swallowed against that plaguey roughness in his gullet. The kitchen was empty and he snatched up the gin bottle, carried it into the pantry and shut the door after him. With the bottle upended over his jaws, he squinted up at its butt end until he saw four bubbles rise, then lowered it and gasped. Gin and French? He sniffed the glass the Beeb had given him, but the scent was unenlightening. He fixed a gin and tonic with a lot of ice and headed back toward the front of the flat. En route he toppled a tower of bowler hats from the hall stand, made an abortive move to gather them, then decided to let them lie. Deep in conversation with Big Brother, Thracewell took the drink unconsciously and tasted it without looking. Alf watched his mouth shrivel to the surface of the glass, and at that very instant the vast bubble of gin he'd swallowed burst inside him with a soft explosion.

"*iirrrfffooorrrffffaaarrrROOOOORF OOOO OOOO!!!*" he howled. All around the room he could hear vertebrae popping with the speed of the turning heads.

"Your *younger* brother this is, you say?" Mr. Thracewell murmured. "My word, a most original chap."

The Spanish holiday did not materialize and now that school was out Alf was at looser ends than ever. Though the weather had turned generally fine, he tended to loiter around the flat, tracking Hazel from room to room till she was inspired to invent some errand for him. He went down Elystan Street to the newsagent on the little square and joined the queue of all the old ladies of Chelsea, each waiting patiently for a lovely chat with the brick-faced woman behind the postal grille at the rear. Often he came here to buy stamps for Hazel. The fat lady behind the candy counter glowered at Alf and only Alf, who was a foot taller and forty years younger than anyone else present, the only man and, to be sure, the only foreigner. He shifted nervously from leg to leg, trying not to think of how soon Big Brother was likely to discover that he had set foot in the London School of Economics only once or twice ten months before. The tiny lady immediately ahead of him, ancient and brittle as a bit of dry-rotted antique lace, had with the help of a complicated-looking walker made her way up to the grille. She conducted some sort of savings transaction and asked for a television stamp. Television stamp? Alf rocked forward and peered to see what that might be.

"What do you *mean?*" the brick-faced woman hissed. "Turn round, you. Turn *right* round. I shan't go on till you turn right round."

Alf unfroze himself and turned around and stood staring out over the heads of the others behind him, into the blinding square of sunlight at the door. When permission was given to approach, he made his purchase wordlessly, fumbling the change with his slightly trembling fingers, and went out. Halfway back up Elystan Street the enlargement of his throat surpassed containment.

"wurf! Wurf! WurrrfffaaarrrhhOOORRRHHHrrrr," he barked. A bobby looked at him sternly from the opposite side of the street. With an additional swallowed snarl tightly wrapped around his tonsils, Alf averted his eyes and went resolutely on.

Hazel seemed to grow a little restless too; she swept more and more activities into her schedule, adding to the watercolor sessions a class in yoga and another in French conversation. Her shopping expeditions moved farther afield; she undertook riverboat trips and excursions to outlying villages. Alone in the flat, Alf turned the television on and off, flipped through books and magazines and furtively prowled from room to room; the areas he found the most attractive were those where he had no good reason to be. A time or two he breached the sanctity of Big Brother's electronic office, tiptoeing in and standing on the little throw rug before the desk. All around him on their long shelves the machines blinked and flickered, pooped and wheeped, and every so often they spontaneously crunched out some document. Alf could not rid himself of the superstitious fear that somehow they were recording his own activity to report to Big Brother on his return.

In the bedroom, Hazel and Big Brother's bedroom, there was an indefinable smell of lilac, a natural scent as from dried petals, though Alf could find no bowl of potpourri. Atop the bureau was a wedding picture in a silver frame. Big Brother's long neck was loose in the high stock of his tuxedo; he looked a little frightened, perhaps startled by the flash, but Hazel wore an easy, merry smile, and looked straight out of the frame at Alf, who set the picture down. He opened a drawer at random and discovered Big Brother's starched white shirts laid out in rigid rows. Another held a tangled nest of Hazel's jewelry.

The bed was a platform on short legs, low and broad, with two unremarkable nightstands on either side of it. On Hazel's was a ragged copy of *Time Out*. Big Brother's was bare except for the coaster where he set his water glass at night. The bed was spread with a quilted eiderdown, emerald green, with feather pillows mounded on it at the headboard. When Alf leaned down and touched the surface of the quilt, his fingers somehow would not come away. He was drawn farther, farther down, his shoulder tucking as he dropped. He curled up on his side and dreamed.

"I don't know why," he said. "I just don't know." His arms were pasted to the leather arms of the deep dark chair, his head lolled, his eyeballs spiraled behind their lids.

"You know," the hypnotist murmured softly. "Oh yes, you know very well."

"I didn't *want* to know," said Alf. "What would have been the use of that?"

"Knowledge is power," the hypnotist suggested.

A galvanic shudder emerged from the reaches of Alf's autonomic nervous system and shook him to his finger ends.

"No it's not," he said loudly. "Not when you know everything and can't change any of it."

No matter how deep his daydreams took him, Alf remained alive to the sound of Hazel's key entering the downstairs lock. He'd roll from the eiderdown, land on his hands and knees and scamper out, coming erect again some distance down the hallway toward his own bedroom. Until the day some deeper sleep overtook him and he woke to find Hazel standing in the doorway, looking down. She wore her loose black sweatsuit, her face was patchily flushed from yoga, and a forefinger pulled down her plump red lower lip in her familiar gesture of perplexity.

"oooOORF!" barked Alf in sheer alarm. He flipped from the bed onto all fours and barked again, "urrrrrffffff-OOOHRRRFF *RRAAAARRFFFF!*"

Hazel's eyes lit up, she swirled in the doorway and ran down the hall. Alf pursued her as quickly as he could on his knees and elbows, barking happy ringing barks. She ran a little awkwardly, her loose hair flagging out behind her, looking back over her shoulder in mock fright. He chased her around his room, back down the hall and down the stairs and up again, yapping hysterically at her heels. Hazel fled back into her bedroom, dove onto the bed and rolled onto her back, shuddering with wave upon wave of laughter. Her knees drew up toward her stomach, her sweatshirt rode up to the bottoms of her breasts, her head thrashed back and forth on the wide silky spread of her hair. Too breathless to bark anymore at all, Alf put his forepaws on the quilt between her feet and raised himself to look at her. She was warm with a radiant heat, an intoxicating scent poured out of her, she was rich with her own beauty (he put his hind paws on the bed and bunched himself for his next move)—she was *his brother's wife*.

Hazel turned stone pale and sat up quickly on the edge of the bed. She clapped her knees together, wrapped her arms around herself, bit down on her lip till it went white, and began to shake all over. Alf got up too and stood with his hands hanging, dead little lumps against his thighs. After a moment he picked up her hairbrush from the bureau, turned her slightly with the least touch on her shoulder and started to brush her hair. Supporting the whole sweep of it over his left forearm, he brushed it out till every auburn highlight gleamed beyond perfection. After a few minutes her back loosened and her breath began to ease and deepen.

"Thank you, Alf," she said. "Thank you, that feels good. That was very nice. You can stop now, please."

Alf walked away and set down the brush, turned and propped himself on the bureau's edge. Hazel gathered her hair in one hand and drew it forward over her shoulder. She put an end of it into her mouth and wet it into a point, then took it out and stared at it round-eyed.

"I'm thinking of getting all this cut off," she said.

"Don't do it," said Alf. "What for?"

"It's a lot of trouble to take care of."

"It took you twenty years to grow it."

"Neddy said he'd style it for me free, said he'd come to the house and do it."

"What, that slimy little shrimp? Don't you let him touch your hair."

"*He'd* like it if I looked a little more contemporary," Hazel said, jerking her head toward Big Brother's nightstand.

"Don't do it," Alf said as he walked out of the room. "You'll be sorry if you do." He hadn't been so sure of anything all year.

. . .

Big Brother had been working too hard—well, that much was no secret. But Hazel wanted a good night out, she wanted a date with her husband, in fact, and that wasn't so unreasonable, was it, once every couple of months or so? They went to the theater and to a champagne supper afterward. Alf fell dead asleep on the eiderdown and didn't wake up till he heard them giggling outside the bedroom door.

There was time, just barely time, for him to make it under the bed. He lay frozen in a mummy's pose, admiring its simple but ingenious construction. There were many slender wooden slats, and these were surely what made it so comfortable to lie on. He heard the sound of buttons and zippers, drawers opening and closing upon articles put away.

"Love?"

"Yes, Love . . ."

A great soft weight settled itself over him. He began a mental chant: *Don't bark, Alfie, you mustn't bark, quiet now, good dog, good dog* . . . and by some mercy this drowned out every sound. Three fifths of the way down the length of the bed, a group of slats began to flex, slowly at first, then faster and *faster* and FASTER . . . Then it stopped.

Big Brother unlocked the door, came in, set down his sharkskin briefcase, locked the door, picked up his sharkskin briefcase and snapped his fingers. Alf, who'd been basking in the glow of the BBC in the front room, raised his head slightly from a couch cushion.

"A word with you, young Alfred," Big Brother said brittlely. "Upstairs, if you please."

Alf stood on the little throw rug in the glow of the various video terminals. The phrase "called on the carpet" distantly presented itself to his mind. Big Brother, strangely inarticulate, swiveled to and fro in his desk chair, compulsively flicking the edge of his sharkskin calculator case with a fingernail. Finally he stopped in midrotation and stared up at Alf.

"My hair is brown," he remarked. "Yours, on the other hand, is black."

"This much is true," Alf said. "Always the wizard of perception, Bee Bee."

"I have a name," Big Brother said bleakly. "My name is Tom. You are familiar with it, I believe. Why don't you ever call me by my name?"

After the ensuing silence had accomplished itself, Big Brother spoke again.

"Well," he said. "Right." He reached into a tea mug on his desk and pulled out a little snarl of something. "This is hair."

Alf nodded.

"Black hair."

"That's so," said Alf.

"There's quite a bit of it, wouldn't you say?" Big Brother said. "I've been collecting it for about a week. Off my pillow, in point of fact."

Huskily, Alf cleared his throat.

"Well then, I'd like to know what you've been playing at."

"When exactly was it you started talking like a freaking Englishman?"

"When in Rome . . . ," Big Brother said. "Don't try to change the subject."

"Okay," Alf said. "You're concerned that I've been climbing on your furniture."

"Yes, I suppose you could put it that way."

"At least I'm housebroken," Alf said. "That's something to be thankful for."

In the weird light of the computer screens, Big Brother's sudden change of complexion looked purely fantastic.

"What the hell is the matter with you?!" he cried, half rising from his seat. Alf barked at him several times and left the room.

He sat with his elbows on the table, watching a bug walk around the little blue squares of the oilcloth. They didn't have cockroaches in the flat, and this bug didn't much look like one; however, it didn't look much like anything else either. After a long time Hazel came down and made a pot of tea. When she brought it to the table, Alf could see the dark circles around her eyes.

"It's been a tough year for him too," she said. "You need to try and understand that, Alfie. He's more of a small-town type of person, really. We all are, I suppose."

Alf leaned back and raised his eyebrows toward the ceiling.

"I had to make him take a pill," Hazel said. "Zonko."

"I see," said Alf. "Well, here we are."

"It's really hard for him at work," she said. "The English snub him all the time. But they don't know *any* of the stuff he knows. Till this year they did their whole stock market with pen and ink and big black books, supposedly." She gave her braid a yank and dropped it. "But it worries him that he doesn't fit in. *He* thinks *they* think *I* look like some kind of a pioneer woman off the prairie . . ."

Alf scalded his mouth on a gulp of tea.

"You two were close when you were children, I know that," Hazel said. "He used to talk about that a lot."

"That's right," Alf said. "But ever since we got to London he's been acting like a goddamn microchip."

"He's really scared about it all sometimes," Hazel said. "He's afraid the whole balloon is going to pop. He says people used to worry when their assets were only on paper, but now they're not even on *paper* anymore."

Alf watched the bug walk over the edge of the table out of sight.

"He's worried about you too, Alf," she said. "He's pretty upset about you, in fact."

"He doesn't think—"

"No, not that. Thank God, he never even thought of that . . . He knows you didn't go to school, though. But he doesn't know what to do about it."

The bug reappeared in the vicinity of Alf's tea mug. He

turned the mug around and around and watched the amber liquid swirl.

"He's worried maybe you're going nuts," Hazel said. "He doesn't know how to handle that either. Alfie, you know he'd do anything for you, but what is it he can do?"

Alf reached over and snapped his finger at the bug, which rebounded from the Delft tile around the kitchen fireplace and fell down into the shadows below.

"He was crying, actually," Hazel said.

"roorrrfff!" said Alf. "aaaarrhhhhwwwOOOOOORFF-OOOOOOOOO!!!"

"For God's sake, will you stop that ridiculous barking," Hazel said, and slammed her palms flat down against the table.

As he retreated further and further into the world of the canine, Alf's sense of smell became increasingly acute, so that on the final day he was faintly apprehensive of disaster from the moment he got onto the lift. The aroma, at first indefinable, became more vivid and more complex as soon as he had entered the flat. Hanging over everything was the odor of neutralizer and the bright ammoniac smell of the perm fluid. Mingled with this was a whiff of Neddy's after-shave and, most alarming of all, the smell of Hazel's tears.

He went down the hall with his hackles rising. Hazel, barely recognizable by sight, sat at the kitchen table, weeping over a small square mirror. The inch or two of hair remaining to her had been strangled into tiny ringlets which resembled scrambled eggs. The balance of her face was wrecked and her features looked heavy and bovine. It appeared that she had been crying for a long time without even trying to wipe her face. Her eyes were ridged with stiff red veins and her tears were pooling on the mirror.

"Well, there's no need for you to keep grieving so," Neddy said a little crossly. He had stretched Hazel's severed hair out on the table and was securing each end of it with a bit of black ribbon. "What if it *is* a little tight? It'll relax in a day or so, you'll see if it doesn't . . ." He took a cloth tape from his pocket, measured the coil of hair and tucked it away in a leather bag. "And if you *really* decide you don't fancy it, why, in just a few years you can grow it all back. So brace up, eh? There's a duck . . ."

Alf dropped to all fours on the kitchen floor and bounced springily on all of his paws.

"Here now, Hazel, look who's come," Neddy said with a nervous titter. Hazel cried intently on, as if she were incapable of hearing.

"It's your little brother who's mad," said Neddy.

"*rrrrRRRRRR,*" said Alf. He bristled. His lips pulled back from his incisors.

"*Hazel,*" Neddy said. "Your brother's off his bloody head—"

"*rrrrRRRRR,*" Alf said, and moved a little closer in, his hindquarters taut and trembling. Neddy took a long step backward into a complicated corner of the fireplace and the kitchen walls.

"Here now, Alf," Neddy said. "Let's be reasonable, old chum. There's a good fellow, I mean, *keep away, you! Just you keep off!*" But Alf was no longer able to hear or understand his speech. In fact, he was aware of nothing at all but the vibrating fabric of Neddy's trouser leg and the odor, texture and taste of the blood and meat inside.

"No," the hypnotist said thoughtfully. "No, I do not think you can believe that you were justified. Undoubtedly what you did was very wrong. And it is true, as you have heard, that human bites are very dangerous . . ."

Limp in the deep dark chair, Alf commenced to twitch and whimper.

"However," the hypnotist went on, "you will remember that it has all been satisfactorily resolved. The gentleman in question has accepted your brother's settlement. Moreover, he has not been lamed or hurt in any permanent way. It is *not* true, and never was, that you have rabies. And so, though naturally you will regret your unwise action, you will feel no permanent guilt. You will forgive yourself for what you did. Indeed, you have already done so."

Alf twitched again and faintly yipped a time or two.

"And now," the hypnotist said, "and *now*, you are let off your leash. You have slipped your collar, Alfie, you are free. You are running away from the house and into the barnyard. You feel the soft damp grass of the lawn between your toes, you feel the dust and the little stones of the barnyard. When you have run into the hall of the barn, you pause and sniff—you smell the hay, you smell the grain . . . and something else too, another odor. Rats, Alfie! *rrrRRRATS!*"

"rirfff!" yelped Alf from the chair. His body tensed and then relaxed.

"You leave the barnyard," the hypnotist said, "and you go into the field. You are capering among the hog huts, you run past the slow and lazy hogs until you reach that farthest fence. Feel the wire rub hard across your back as you squirm underneath. And now you have come through the screen of trees to reach the little pond. You are very warm from the sunshine and from running, and so you splash into the water, you feel the cool water soaking into your hot fur, and you look up and see how the little white duck you startled is flying far away in the blue sky.

"And now you are lying on the warm soft grass, Alfie, with your eyes closed and all four legs stretched out. Feel how the warm sun dries your fur, feel how the little breeze ruffles it. You doze, you are sleeping very deeply, yes. You dream.

"And now you are running into the forest, deeper and deeper into the trees. You see all the woodland sights, you hear all the woodland sounds, and you are in a very special world of *smells*, Alfie, which only you can understand and navigate. There are many, many smells, Alfie, but one of them is more important than all the rest. What is it, Alfie? What is that you smell? rrr . . . rrrrrr . . ."

Alf's mouth came slightly open as he whined; he salivated on the leather of the chair.

"rrrrrRRRRABBIT!" said the hypnotist. "You *smell* the *rabbit!* You smell the rabbit *very* near! And now you *see* the rabbit! And now you *chase* the rabbit!"

Alf's arms and legs began to pump in rhythmic running motions as his neck stretched out and out.

"And now you *catch* the rabbit in your jaws, you *bite* through the fur and skin into the tender flesh and the hot blood, you *crush* the rabbit's little bones, and you swallow every part of it. And now, Alfie, now that you are satisfied, you rest. Rest now, Alf. You are sleeping very deeply now.

"And now you hear voices, Alfie, voices calling out your name from far away across the fields. *Alfie, Alfie,* they are calling. They are calling you to go home to your house, Alf, and you go. You will obey the calling voices, you are going now. On the back porch of your house you see your family waiting for you—your mother, your father, your elder brother Tom, your sister-in-law Hazel, she is there too. It is they who have been calling you, Alfie, because they need you to come home. They feed you your dinner, Alf, and when you have eaten, they pat your head and they rub your ears the way you love it so. They have prepared a soft mat near the warmth of the kitchen stove, Alf, where you stretch out and rest from your doggy, doggy day. You have no worries, Alf. You have no responsibilities at all . . . but still, something is missing. What is it, Alf? What is it that you lack?"

Alf shifted, coming more nearly upright in the chair. He trembled a little, but he didn't bark. His hands settled on his knees and he assumed a posture of attention. The hypnotist leaned a little closer to him.

"*Dogs don't love*," the hypnotist whispered. "They haven't got the capability. They *feel*, yes, but they don't love."

"That," said Alf, "is a debatable point."

"Perhaps," the hypnotist said. "Possibly. But in your case . . . not worth debating, I shouldn't think."

Alf whined and pricked his ears, then let them lower.

"Come on, Alf," the hypnotist said. "Come on, boy. Come on out. Are you coming, now?"

PETIT CACHOU

TON-TON DETROIT climbed the steps to the small square castle which housed the Cocteau Museum, paused for a moment to look back at the rows of white boats floating in the harbor and ducked through the stone doorway onto the shelf that ran along the outside of the sea wall. The sounds of the town waking were abruptly cut off behind him and all he could hear now was the slow pull of the sea. The wall, something more than twice his height, seemed to decline very sharply as it ran west to the short round tower of the signal light that was its terminus. No one else was in sight. Ton-Ton Detroit walked about a third of the way down the pier, picking his way among the numerous twists of dog dung littered along the path. When he felt he had come to the right spot he stopped, unslung his bag and quickly peeled off his jeans. Naked now except for a blue undershirt that came just down to his navel, he stepped out onto the rocks of the breakwater and crouched to evacuate his bowels as quickly as seemed reasonable. While he was so occupied a twig-sized figure rounded the signal light and began to grow larger as it approached, towed along by a dog on a leash. Ton-Ton Detroit fired a powerful thought beam in that direction and the twig person obediently turned back and went out of sight on the other side of the wall. Ton-Ton Detroit sighed and got up and walked surely back over the rocks to the shelf, his long toes curling into cracks of the stones to confirm his balance. It was not his favorite part of the day, but business was slow so early in the season, and he had cut his trips to the public toilet by the harbor to one day a week: Friday, when he'd pay the six francs it cost to also take a shower.

Today was Wednesday. It had been a foggy night but the mist was lifting quickly now, and already he could see down the coast as far as the checkpoint at the Italian frontier. Above and beyond the border post, the mountains were still almost invisible, only a blue mass vaguely drifting in a lightening swirl of cloud. Ton-Ton Detroit groped into his bag and unfurled the long gold-striped dashiki, shrugged it over his head and then put on his sandals. He shoved the rolled jeans to the bottom of the bag and began to take out his samples and string them all over himself: the belts, the bone bracelets and bead necklaces, the snakeskin clutch purses and a couple of the headphone radios. As the final touch he fit one of the radios over his ears and raised both antennae as far as they would go. By the time he was ready, the shapes of the mountains had begun to appear more distinctly out of the dissolving cloud, a jagged pale violet line marking the nearest peaks. Ton-Ton Detroit hitched on his bag and walked back toward the small squat castle at the near end of the sea wall, his eye bent on the ocean. It was low tide and the water was nearly flat, shimmering just slightly with tiny pricks of light. With the sun angled across it so low, the sea was bright and colorless as a crinkled sheet of aluminum. The Kamikaze Club boat, on its way to drop scuba divers at various points east along the coast, cut a neat white line across the water. The boat was too far out for Ton-Ton Detroit to hear the engine, and the ocean made only the faintest sucking sound as it dragged at the bottom of the rocks.

He walked down the stairs inside the wall to the harbor parking and stopped at the bottom long enough to light a

Gauloise Blonde. Fuming blue smoke, he climbed the short grade up from the parking and came out at the end of the Promenade du Soleil, the long concrete walk which swept along the gentle curve of the coast all the way to Cap Martin. Below, the diehard sunbathers had already begun to spread themselves out on the pebbled beach, though it was very early still. A light easterly breeze brought him a whiff of suntan oil. Ton-Ton Detroit reached up to his right ear and flicked the radio on. It was already tuned to *France Culture;* he couldn't bear French pop music. Time for the science program. Ton-Ton Detroit's eyes sank half shut and his mouth softened into a sort of smile. He thumbed the dial so the voices fell to a mellifluous mumble in his ear, blending with his own pitch as he began to move out across the beach: "*Regardez . . . Regardez, messieurs, mesdames . . . C'est pas cher . . .*

Clayton Powell Simpson, commonly known as Clay, had somehow managed to be dead asleep when the bus pulled into the Gare Routière. Even though the trip from Monaco was short and the road was full of sudden twists and lurches, he didn't wake up until the driver kicked the sole of his shoe and bent down toward him, jabbering something way too fast for him to make it out.

"Say what?" Clay said, blinking back sleep. "*Comment?*"

"*Fin du chemin,*" the driver said. "*C'est terminé.*"

Clay had heard that last phrase often enough in restaurants to comprehend that he must have come to the end of the line. He went a few paces away from the bus and stopped to try to slap some of the wrinkles out of his tan poplin suit. Not much of a bus station going here, just the parking lot, a kiosk and a glass-walled information booth. Not even any lockers, which you might take to mean it was just as well he didn't have his suitcase anymore, if you wanted to look on the bright side. In front of him and on either side, there were hills climbing almost straight up. Some buildings were up there, with roads winding up among them, but it didn't look like the most promising way to go. He turned around, squinting into the sun, and automatically glanced at the place on his wrist where his watch should have been, but it was still gone. Didn't matter so much anyhow; there was no place he had to be at any certain time.

He walked out of the Gare Routière on the downhill side. Beyond the railroad overpass, the road opened out into a boulevard with a sort of park between the lanes, with a fountain and palmettos and a lot of vaguely tropical-looking shrubbery. Two blocks down it dead-ended at the front of a cream-colored building with looping letters over the door that read CASINO. Clay practically flinched when he saw that, his mouth pulling tight at the corners. There was a blond chick sitting on a bench smoking a cigarette and he hailed her as he approached.

"Hey, darling, got the mate to that?"

The girl looked up at him, startled and blank, and Clay wiped her away with his hand as he went on by. It didn't matter, there was plenty of traffic. When he saw the next girl smoking he tried again.

"Hey there, sugar, let me have a smoke?"

Again he could tell for sure by the look on her face that she didn't understand one word he'd said. Clay stopped cold and fumbled the bus schedule out of his inside pocket to scope out just exactly where he was. Menton — it didn't look to be that far, but in Monte Carlo at *least* every other person had spoken English.

"Well, I'd call these steps just a little bit skimpy," Martin Ventura grunted, mostly to himself, since nobody else was paying any particular attention. Nadine was still fussing around the car they'd rented in Nice, and Mindy had already started yakking it up with the concierge, or listening to the concierge yak it up, at the foot of the steps in the entrance hall. In fact, the steps were so narrow Martin practically had to turn his feet sideways to get down them, no joke either when he was carrying the two grotesquely heavy suitcases, which weren't even his but Mindy's and Nadine's, of course. Not more than an inch away from a nice fall to a pair of smashed kneecaps and a gorgeous damage suit, though he supposed he'd have to hire help to take it through the French courts, he didn't even own a wig himself. Reaching the level floor at last, he dropped the suitcases with a crash, set his hands on his hips and tried to arch the cramp out of his back. From the far end of the dim hallway he could hear Mindy calling back to him.

"*Daddy*, you be careful with my bag."

"Yeah, yeah," Martin muttered.

Nadine had come to the top of the stairs. "Need any help with those, Marty?"

"From here I can wheel it," Martin said. "Just leave the other one in the car, I'll come back and get it. And try not to break your neck coming down these stairs."

He snapped out the tow handles of both suitcases and hauled them down the curving corridor to the open door at the end of it. The concierge was displaying various features of the little kitchen cubicle to Mindy, who was nodding and smiling and now and then slipping in a word of her own. On her face was a beautiful look of comprehension which Martin knew meant nothing at all, since it was the look she always put on whenever he tried to tell her something she should know.

The whirl of French seemed to daze him a little; he was half stunned already from the flight and, especially, from the drive. He let go of the suitcases and took a turn around the apartment. When you traveled by throwing darts at the map, you had to be ready to overlook a few things and this place offered enough opportunities to practice the technique. There was one bedroom, which he and Nadine would take; Mindy would have to make do with a fold-down something in the living room. The place was thin on furniture, which was just as well given the character of the furniture that was there.

On the walls were some of the worst pictures of boats he'd ever yet seen in any vacation apartment; there might be room for those in a closet somewhere, though on the other hand it might be unwise to expose any more of that wallpaper.

Well, the idea wasn't to spend all that much time indoors anyway. Martin slid back a glass door, stepped out onto the balcony and swore. The view of the sea the agency had promised was a thumbnail of blue at the far left corner, mostly obscured by some sort of scrubby pine tree that had sprouted from just below the building. The main prospect was over the roofs of a few other condos, across the canyon to the hair-raising highway cut into the side of the mountain.

"The French Riviera, *voilà*." Mindy was hanging in the doorway behind him, her arms stretched wide enough to raise the hem of her shirt a good two inches above her little brown bellybutton. "Congratch, Daddy, you found us another real dump. I told you we shoulda went to the Cape."

"I spend all this money to send you to Concord so you learn how to say 'shoulda went'?" Martin said. "Sweetheart, I hope your French is better than your English or we're all going to be in trouble soon."

Mindy swung her head back and a wave of black hair broke over her shoulders.

"So far I'm managing," she said. "Dibs the bedroom, by the way."

Martin laughed.

"There's fold-down beds in the living room," he said. "Take all three of them if you want. You don't need any bedroom anyhow, you spend your life in the bathroom, you know?"

He walked away from her down the balcony and discovered another sliding door that let into the bedroom. Nadine was already laying her things out on a small vanity under the mirror.

"Oh, you brought the other stuff," Martin said. "I was going to go get it."

"Didn't want to leave it all in the car." Nadine rubbed at

some invisible blemish on the side of her nose and stared at the spot in the mirror. "You got both the heavy ones anyway."

Martin stepped into the room and slid the door shut behind him.

"Well, I can't say it's not the French Riviera this time," he said. "You know why, because it *is* the French Riviera."

"I like it just fine, babe," Nadine said. "It's plenty big enough, it's got all we really need. We might just switch things around a little . . ."

"Just don't stand too near that wallpaper," Martin said. "Looks to me like it might be planning an attack."

He opened the door again and stepped back out. The balcony was big, you could say that for it. It ran the length of the apartment and was comfortably wide. From this angle he could look down across a railroad track that must come out from a tunnel somewhere underneath the building. Half a mile down it was the town of Menton.

"Maybe we should go out for a while," he said. "Have a look around the town."

"Sure, if you want," Nadine said. "Just let me get changed into something cooler."

Martin walked back along the balcony, trailing a hand along the rail and looking vaguely out toward the highway.

"Mother Mary," he said, and stopped cold.

"You rang?" Mindy had come out on the balcony.

"Smart pants," Martin said. "I thought they only did that in Italy."

"Did what?"

"You already missed it," Martin said. "Two buses passing on a turn." He shook his head. "What a trip, I think I might be ready for a delayed-reaction heart attack."

"Coulda let me drive, I offered." Mindy shrugged. "Okay, I'm going to the beach I guess, if I can find it from here, that is."

"Forget it," Martin said. "We're going to town and look at culture, we need you for an interpreter."

"So I can drive?"

"Drive what?" Martin said. "I want to see things, we're going to walk."

Mindy cupped a hand around her ear.

"There's a secret to life which you ought to know," Martin said. "If you walk and do exercise kind of things sometimes, you can eat like a human being and still not get fat."

He turned around and went back into the bedroom. Nadine had put on a white sundress with spaghetti straps. Martin bent down to kiss the back of her neck. "You're not going to get sunburned in that thing?" he said.

"I've got the sunscreen in my purse," Nadine said. "Mindy ready?"

Martin exhaled and stroked the side of his carry-on bag to verify that both bottles were still there, unbroken. "Sure she is," he said. "She's ready to give me a pain in the neck."

When the sun had reached a point almost directly overhead, Ton-Ton Detroit stopped and took off his radio. He put on the white hat and crinkled its short round brim up over his ears and put radio back on, on top of it. The puff of air trapped in the top of the hat made a cooling cushion between his head and the sun. Now it was perfectly clear, the sky a smooth bland shade of blue. He could have seen almost as far as San Remo if there hadn't been anything in the way. The next cape westward down the coast was clearly defined against the sea.

A proportion of the morning sunbathers were beginning to pack up their mats and towels and start in for lunch. Those who remained would be too completely stunned by the light and heat to even look up when he went past them, and they'd stay that way for at least an hour, as long as the sun was at its height. He had come all the way to the end of the beach at Cap Martin without selling any more than two bracelets and one of the belts. It was too early in the season, most of the people were French and he had nothing in his display to surprise them. Scattered back across the beach toward Menton, he could see the silhouettes of the other peddlers coming along wraithlike through the shimmering heat. They would be doing no better than he.

Ton-Ton Detroit walked down to the last ripple of stones before the water's edge and stepped out of his sandals there. He raised the hem of his dashiki and walked out till the water was halfway up his shins. The sudden cold sent a pain rocketing up through his bones all the way to his back teeth. After a moment its sharpness was broken and it faded into a rather pleasant ache. The water was fantastically clear and he could still see the bottom plainly out to five feet deep. Odd scraps of seaweed hung suspended at different depths, along with bits of molding paper trash. His own feet seemed to float up toward him, distorted and slightly magnified by the water. There were no swimmers nearby except for a twelve- or thirteen-year-old girl who sat astride a dolphin-shaped float, rocking in the small rollers that came into the beach. She was tanned very brown all over and her brown hair hung in a tangle just down to the bare knobs of her new breasts. The dolphin bobbed continuously, relaying her a molded rubber smile, but she was staring fixedly out over it toward a large sailboat which had anchored some seventy yards out.

Once he was thoroughly cool within, Ton-Ton Detroit came out of the water and walked up the steps to the promenade. He went past the corner *tabac* to the bakery and bought a loaf and then a tomato from the fruit stand outside. Turning uphill, he went to the Escalier de la Plage and climbed enough steps to reach a shady spot, where he sat down. Dozens of doves were softly hooting, hidden in the trees and shrubs all around the long concrete staircase. Ton-Ton Detroit sliced the tomato onto the bread and ate it very slowly. The bread was fresh enough to be just slightly warm. When he had done he stayed there long enough to smoke two cigarettes and in between them he dozed for half an hour.

After his second smoke was finished he got up and went back down the stairs and out to the promenade. It was still very hot but there was a breeze bringing a cool air current in off the water. He rearranged his display across the front of the dashiki and began to walk at a steady pace toward the cafés that were scattered across the promenade all the way back to Menton. Above the town, the mountains could now be most plainly seen, the bald rocks thrusting out through gaps in the skein of trees.

Sometime a little after noon, Clay got just too played out to keep moving anymore. Already he could feel big liquid blisters rising on the balls of his feet just back of his big toes. Slick patent leather wasn't good for this much rough walking up and down. He went among the cafés on the promenade, looking for a likely one. The place with the cushioned swings facing the water was irresistible, even though he supposed it might be more expensive than the others. When he sat down a girl with birdlike eyes shining from a mass of curly hair appeared, holding one of the round high-walled trays.

"Uh bee-are," Clay said.

The girl receded. Christ, he hoped he wouldn't end up with a lemonade or something. Already it had been a bad day, and he had not yet eaten. Everybody around here seemed to be white, though that wouldn't have bothered him if he just could have talked. The girl came back with a stemmed glass of lager. Clay handed her a fifty-franc note and she gave him back four of the fat brown ten-franc coins along with a little silver. Oh God, now he was down to nothing but change.

He sank back into the creaking swing and tried to smooth his mind completely blank. Under the sunshade he quickly grew cool, but his stomach would not come unknotted and he couldn't keep his eyes shut tight. When they came open he saw one of the guys in the muumuus starting to work the tables in his direction, a tall lean dude with a scruffy white beard that scrambled over the jet-black ridges of his face. Clay's eyes fastened on the cigarette clamped in the corner of his mouth; he hadn't had a smoke all day either. Nobody spoke English but waiters and barmen, and with them nothing would ever be free. As the old man came closer he began to compose a sentence in his mind.

"Voo — Voozahhh—" He gave up. "Cigarette," he said hopelessly. "Cigarette, see voo play."

"Say you want a cigarette?" Ton-Ton Detroit said. "First one's free."

Clay's tortured mouth muscles went marvelously slack.

"Hey, you talk English," he said. "Come on and sit down a minute, tell me your name."

"Ton-Ton Detroit, you know, man, like Uncle Detroit." The peddler dropped into the swing beside him. He smelled a little high up close but Clay was in no mood to mind it.

"Clay, uncle," he said, reaching for the cigarette. "You sound like an American. Where you from?"

"Cleveland," Ton-Ton Detroit said. "You?"

"New York." Clay lit his cigarette off Ton-Ton Detroit's and held the first drag deep. "Man, that goes down good right now," he said. "Hey, lemme ask you something, how come they call you Ton-Ton Detroit if you from Cleveland?"

Ton-Ton Detroit smiled with long brown teeth. "People round here can't wrap their lips around Cleveland too good," he said. "It just makes things more easier. Where'd you blow in from yourself?"

"Monte Carlo was the latest."

"Been losing?"

Clay followed the old man's eyes down to the elbows of his jacket and saw they were all scuffed up from when he'd gone skidding down the sidewalk trying to protect his face. Hadn't even noticed that before. To take his mind off it he drew the three bent playing cards from his breast pocket and began to rearrange them swiftly across the tabletop, touching them just lightly by the edges with his long slim fingers.

"I had a blackjack system," he said.

The old man's eyes darted as he tracked the cards. "Don't tell me it was one like I see," he said.

"Uh-uh," Clay said. "I'm just a counter."

"I thought counters were supposed to make out."

"Musta lost count," Clay said. "I can run monte too, though. I'm what they call multitalented. You know where they'd be a good pitch around here?"

"Nowhere," Ton-Ton Detroit said. "I wouldn't even think about it, son, the *flics* around here can hear you think."

"Is that a fact?"

"I wonder did you ever see a *matraque?*"

Clay looked up.

"It's like a rubber billy stick with weight loaded in the hitting end. Got nearly a foot of flex to it when it goes *wong wong* upside your head and knock all them bad thoughts clear out."

"I get it." Clay slid the three cards together and held them covered under his hand. "Don't suppose you could use any help with your thing, could you?"

"Not unless you want to buy something," Ton-Ton Detroit said. "I'm barely making it one day to the next right now."

"What about all them other cats I see, they all from Cleveland too?"

"Uh-uh. They North Africans mostly. Maybe one or two from Haiti." Ton-Ton Detroit shook his head. "I'd leave 'em alone, they mostly crazy. Don't bother with 'em too much myself."

Clay shoved the cards back into his pocket and stared off along the line of swings. People sitting at the other tables were starting to get served plates of food. A plump boy with olive skin was weaving among the tables, trailing behind a black toy poodle on a thin red leash. The kid was so out of it he let the dog drag him to bump into people without even noticing; all he did was hum to the dog in a kind of whiny singsong.

"Man, I think I got my tail in a crack," Clay said. "I thought they was gonna be tourists here talking English."

"You just a little bit early for that," Ton-Ton Detroit said. "Right now it's mostly just the French."

"You looking for it to pick up soon?"

"Praying, is what." Ton-Ton Detroit stood up. "But it's apt to be tight another two, three weeks."

"You kidding me," Clay said. "Man, I just got to find some kind of thing to get into."

"Luck to you," Ton-Ton Detroit said, moving away.

"Hey, thanks for the smoke," Clay said. "Maybe I'll see you."

"Look careful," Ton-Ton Detroit said, and walked out of the area of the café.

When she had finally dragged herself to the top, Mindy turned around to look back down the zigzag staircase that climbed to the small irregular square before l'Église Saint-Michel. The patterns the black and white pebbles made on the landings were kind of neat looking from up here, though it wasn't really worth it when you considered she'd felt every one of them right through her shoes on the way up. One thing she was already sick to death of was climbing up and down all these steps; it seemed like everywhere was either straight up or straight down. There were a hundred and seventy-seven steps down to the beach from the dump they were staying at, which was going to really be a bitch, and it was a lot longer if you tried to go around by the road, so forget it. If she could talk Daddy into letting her rent one of the little mopeds all the French kids in town seemed to ride, life would start getting a little bit easier.

"Mindy," Nadine was calling, "come over here a minute and read me what it says on this sign."

Mindy turned her head partway around and then switched it back, remembering to pretend she hadn't heard. Another thing she was already good and sick of was being everybody's interpreter all the time. It was just a scam of Daddy's anyway, to keep her tied to them every minute; she was pretty sure he could at least read French himself—anyway, he'd read through all that stuff the goddamn apartments sent him. She stared out past the highway below; the view of the beach from here was great. One thing the place had going for it was that the water looked fantastic. From up here its color was almost turquoise, and it was so clear that she could see all the way to the whitish bottom for quite a good way out. Just before the line of yellow buoys that marked off the swimming area, the water changed sharply on a clear line dividing the pale light-flooded water from the deeper opaque blue. Barely beyond that drop-off point floated the white square of a diving raft with five or six miniature figures splashing around it. She just hoped the water was as warm as it looked.

"Oh, *Mindy*," Martin was calling, "why don't you just hotfoot it on over here right now and have me a look at this sign."

Mindy made her slow-motion turn and arched herself all the way back with her hands on the balustrade for support, so far back her hair hung straight down and she saw the sea where the sky should have been. All those people swimming upside down: it was a wonder they didn't fall out. When she straightened up she peeped through her hair to see if she'd scared him, but he didn't seem to be paying her any attention. She smoothed her hair back over her shoulders; it had got sticky in the heat. In a patch of shade by an angle of a building, some little brown-skinned kids were bouncing a dirty white ball up and down. A short way from them a bigger boy was letting a tiny black poodle lead him around at the end of a red leash. Otherwise there was no one around but her parents, standing in the doorway of the church. Mindy shrugged and went over to glance at the descriptive plaque.

"It says it was built in sixteen-whatchamajiggy," she said. "It says it's very old and very boring. A bunch of Catholics used to come here and pray after they got through burning people at the stake."

"I would call that kind of a free translation," Martin said, a slight edge to his tone. "Care to try to tighten it up a little? You know, like pretend it's on an exam."

But Mindy turned away from the plaque and moved toward her mother, who was backing away to get a better angle on the rise of the church's façade. When she had backed nearly to the head of the stairs she twirled herself around, arms spreading wide and her purse flying out to the end of its long strap, and then leaned forward, braced on the wall.

"If that isn't the most marvelous view," she said. "Wonder if you ever see whales out there."

Between Mindy and Nadine, the boy was meandering in slow circles after his dog, who seemed to be following some invisible but intricate trail around the patterned pebbles of the court. The boy looked to be about eleven or twelve and was rather fat, with plump rolls of flesh pushing into every fold of his clothing. He had a mop of dark curly hair and a face shaped a little like a sheep's and his eyes were large and liquid brown. All his attention seemed to be buried in the dog, to whom he sang little rhyming endearments in a high sweet voice.

"*Viens ici, petit jou-jou . . . Vas-y, mon chou, petit cachou . . .*"

Mindy walked around him and came to the wall to check out the view again herself. She couldn't see any sign of a whale but there was a nice-looking red speedboat ripping a high wake across the water. She wondered if people did much water-skiing around here. Daddy had peeled himself off of that sign finally and was headed their way, taking a detour to clear that kid with the dog, who seemed almost incredibly out of it, totally unaware that anything else was going on around him. Within the ring of smaller children, the ball kept thumping steadily; the whole group was starting to drift their way. Mindy propped her hip on the wall and adjusted herself with a hand on her mother's shoulder.

"Ouch! Careful," Nadine said. "What have you had your hand on? It feels sort of hot."

"What?" Mindy said. When she took her hand away she

could see pale finger lines against a faint rose flush just rising on her mother's normally ice-white skin. "Oh, Mom, did you get burned again? You forgot the sunscreen, right?"

"Oh no, I didn't forget," Nadine said. "I have it right here in my purse."

"Yeah, but did you, like, put any on your *skin?*" Mindy said. "I mean, it actually doesn't work too well down there in the bottom of your bag. I can't believe how you always do this."

"Well, I like to get a *little* sun," Nadine said. She pressed her fingertips to her lower lip and lowered her eyes. "I *think* I put some on," she said. "Didn't I?"

"Not a chance," Martin said as he came up, "not unless you did it in secret some way or other." He turned sideways, stumbling a little. "Hey, watch where you're going there . . ."

Nose tight to the pebbled pavement, the little poodle had snuffled its way into the space between the three of them, and the red leash was sawing against one of Martin's legs. The boy jostled into him and came into the center of the group, looking up wide-eyed into all their faces as if he'd just that instant realized they were there. At the same moment Mindy saw his free hand dip into Nadine's open purse and spirit away the long leather wallet that held her traveler's checks. She had to play the whole scene back to make sure she really had it right: the kid looking up so sweetly at all of them while that pudgy hand flicked into the purse like it had a mind of its own. By the time she had started to try to think of the words for "stop" and "thief," he had already started moving away. She made a dash after him, shoving Martin to one side, but the boy and dog had faded out through the knot of smaller children to slip into the mouth of a hidden alley, where, she could tell, they'd be long gone.

In the early evening after he had eaten, Ton-Ton Detroit walked back out to the promenade and moved in the direction of the castle at the harbor's edge, aiming for the bench below the wall, where he could see the Haitian was already sitting. The Haitian shifted a little to make room for him, exposing a thumbnail-sized packet of foil that had been hidden under his thigh. Ton-Ton Detroit vacuumed the shiny square speedily into his dashiki sleeve and reached across to shake hands with the Haitian, transferring a bill folded in accordion pleats into the center of his palm. The Haitian enunciated a rather long sentence in his impenetrable Creole.

"*Ouais*," Ton-Ton Detroit said, not having understood a word.

He offered the Haitian a cigarette and sat beside him, smoking. Now and then the Haitian said something more and Ton-Ton Detroit said *ouais* again without knowing what he was agreeing to. When he was done with his cigarette he got up and went up the steps on the far side of the castle and through the doorway onto the outer sea wall.

Out among the rocks of the breakwater were two flat-topped stone pillars of unknown function and Ton-Ton Detroit vaulted up onto the top of one of these. He changed from his dashiki into his jeans and packed all his other odds and ends away into his bag. The sea was a little rougher than it had been in the morning, slapping and tugging more hungrily at the rocks. He sat down cross-legged and carefully unwrapped the chip of hash, then doubled the foil and rolled it tight around a pencil and slipped the pencil out. Once he'd pinched a right angle in the short tube he'd made, it was good enough for a one-shot pipe. He snapped a kitchen match alight with his thumbnail and drew in a long sweet draft of smoke as deep as it wanted to go. The sea had turned a solid blue all the way up to the rocks it chopped at. Far, far out, a tiny triangle of a windboard bounced along in the rising swell, but otherwise the horizon was blank. Ton-Ton Detroit let the fire in the hash go out and reached into his bag with his other hand to find his fisherman's sunglasses. Aided by the filtered lenses, his eyes cut into the water to find a school of silvery sardines hovering just a foot deep.

Watching the fish, he struck a match to the pipe and drew on it. The foil heated up just enough to scorch his lips a little. He had just begun to think that he might save the other tokes for later and put his hand on his flute right now when he saw the New York kid with the straightened hair coming up the steps toward the doorway. Automatically his thumb flattened the pipe bowl and crushed the spark out of the hash. He had done that so many times before he had a callus there, so he felt no pain. The *flics* barely tolerated him and the other peddlers, and even the most minor kind of drug arrest could alter his life quite seriously for the worse. If he had not had his sunglasses on he would have tried to flatten the New York kid with a thought beam. Now and then it was nice to hear a voice from home, but Ton-Ton Detroit had one of his special feelings that this boy would be more trouble than fun, and he had never liked New York people all that much in the first place. He rolled the foil to protect the hash and slid the little lump into his watch pocket.

"Anything shaking, uncle?" Clay said as he came up. "This the spot you like to hang?"

"Sometimes," Ton-Ton Detroit said, looking out over the water.

The windboard had disappeared somewhere, and a long white yacht had just rounded the point from the Italian side, pointed toward Monte Carlo. Down under the surface, the sardines scattered in a flickering star pattern as something long and indistinct approached them from below.

"Cool place, real quiet," Clay said, and wrinkled his nose. "Little bit rank, though, I have to say. They's a whole lot of dogs around this town, you notice?"

"Sometimes," Ton-Ton Detroit said. Clay moved up a little closer but Ton-Ton Detroit was sitting right on the edge of his post, so it was not really possible for Clay to hop out there and be with him.

"I been kinda wondering something here, uncle," Clay said, lacing his fingers together in front of his crotch. "Like if you could maybe let me hold a hundred francs, you know, just until tomorrow?"

Ton-Ton Detroit said nothing at all.

"Fifty?" Clay said.

Ton-Ton Detroit's lips drew back to show how tight his teeth were clenched. After a second he relaxed his jaws.

"You dead out of luck, son," he said. "I hadn't touched fifty francs this week myself."

"Didn't mean to bother you," Clay said hurriedly. "Well, I guess I'll just go on and leave you to your thoughts."

He turned and went back through the doorway and down the steps. When his head had bobbed down below the level of the sill, Ton-Ton Detroit and the ocean let out a long sigh together. Then he got the foil out of his pocket and began to shape it back into a pipe.

Clay was taking the walk back toward Cap Martin because he couldn't think of anywhere much else to go, no matter he'd nearly worn a rut pounding that same pavement back and forth all day. In another hour it would be dark and he wasn't a step nearer to a full meal or some place to stay than he had been when he got off the bus that morning. Reaching the point where the cape began to turn out to sea, he went down a set of steps to check out what the beach might look like to sleep on. The rocks seemed pretty hard and lumpy; he guessed that was why so many of the beach babes lay on those little cushioned mats. He picked up an egg-shaped stone and tossed it up and felt it join his hand again with a meaty slap. One thing was sure enough right now: the time for subtlety had passed.

At a turn about halfway up the Escalier de la Plage, there was a break in the left-hand wall that let into a little scrabbly place in the undergrowth which none of the condos quite overlooked. Clay had swaddled the rock in both of his socks and he was crouching down behind the wall, rolling it from one hand to the other. The corner smelled sweetly of honeysuckle and somewhat more dimly of dog mess and urine. Some kind of birds were hooting in the twilight all around; he wondered if they might be owls or what. Near him some nits hovered in a cluster just under a branch, all keeping the same precise distance from one another, like they were stuck to something invisible and couldn't get free.

The first person up the stairs was a fat lady with groceries and Clay let her go on by, on the assumption she'd probably already shot her wad at the store. He had to wait nearly twenty minutes for the next one, but when he came along he looked just right: a thirtyish dude in pointy shoes, tight pants and a barf-yellow shirt, swinging one of those purses Frenchmen liked to carry from a little strap on his wrist. When he had mounted the step just past the gap in the wall, Clay snatched him back with a hand clamped over his mouth, conking the padded rock on the side of his head at more or less the same time. The dude went soggy on the second clobber and Clay dumped him face down in a tangle of dry vines, then turned him over for a quick check-out he wasn't maybe going to die. Four minutes later he was walking the promenade back to Menton and taking his easy time about it. He hadn't looked into the purse just yet, but it felt fat and promising, snugged into his waistband under his shirt, and he thought the town was starting to look kind of pretty, now that the lights were coming on.

Well, just thank God she had her father's heavy-duty skin, was what Mindy was thinking as she walked back toward Menton. It would be tough to be Mom on a trip to the beach; still, there was something really amazing about how she *never failed* to get herself fried to ashes the very first day they went out anywhere. By the time they'd got back to El Dumpo, she'd been completely broken out in welts. Which meant she'd spend about the next two days in bed gobbling anti-histamines and aspirin and slithering around in practically a tidal wave of cortisone cream. Well, you couldn't say that she wasn't the one who always did it to herself. On the plus side, though Mindy was sorry about the sunburn and all, that along with the whole pickpocket episode had created enough confusion to buy her some time on her own.

Traffic on the street she was walking was really kind of incredible for such a small town. The little motor scooters whirred in and out among the cars, droning away like big fat wasps. It would have been a lot more fun to be riding on one than to have to keep dodging them on the crosswalks. Have to try to do something about that, the next couple of days . . . but for now she was happy enough just to be out by herself for a little. Daddy had given her money to eat, but she didn't really feel all that hungry. The thing to do would be sit down somewhere and see if she could get a drink. Just up ahead was the town casino, which didn't look like too bad of a place. There was a sign flashing over a side door that said DISCOTHÈQUE, but the guys in the tuxes there in the hallway looked like they were probably bouncers and she doubted they would let her in, not the way she looked right now. In Vegas you had to be twenty-one to crack a casino, and she couldn't pass for that without different clothes and a lot of makeup and some more help from dimmer light than this.

Of course it might always be different in France, but she didn't really feel up to a hassle. She walked a block or two on past the casino, swinging her purse on its braided strap and peering into the different cafés that sprawled out on the sidewalks. The trouble was, they were all kind of small and she would rather have gone in somewhere she wouldn't be noticed while she tried to decide what she wanted to get. A half block ahead she saw one that looked bigger, with tables outside on a concrete apron that broadened into the junction of the two side streets. The banner over the front door read LA RÉGENCE.

Inside, the place was a little queer, kind of run-down and grimy, but plenty big, one huge room with such a funny zigzag shape you might have taken it for three. There was a little bit of everything: in the back a cafeteria type of restaurant, in front a long metal bar and in the narrower space that divided them there was even a kind of a newsstand. Mindy stood there for a couple of minutes, turning a rack of moldy paperbacks while she tried to figure out what she wanted to order. Beer made you fat and she hated bar wine and she didn't know how to say mixed drinks in French—besides which, she had heard they were really expensive. At the bar were mostly middle-aged Frenchmen drinking Pernod, but she couldn't stand that thick licorice taste. After she watched for a while she saw a guy at the bar get served with something that looked like a Tom Collins. Before he could carry it off she lunged into the space beside him.

"*Un comme ça*," she said, and pointed as the bartender caught her eye.

"*Un long-drink*," the guy said to her, smirking. "*Vous voulez un long-drink?*"

"*Bien sûr que oui*," Mindy said, picking up a little speed. *Long-drink*, hey, she could pronounce that no problem. The guy was maybe a bit of a jerk but at least there hadn't been any hassle about proof. She took the tall glass out on the patio and sat down at a round table with her back to the show window. There were all kinds of kids swarming around the other tables and she put her sunglasses on, even though it was almost dark, so she could spy on them a little without being noticed. One thing she could pick up right away: if she wanted to fit into this scene very well, she was going to need about another suitcase full of clothes. The stuff she had brought would be fine for the Cape but it was going to look too loud around here, the way everybody was so deep into pastels. Not that her heart exactly cried out for a pair of turquoise tennis shoes or anything like it, but she didn't want these people to think she looked queer.

But all of a sudden she was feeling eyes on her; somebody must think she looked okay. Covered by the sunglasses, she looked over—it was a guy in a wrinkled tan suit going by on the sidewalk, dark-skinned and really very good looking. In fact, he even looked a little like Prince. She would have smiled back at him but he went by too quick. The *long-drink* didn't taste all that damn strong but she could tell by the way her thoughts were getting a little soupy that she'd probably got her money's worth on it. Better slow it down a little, maybe; the drink was so cool and she'd been so warm she'd already killed more than half the glass without noticing. Three French boys sat down one table over from her, one really cute one with sun-bleached hair and a coffee-rich tan, and she switched her chair around halfway toward them to see if she could eavesdrop some. But she couldn't seem to hear them very well at all; it was like her ears were stopped up or something. It took her a minute to realize that she could *hear* them, sure enough, she just couldn't understand a word they said. French in France was not working out to be quite the piece of cake she had expected. She'd always ripped through language lab like a comet, but the guys on those tapes spoke like very slow retards compared to the way it went over here.

Her glass clinked back on the tabletop, empty. Man, that stuff had a pretty good punch, whatever it was they were putting in it. She felt warm and happy and ready for another one, though until she got a better grip on the language problem, she might just be better off on lemonade. No doubt Daddy had managed to come up with a place where no other Americans would ever turn up in about a gazillion years, and she needed to be able to meet people *somehow*. Still, another *long-drink* might have gone down fine, but Daddy was supposed to be meeting her with the car. Most times she wouldn't have let that stop her, but she wasn't quite sure what went in those things yet, and if her toes were twinkling too much when she got back, she might have more trouble getting out next time.

It was getting fairly dim outside and Martin had drawn the curtains, so it was almost completely dark inside the bedroom. Nadine lay face down on the bed, uncovered, her back speckled with ghostly white daubs of cortisone.

"God," she said, "I don't feel too sharp."

"I don't blame you." Martin knelt and felt in the side pocket of his carry-on for the bottle of Ricard, which he'd put on the top. "Anything I can get you to drink or whatever?" he said.

"No thanks," Nadine said. "I just feel like I want to turn over on my back, but I bet I wouldn't like it if I actually did." From the drifty tone her voice had, he could guess she was probably a little feverish. "I don't know," he heard her mumble. "Maybe we *should* have gone to the Cape."

"They have sunburn on the Cape too, remember," Martin said. "Also, if we went to the Cape again, I'm afraid by the end of the trip our daughter would be a pregnant dope addict with five different kinds of venereal disease."

"You have a way with exaggeration," Nadine said.

"I'm a pessimist, it's always worked for me in court." Martin strolled to the side of the bed. "Where can I touch you it's not going to hurt?"

"Try the inside of my hand," Nadine said with a weak laugh.

Martin stroked her palm for a moment and then spread her fingers back on the pillow. "Well, I'll be right outside on the porch here," he said. "I'm leaving a crack in the door, so just call if you want anything, okay?"

"Thanks, Marty," Nadine said. "I think I'm just going to go to sleep, probably."

Martin inserted himself into the tiny kitchen and took out the pitcher of water he'd put in the fridge just before he went out to call American Express. His theory of vacations was that a certain amount of catastrophe was always sure to be included and he wasn't so unhappy to have got this much of it over with so early in the trip. Nadine's sunburns were a given, you could write that off before you left home, and she hadn't lost any money or credit cards, only the packet of traveler's checks and the cheap wallet that held them, so the damage control looked fairly efficient so far. There was nothing on the agenda now but to make a little run for some food to bring back and pick up Mindy on the way—speaking of which, he was happy enough to have a couple hours off from being her parole officer, not a job that suited him too well in the first place. He doubted her French was really good enough to get her in serious trouble here. Not the first evening, that was a bet. He dropped an ice cube into a short glass and carried the bottle and pitcher through the front room and out to a small white table by the balcony rail. The tin cap of the Ricard came off without cutting him even a little bit—nice work there, Marty; things were looking up. He liked pastis but drank it only on vacation, kind of a reward for surviving the journey to wherever it was. The amber syrup streaked misty green where it touched the ice cube, and when he poured the water in, it clouded up to the brim. Martin took a hard enough belt to numb his teeth slightly, looked up and discovered the mountains.

He couldn't think where they'd been that morning; maybe he just wasn't paying attention, or they might have been covered up with cloud. In the twilight the highway was no longer noticeable. It had turned very quiet, and beyond the canyon the mountains were bathed in silence and in the light, which remained wonderfully clear even as it faded. As the light receded on its slow smooth curve downward, the mountains began to lose dimension, flattening away into a deepwater blue distance, the rangy line along the peaks forsaking its distinction to evaporate into the darkening sky. Suffused with a calm so unfamiliar he could not recognize it, Martin raised his glass to the mountains and smiled.

When morning came it was the kind of morning which Ton-Ton Detroit did not like. Inshore it was clear enough, though the mountains had been decapitated by cloud, but out on the water it was so hazy that the horizon had disappeared altogether and there was nothing where it should have been but a rolling band of zero-colored vagaries. The sun was not shining from any definite direction; only an evil-seeming radiance whirled down into that amorphous zone that might have been either sky or sea. Ton-Ton Detroit went grimly through the trial of his morning ablution, then picked his way back across the rocks to his bag and began to worm into his dashiki. When his head emerged from the neck hole he was horrified to see that that New York kid had managed to slip up on him while he was blinded by the cloth.

"Well, uncle, I'll say we must be two of a kind." Clay grinned at him. "Both of us be getting up with the birds."

Ton-Ton Detroit said nothing at all. Mechanically, he went ahead with his preparations for the day, making a prodigious mental effort to annihilate the other's presence from his mind. When his wares were arrayed down the front of the dashiki, he fitted the horned radio over his ears and turned on *France Culture*. Time for *les informations*, and on a day like this one was shaping up to be, he wouldn't doubt the news would be all bad. Clay walked a little way down the sea wall, stretching and bouncing on the balls of his feet, then turned around and started to come back.

"You know what I used to believe, uncle?" he said. "I used to honestly think that people in Europe still carried real *money*. But I want you to just look here at how bad I been fooled."

From between the bottom two buttons of his shirt Clay produced one of the flat leather purses the younger Frenchmen sometimes carried and stuck it out at Ton-Ton Detroit at the end of both his arms. Ton-Ton Detroit moved to turn up his radio and drown out whatever Clay might be going to say next, but by some cursed accident he touched the wrong dial and instead was caught listening to a blurry French cover of some American pop tune he knew he had always hated even without being able to completely recognize it now.

M'enlève pas ma yunyunyah . . .
M'enlève pas ma yunyunyah . . .
M'enlève pas ma yunyunyah . . .
oooh-ahhhh . . .

He flinched, his teeth squeaking together, and turned the radio off. All things considered he was not particularly surprised by this development. He had had ominous dreams all night and the *flics* had already flipped him upside down and shaken him this morning on his way out to the breakwater, turning all his gear out onto the asphalt of the parking and leaving him to scrape it back together when they were done. They knew that he knew that they knew that he had had nothing to do with the mugging at Cap Martin, but whenever anything of that kind happened they liked to throw a little scare his way in case perhaps he might inform, though up to now he never had. Clay pushed the zip of the purse back with his thumb and spread it open across his palms.

"What do you think, uncle?" he said. "Don't try to tell me that's not pitiful. A guy carries around this fat old bag and nothing inside it at all but what?" He gave the purse an angry shake. "Suntan oil. Address book, okay. Pictures of babes, man, this cat knows some *ugly* women. Here we got a bracelet of some kind of worry rocks or something, I don't know what. And five different kinds of credit cards, three of which I never even heard of. And not enough cash for a baby mouse to make a nest in."

Clay shook the bag some more, jogging the contents up and down. Ton-Ton Detroit put on his fisherman's sunglasses but the inside of the purse didn't look any different under polarized light.

"I tell you something, uncle," Clay said slowly. "You just about the best friend I know in this whole town. Man, I know you got to know somebody can help me move this plastic."

"*Je balance pas,*" Ton-Ton Detroit said. *I don't rat.* But maybe it was time he changed his policy.

"What's that you say?" Clay said. "You know I don't talk all that much frog."

"I can't help you any, son," Ton-Ton Detroit said. "You might just as well be showing me a nice handful of radioactive rocks."

"That bad?" Clay fanned the credit cards out like a hand of five-card draw and then folded them together and stuck them in his top pocket.

"You ought to get rid of that mess, boy," Ton-Ton Detroit said. "I can tell you from here it won't bring you any happiness at all."

"Well, you know I *want* to get rid of them," Clay said. "But I was like counting on you to show me the way how. Come on, uncle, I *know* you know *somebody.*"

Ton-Ton Detroit forced out the bottom of his breath and turned himself to stone. Clay took a few nervous steps back and forth along the wall and then slapped his coat pocket and took out a box of Marlboros.

"You like one of these, uncle?" he said. "Go ahead, I owe you one."

"I like my own brand," Ton-Ton Detroit said. "You find them in that pocketbook?"

"Ah well, what if I did?" Clay said. "Still not enough to take me very far." He poked a cigarette in his mouth and dropped the box back in his coat. "While we at it, you got a light?"

Silently, Ton-Ton Detroit handed him a single kitchen match. Clay looked at it a second and then struck it on the wall and lit his smoke. After he had flipped away the matchstick he scooped out the contents of the purse with the motion of somebody seeding a cantaloupe and dropped everything off the edge of the breakwater. Then he zipped the purse back shut and began to fondle the smooth brown leather.

"Nice Spanish leather we got here, uncle," he said. "Quality workmanship too, all handmade, just look at that stitching, it's made to last. I wouldn't doubt it would bring you two, three hundred francs at least if you wanted to hang it on your rack. People around here go for this kind of thing."

Ton-Ton Detroit reached for the purse, held it close to his eyes for a couple of seconds, then turned and flung it out over the water as far as it wanted to go. It traveled a wide arc against the blurred zone where the horizon should have been, spinning horizontally like a plate, and landed far enough away he couldn't hear the splash. When he turned back, Clay's face had drawn so tight the bones were sticking through the skin and Ton-Ton Detroit made ready to trip him off the breakwater if he decided to lunge. However, in a few seconds Clay had relaxed.

"They put a *flic* on l'Escalier de la Plage already," Ton-Ton Detroit said. "I wouldn't be surprised if you found one just about anywhere else it might occur to you to try."

Clay sagged back against the wall, crossing his shiny black shoes in front of him. He took the cigarette out of his mouth and stared at the long tube of ash on the end. There wasn't even enough breeze to blow it off of there.

"All right, uncle, it's your beat," he said. "If you think the thing's too hot, it's too hot, I guess. Can't be too careful in this business, right?"

Behind his sunglasses, Ton-Ton Detroit squinched his eyes tight shut. Clay pushed himself upright off the wall and brushed a little white dust off the tail of his coat.

"Dig you later, uncle, I guess," he said. "And just keep me in mind if you have any ideas."

When Ton-Ton Detroit still did not answer Clay shrugged and started away toward the harbor with his head tucked in and his hands pushed deep in his pockets. Once he was good and gone, Ton-Ton Detroit lit a Gauloise Blonde, but it tasted stale and gritty to him now. It was already hot and the day was still suffocatingly calm. When he looked up for the mountains he saw only a blank. He readjusted the radio, gazing out over the pale tinny water. Time for the science program; *les informations* had passed. He hoped that the purse wasn't planning to come floating back up to the breakwater; it would give the *flics* an edge on him if it did, since they knew he hung around the place.

Mindy had come to the conclusion that until she managed to get to a store, her white beach pajamas were the best thing she had going. She didn't bother to put a top on underneath. Daddy gave her the *oh God* look when she went out the door but she didn't think he'd really noticed or he would have pitched more of a fit. That was it, she was cool till lunch or later, since he'd have to stick close to Mom all day.

So naturally *all* the beaches were pebbles, of course they wouldn't have heard of sand yet in France. She explored a little way down the shore, but let's face up to it, rocks were rocks, and there really wasn't any place better than the section below where the stairs came out. You could rent time on deck chairs here and there, she saw, but her cash flow was a little constricted at the moment and she'd rather hold on to what she had for maybe a couple of *long-drinks* that night. It wasn't particularly crowded and she found a decent-looking spot and spread her towel on it, pounding the gravel in a few key places as if that might make it a little softer. Actually it wasn't as bad as it looked once you got it all kind of adapted to your bod. She stepped out of her white trousers and folded them neatly for later and then sat down and rolled off the blouse. *Shazam*, first time ever on a topless beach, not counting skinny-dipping at night, but it didn't look like any applause was going to start up right away.

She put the blouse away in her bag and started giving herself a long slow coat of cocoa butter, checking out the area on either side while she rubbed it in. You could tell the French women must come here all the time because none of them had the ghost of a strap mark, but apart from that Mindy felt well ahead on points so far. Most of the others had stretch marks if you looked close enough, and seemed at least a little droopy up top, and they all seemed to have little kids along with them, which probably explained why they looked a little run-down. The guys, well, first of all most of them looked like husbands, and none of them were that great to start with. The basic trouble with French guys was like hardly any muscles, they all seemed to have those little chicken-wing arms, not that it seemed to slow them down much. Actually there were a couple of hunkier ones stretched on platforms back up by the steps, but some way or other they seemed kind of out of it, lying there still as statues carved out of meat.

Maybe they were all gay or something; anyway, it was pretty early still. Mindy stretched out on her back and shut her eyes, breathing in the sweet smell of the warm cocoa butter. The sun seemed hotter on her breasts than anywhere else, if she wasn't imagining it, and for a minute she felt just a little self-conscious, but pretty soon she forgot all about it and started to daydream. When she woke up she'd broken a sweat from the sun and she sat up to check for sure she wasn't burning; she had an okay poolside tan from California but it would be dumb to end up with a pair of blistered tits. Time to see what the water was like, but hey, walking barefoot on these rocks was no joke, she didn't see how the French people could hack it. Way out near the line of buoys were some people lying on another diving raft, but Mindy was only a couple of steps in before she knew she'd never make it, man, it already was making her eyeballs hurt and she was barely up to her knees. She could tell the shelf dropped off a few feet more right in front of her because there was this fat lady swimming right by, with a bathing cap on and also a pair of flip-flops—so that was how you got over the rocks. Farther out, a guy with a snorkel popped out of the water, and he was also wearing a wet suit, and she would bet he needed it.

Well, okay, forget about swimming. Blue had never been her color. She turned around and went mincingly back toward her towel. More people had showed up while she'd been napping, but they all still looked like little families and stuff, and surprise! but all of them were French. Nobody seemed to be cruising at all, it was kind of an antisocial scene, everybody just rooted to their own patch of gravel. The French boys seemed to all hang out up there on the promenade, slouching around on their bikes and like that; she wondered how they kept those great tans without ever coming down to the beach.

Well, once she had her moped she could probably make it to Monaco, for sure there'd be something more going on there. Mindy dropped to her knees and then stretched out on her stomach, but it was tougher trying to lie on that side, every little rock seemed to be out to get her from under the towel, and after a minute she had to sit back up. Yep, she was starting to get just a little bit bored, should have brought a magazine or something, she wished she'd remembered the radio. Back home she had a mini-TV, but she'd been told it wouldn't work over here for some reason. She stared down the beach; even with sunglasses it was getting too bright. One of those black street peddlers, or beach peddlers, whatever, was coming along the strand her way, repeating a phrase in a kind of low grumble.

"*Regardez-moi ça, messieurs, mesdames, c'est pas cher, regardez, c'est pas cher . . .*" Ton-Ton Detroit came to a halt, his sandals about an inch back from the fringe of Mindy's towel.

Mindy rose to her knees to peer at his stuff. The jewelry was okay but too heavy for her, and though the radios were kind of neat she already had a radio back in the apartment. She couldn't quite remember the French word for "purse."

"Uh," she said, pointing, "*montrez-moi ça.*"

"Ees a booteeful purse," Ton-Ton Detroit said, turning up his French accent as far as it would go and unhooking the thing from its little strap.

"Hey, you speak English?" Mindy said.

When she all of a sudden remembered she was topless she almost blushed, but she didn't think she had all the way, and she was tan enough in the face she didn't really believe it would show all that much.

"Onlee a leetle," Ton-Ton Detroit said. The Americans usually liked it better that way. "Vayree good deal, onlee one hundred frawncs." He grinned at her from one ear to the other.

Mindy snapped up the flap of the purse and peeked inside at the lining. Cute idea, snakeskin, but it looked fakey close up and she could tell at a glance the stitching was junk. And a hundred francs was practically twenty bucks, for God's sake. She didn't feel a bit embarrassed anymore, she felt sort of cool and Continental, and she knew she was maintaining just fine.

"*Non, merci,*" she said, flopping back on her towel. "*Je ne l'aime pas.*"

In spite of all the omens, Ton-Ton Detroit had sold more this morning than the morning before, though that didn't make him feel any better, since he now had to look for the bad luck to strike him from some unknown direction. By noon he was still not very hungry and he walked back toward Menton on the street behind the hotels, hoping his appetite might improve. On his left-hand side the *midi* rush hour traffic buzzed and roared, all the people fighting their way back home for lunch. Since he had a little extra money Ton-Ton Detroit went into La Régence and ordered one of their cheaper salads, but his mouth remained obstinately dry and he might as well have been kneeling down to eat grass for all the taste the lettuce had. On his way out he paused at the *zinc* for a glass of red wine, which made him feel a little better by the time he reached the street.

The heat was at its maximum but he felt too listless to try to evade it. It was not the right time of day for people to buy things, so he climbed to the stone catwalk inside the harbor wall and spread himself like a lizard in the full glare of the sun. The heat of the wall soaked into his back, and as he began to feel more comfortable and sleepier he let his feet slide slowly forward until they dangled slackly between the posts of the steel railing. In the shade of his sunglasses, his eyes narrowed to slits. The entire spread of the harbor was almost too bright to be visible, and on the beach beyond it the sunbathers lay fixed to the ground as though particular beams of light had nailed each of them down.

The only movement was a steady trickle of people going back and forth along the concrete ramp that led up into the town, and there was a place where it was blocked by a lump of people clogging an area shaded by several trees. Ton-Ton Detroit's eyes came open a little wider when he saw that Clay was at the center of this thickening crowd. The boy had set up a stack of old boxes and his hands were flying across the lid of the top one, light and nervous as a couple of bats. His movements were so rapid and ardent that from this distance his whole body seemed to shimmer. It looked like he might be doing pretty well too; at least he had a good enough crowd to draw pickpockets.

Ton-Ton Detroit leaned forward a little more, hooking his elbow up around the guardrail. For Clay the game must just be starting to get sweet. The cards spun and flashed crazily along the lines his fingers stroked, catching the light when he turned them face up. A hundred-franc note looked almost pink at this distance and Ton-Ton Detroit thought he could see quite a few of them changing hands. The boy might make out all right if only he knew when to quit. Ton-Ton Detroit would have given him about fifteen more minutes, but as it turned out he got almost twenty before the *flics* arrived. The shovel-nosed car rolled slowly to the end of the parking and stopped just in front of the Cocteau Museum. It was the same pair who had rolled him over early that morning — the one who'd dumped his bag was slightly bowlegged, the other tall and razor-faced. Both wore short-sleeved white shirts with little pleats on the pockets, and their browned forearms swung out to a stiff clicking beat as they moved up toward the edge of Clay's crowd. Still caught up in the heat of his game, Clay didn't seem to have noticed them yet. Ton-Ton Detroit thought in an abstract way of giving a shout, but he didn't think his voice would carry so far, and besides, he doubted he was going to miss Clay all that much either, if something should happen to cause him to leave.

What Clay could have used was a whole boatload of things he just hadn't got and didn't see coming: a fresh jacket with no scrape marks down the sleeves, a crowd that spoke English, more money to lose and above everything else some kind of a partner, a dude to get the betting started and then watch down the street once the action warmed up. But the only one he'd been able to think of was old uncle, and the man didn't appear inclined to be helpful, so Clay hadn't even felt like he wanted to ask.

This would be as close to the bone as he'd ever cut it, and he'd had some doubts about whether he should try it at all, but the short of it was, he didn't have all that much left to try. If that one guy he'd already hit was average, he'd need to do around ten more like him to make enough for a flight, and it did seem like that would be really pushing it. He'd figured out that you probably didn't need all that many words to run a simple game of three-card monte, and he'd spent a few minutes with a dictionary, standing up in a store, to check out the couple he thought he should know. After that there was nothing much to it but grab a few boxes out back of a restaurant and stack them waist high in the likeliest spot.

"*Trouvez le rouge, trouvez le rouge.*" Clay figured he could get by with that and *Pariez cent* and handle the rest in pantomime. It should work out if he could just get it started, but now was the moment he most needed a shill. If he looked up, he could see old uncle perched high up there on the wall of the harbor; why couldn't he come down here where he might be some use? Clay made the cards flash and flicker and dance, finding the rhythm, fondling the beat. People were just glancing at him and going on by, man, they must think he had time enough to stand there all day. There were enough of them, but none of them stopped, and it was hot as the devil even here in the shade, his face was already running with sweat.

"*Trouvez le rouge, trouvez le rouge . . .*" Okay, so it wasn't the most exciting line of patter. But stop for me, somebody, come on, just one. He faced the cards up, aces all: the spade, the club and the lucky diamond. A couple had just now halted in front of him — thank you, Lord — old lady in a blue-striped cotton dress, old guy with gold teeth in a cockeyed denture and silver hair swept back in a sporty wave. Come on, sport, bet me one.

"*Pariez cent.*" Clay spread a hundred-franc note on the box top behind the cards, smiling steady as a corpse as he felt a fresh wave of sweat break over his forehead. The old cat smiled back at him, half his top teeth sliding the opposite way from the rest, but he wasn't showing out any money. Oh man, Clay thought, if I had some more *words*. He flourished the cards as eloquently as he knew how to do it, still no action, but one more guy stopped, big heavy dude with a face that looked like it might just have been stepped on, black wraparound sunglasses hiding his eyes. He had a white bulldog hooked to him on a chain, and one fat mother dog it was too. Clay watched it sit down on the toe of the guy's shoe and start licking all over its own smashed-in face, foaming clear slobber from the hot-pink inside of its mouth.

"*Pariez cent.*" A fresh breeze levitated his bill from the box and Clay caught it under his elbow, still working the cards. The guy's face was like rock, but he was getting the message — thank you, Jesus — he was pulling out a bill. Clay nodded to him, stopped the cards and let him have the first one, gave him the red diamond his thick finger had pointed out.

"*Pariez cent.*" A couple more people had already stopped and behind them he could see there were more slowing down.

Clay let the meaty guy have a second bill. He'd fibbed a little to old uncle back then; there'd been four hundred-franc notes in that purse, though he'd busted one for smokes and food. He'd thought of running the game on fifties but the problem was it would have been much too slow, when something like three thousand francs was the best deal he could find on a flight to New York. He beat the guy back for the middle bill and then let him get it again on the next play. Up to ten people were standing there now, but still, this could get boring quick. Then he saw the silver-haired guy unwinding a bill from a money clip and at the same time another one landed on the front of the box, mashed under a hand he hadn't matched with a face yet. Finally, they were catching on. He lost the first one and beat the next two, kicked back and started making his money.

The main thing on his mind now was time. Old uncle said the game wouldn't go over at all around here, which made Clay think that at least he didn't want to get caught. He thought he'd be good for a half hour or so of fairly fast action and then he'd be a lot better off gone. When he'd guessed the time was nearly up he checked his wrist, but still no watch. Letting the cards stop for a second, he looked up to see if there might be a clock on a building somewhere, but he was facing the harbor and there was nothing that way but Ton-Ton Detroit, still roosting on the wall like a vulture. The old cat was in the perfect position; Clay only wished he had him signed up as a lookout. The silver-haired dude had a watch on anyway, and it said about ten after one. The crowd was good and thick and wrapping the whole way around him now, so anybody coming through it wouldn't be able to see him right away. He thought he could give it five or ten minutes yet before he blew.

He'd been pushing the money down in his back pocket, where it was easiest to stuff it in quick. How much he had in there he had no idea, but a few more minutes and he'd get off somewhere and count. If it wasn't all he hoped for, he'd take the train to Nice and see what kind of a thing he could put together over there. The crowd was packed in tight around the box now, it was getting hard to keep a handle on it all, every couple of minutes he had to wave them all back to make room for himself to breathe and keep working. The only one that wouldn't move out was some kid that wasn't even betting, a moon-faced brat with a little poodle strapped to him by a red leather leash. Clay had a foggy feeling he'd seen him around somewhere before, but he sure didn't need to be seeing him now.

"Beat it, kid," Clay said, wishing he'd looked up the French for that. "Go on, take off, get out of here."

He made a disappearing gesture right under the kid's nose, but the kid just stared up at him with his soft stupid eyes. He was mumbling some kind of I-don't-know-what right along, though Clay had the feeling he was just talking to his dog. Where was that bulldog when you wanted him? It could have finished off this fluff of a poodle in half of a mouthful. The poodle had drifted around the corner of the bottom box and started licking its way up the side of his shoe. Clay gave it a light kick in the chops and the dog sat back on its haunches with an outraged yelp. Maybe that would get rid of the pair of them. When he turned his attention back to the game he could see a wedge opening in the rear of the crowd. What was coming that way he couldn't quite tell, but people were making room for it like swimmers for sharks, and that was convincing enough for him. He kicked the stack of boxes over, letting the cards go flying with them, and took a couple of long strides back into the crowd behind him.

People back here had all been trying to peer over one another's shoulders and they were still trying to see past one another now; they didn't quite know he was what they were supposed to be looking at. The center of the ring had dissolved by this time, but Clay could see the two cops moving in the area right where it had been. He didn't see those rubber sticks he'd been hearing about yet, but he still didn't feel like he wanted to be spending much time with them. But for the moment he held his ground. Nowhere to run to anyway, and if he got lucky nobody would point him out. The cops were saying some kind of stuff, asking questions or giving orders, he couldn't be sure. When the people around him began to move off, Clay turned and started to drift along with them. Right away he felt eyes drilling into the back of his head, but he wasn't going to turn back to see if it was his imagination or not. Once he'd made it a few yards into the regular foot traffic, the feeling passed over and he thought he was cool, but it was right at that moment that something tripped him. His stomach seized up on him as he whirled around, but it was nothing but that same fat kid again: he'd got his foot hung up in the dog leash.

"Little bastard," Clay snapped at him, kicking free, and remembered he probably wouldn't know what that meant. He threw a slap toward the kid's head, but somehow he misjudged the distance, and by the time it got there the boy was long gone out of range.

Martin had always liked to take his vacations on the beach, even though none of the conventional beach amusements attracted him all that much. He was not a great swimmer and had no interest in the other main water sports. As he liked to tell people, he was naturally tan and didn't have to go fry on a field of hot sand to achieve it. If fishing was proposed to him, Martin's line was: "Life is boring, fishing is worse." What he did like was walking on the shore or near it, and sitting somewhere he could look at the water. Whenever Nadine had one of her sunburns he fell back hard on the second pastime.

It was a really bad one this time around and it didn't look like it would get much better before day three. On day two she didn't wake up until midmorning, when Mindy had already gone to the beach, which was good luck for her, or so Martin thought. He gave her a fresh coat of cortisone cream, fed her her pills and brought her a tall glass of orange juice when she kept on saying she didn't want to eat. A little later he left her lightly dozing and went out to see what was new on the balcony. The glass water pitcher still stood on the white table where he'd forgotten it the night before, and it seemed extraordinarily noticeable to Martin somehow, though at first he couldn't have told why. The water had caught no particular ray but it was nonetheless so full of the sun that it glowed inwardly, swollen with light. He went into the kitchen and brought back a glass and poured it brim-full of the water. When he had sipped from it and set it back down, it became at once another such jewel, a crystal absorbed in a quiet inner radiance.

On the other side of the highway there was still dense fog and where the mountains had been was now nothing but cloud. The fog smoked and moiled and formed itself into phantasmagoric shapes as it peeled away layer by slow layer and burned off into the upper air. Behind it, within it, the mountains took on line, then form, playing across a scale of color from the dimmest blue to a patchy gray and green. At last the fog had been all sucked away into a sky that was now an uncompromised ultramarine; in the small corner which Martin could see past the pine, the ocean had begun to reflect it. Down in the town, some reflecting surface had caught the sun and flung it back with nearly a laser's concentration. Along the skyline ridges of the mountains, the conifers stuck up like little hairs. On the table before him, the pitcher and glass shone forth a brilliant diamond light.

When he finally got up he felt he was starving and he went into the kitchen to cook some spaghetti. Mindy would be staying out for lunch or skipping it, probably—well, never mind. He carried a bowl into Nadine and found her sitting up crosslegged on the bed, flipping desultorily through a copy of *Palm Beach*. Trying to find a good part, she said. They ate together without saying much, and when they were done Martin greased her back again and went into the kitchen to clean up. Back on the balcony, the light had tilted, becoming a little less bright, more blue. He sat in a deck chair with a magazine opened across his knees, but his jet lag was still dragging at him and in a few minutes he dropped into an echoing sleep.

He woke feeling calm and only slightly bemused. Once again Nadine had outslept him; she moved uneasily on the bed when he looked in on her, but did not quite wake up. Passing through the front room, he could see no sign that Mindy had been back through there yet. He took the bottle of Ricard out to the balcony and poured his first drink, ceremoniously slow. The water struck the liquor in a smoky explosion and Martin continued to look out and up.

The trees had faded away from the ridgetops now, and the mountains were floating off down their deep well of blue. The swallows had just begun to come in, darting and flickering, then freezing to soar, their crossbow silhouettes slicing long strokes on the sky. When it was almost too dark to see them anymore, Martin noticed that a crescent moon had appeared, stained rose by the last falling light of the sun. Beside it was a jet trail, also red, raking its way across the purpling sky, progressing so slowly he had to strain to see it move. By the time the jet trail had dissolved into the dark, the moon had turned more crimson and was dropping speedily into a cleft of the ridge. When it had gone Martin could no longer distinguish the top line of the mountains, though a net of colored lights was creeping up the hollows toward the spot where it had disappeared. The air had grown cooler, almost cold, and Martin shivered with a pleasant tingle. It came to him that Mindy had been gone so long now that ordinarily he would have been crawling the walls, but here he felt so completely at ease that the worry was more a prick than a shock; he felt that it hardly could reach him at all.

In the evening Ton-Ton Detroit encountered the Haitian in the Eden Bar. The Haitian had bought a handful of peanuts from a little machine that stood on the counter and was feeding them one by one to the parrot who lived behind the metal grille fixed in the wall to the left of the door. The parrot hung sideways with his wrinkled feet clamped to the wire mesh and accepted the peanuts singly into his sharp curved beak, turning his head one way and another to examine the Haitian out of each of his round eyes. The Haitian spoke to him in a guttural murmur and the parrot responded with sirenlike whistles. When Ton-Ton Detroit came in the Haitian offered him a peanut to feed to the bird. Ton-Ton Detroit separated the nut from the small foil packet that had come with it and proffered it to the parrot's beak, holding it in such a way that the bird had next to no chance at his fingers. The parrot took the peanut delicately and after eating it let out such a piercing shrill that Ton-Ton Detroit started a couple of feet back. He shook hands with the Haitian in their usual way and then went down the hill to the breakwater.

An unlucky wind had brought a quantity of trash to float sulkily in a foaming line along the lower edge of the rocks. Without trying he could find a light bulb, a juice carton, a wrinkled hot-pink condom, the front panel of a cheap note pad and a great many other things too rotten or broken for him to identify. The water seemed to be staining the rocks as it licked them and from below the post where he was sitting there rose a dense and fetid smell. He smoked assiduously to cut off the stench from his nostrils, but the hash seemed to darken his mind much more than it relieved it. This evening there were no fish to be seen. Just under the surface of the water a variform patch of seaweed several yards across expanded and contracted in a dull sickly movement like the hand of a drowned man opening and closing with the shifting of the tide. When Clay came popping through the door to the sea wall, Ton-Ton Detroit discovered that he was not at all surprised. He let the boy scramble up on the post beside him without doing anything either to help or prevent him. Clay walked to the edge of the post, scratched his head, turned around, snapped his fingers and finally sat down.

"Listen, uncle," he said. "I know you got to have something, man. I *know* you holding some kind of something because there wouldn't be any reason for you to hang in a place like here if you weren't."

Ton-Ton Detroit sat perfectly still, staring out at the place where the sky met the sea. It had cleared enough for him to see the horizon now, though it was no more than the palest blue line.

"Come across for me, uncle, come on," Clay said. "I'm telling you straight, my head needs some help."

Mutely, Ton-Ton Detroit unpalmed the tinfoil pipe and held it out. There wasn't a lot left in there and it didn't seem to have been doing him all that much good, either.

"That's a little more like it," Clay said, stretching his hand out for the pipe. And while you're at it—" He cut himself off.

Ton-Ton Detroit already had the lone kitchen match sticking straight up under his nose. Clay scraped it into a little blue blaze on the stone and held it over the crumpled pipe bowl and sucked down hard for a very long time. Ton-Ton Detroit saw the line of his mouth tighten when the foil got hot but he did not stop drawing until the hash had burned down to a smear of greasy ash. After he had lowered the pipe from his lips he sat for some time more without breathing, and when he finally did exhale there was no sign of any smoke escaping.

"That's fine, uncle. Thanks a whole lot."

Clay snapped the matchstick in two and let the pieces fall over the edge of the post into the rest of the litter floating dully below. Ton-Ton Detroit peered down after it; he kept thinking he saw that purse drifting with the rest of the trash, though so far he'd been wrong.

"One more thing I hate about this place," Clay said. "Not even a pack of matches is free. Hey, you not carrying any more of that, are you?"

"No," Ton-Ton Detroit said.

"Oh," Clay said.

For several minutes he stared out at a point on the horizon

beside the one that Ton-Ton Detroit was staring at. Then he balled up his fist and smashed the stone surface of the post three or four times with the meaty side of it. On the last smash the fist bounced back at a funny angle and Clay uncurled his hand and looked at the raw edge of it.

"Now I skinned my hand on top of everything else," he said.

"Yes," Ton-Ton Detroit said.

Clay's face crinkled up as though he might start to cry and Ton-Ton Detroit shifted to another angle so he wouldn't have to watch it if he did. But after a couple of seconds Clay just began to curse. He seemed to know a lot of words but he was jumbling them all together in a nonsense sort of way. The one that seemed to please him most was "bastard."

"That little bastard," Clay said, and paused for breath. "He got away with all my money, man, I didn't even get a chance to see how much it *was*."

"Yes," Ton-Ton Detroit said.

Clay raised his head and stared at him hungrily. "You *know* him, uncle, is that right? Then why didn't you ever let me know about him?"

"I try to let you know about a number of things," Ton-Ton Detroit said.

"Well there's just one thing I need to know now. Where's he live at? What's his name?"

"He don't really have a name in particular," Ton-Ton Detroit said. "The people just mostly know him by that little dog of his."

"Yeah, that sweet little son-of-a-bitching dog," Clay muttered. "He talk to it like it was a baby or something . . . Man, but all of my money is gone."

"I understood it you didn't have any money," Ton-Ton Detroit said.

Clay did not appear to have heard him. "Uncle, I swear you the best friend I got," he said. "Don't you have some kind of a thought about what I could do?"

Ton-Ton Detroit lit himself a cigarette and smoked a fair

portion of it down. He waited for Clay to ask for one too, but the boy just gazed at him out of sad baggy eyes.

"Come through for me, uncle," Clay said. "I need somebody to tell me my fortune."

Ton-Ton Detroit licked his fingertip and dampened his cigarette where it had begun to run down one side.

"I think you be better off leaving this place," he said.

Clay snorted, then rocked back and moaned. "Now just what you think I been trying to do? The one thing I want now is get back to New York. But I can't even raise the fare for a bus across town."

"I don't see why you don't go to Italy," Ton-Ton Detroit said. He twisted the top of his body to point farther down the coast where Italy began. "You can just walk over the border. It's not more than about a mile."

"Yeah, but you know, I don't speak Italian," Clay said with a frown.

"You don't speak French either," said Ton-Ton Detroit.

"But I hate to leave here where I got my good friends," Clay said.

"If you turned yourself in, they might just deport you," Ton-Ton Detroit said. "Of course, on the other hand, they might not."

"If that's the best you can come up with, don't bother trying anymore," Clay said. He made a move to pound the stone again, but changed his mind and only smacked his thigh. "Man, if it wasn't for that *little bastard*. That oily little bastard, I'd swear he even had greasy eyes. Man, when I once catch that little bastard I'll rip him into little pieces and feed him straight to his own damn dog."

Ton-Ton Detroit reached up to his ear and turned on *France Culture* as loud as it would go. It was time for the music now, and he'd struck it lucky, they were playing Ornette.

"You go ahead and do that," he yelled at Clay over the mad squall in his ears. "Then just work in a rape and you'll have done everything."

. . .

In the beach pajamas and her red espadrilles, Mindy felt a little bit more on the beat, swinging back into La Régence like an old *habitué* and whistling up her *long-drink* from the bartender, who served it this time with a little bit more of a smile than a sneer. She took a good long slug from the glass on the way out to the same table she'd sat at last night. Outside, the place was busy again, and she thought maybe she recognized a few of the same people she'd seen before, though actually they were all beginning to run together just a little. She was a touch woozy from all the sun she'd had today, and the warm rasp of the loose fabric over her skin was letting her know she'd stayed out in it right up to her absolute limit. From the looks of her arms she thought she could tell her tan was getting really deeper, though of course it would show up the best against white. She crossed her legs and rocked her free foot, admiring how brown her ankle had turned. A young guy coming in from the street shot her some question or sudden remark and paused to see what she would answer, but Mindy was so startled she just drew a blank. The guy flicked her away with one hand and went on inside the bar, leaving her sitting there with her lips still slightly parted.

Man oh man, one lost opportunity. She dipped into the beach bag and put on her sunglasses; next time it happened, at least no one would be able to tell if her eyes started to bug out or anything like that. If they'd talk right to her, she thought she'd understand all right, that's if they gave her a few seconds' warning before they were planning to start. With luck she'd get better in a couple more days, because she wasn't too socially brilliant like this. There were gangs of kids at two tables near her, and she tried to tune in but she couldn't quite concentrate. It all could just as well have been bird sounds to her right now. She hit the bottom of her *long-drink* and closed her eyes behind her glasses, feeling her mind beginning to coast. She hadn't eaten much all day, not that she felt hungry now; it was just a sort of buoyancy, a dizziness too slight to be unpleasant. When she got up she could tell the booze was getting through to her fairly quick too, but still she felt like she was definitely good for at least one more.

Back inside the bar, she crossed over to the tobacco counter. Normally she didn't smoke, but she didn't mind one with a couple of drinks. A bullet-headed guy behind the counter gazed blankly through her as she scanned the shelves behind him for anything menthol, but there was nothing in sight and she didn't really feel up to phrasing a question, so she settled for a square blue pack of Gauloise, then cruised by the bar for another *long-drink*. When she got back to her table she did a slow careful job of tamping the pack—no use getting tobacco flecks on her teeth. The cigarette was almost as fat as her finger, and it smelled more like a cigar when she passed it underneath her nose. She stuck it in her mouth and riffled through her bag, but of course she'd forgotten to get any matches.

That left the oldest ploy since the invention of smoking . . . The table with the two guys and one girl looked the best. Now just be careful you don't ask for a light bulb or a forest fire or something. What was the word for matches again? She stepped over and nudged one of the guys on the shoulder.

"*Avez-vous une allumette?*"

The guy looked up at her, slightly surprised. His eyes were the light blue of a thin pane of colored glass. After a second he flicked his Bic and Mindy dipped her cigarette down to the flame.

"*Merci*," she said, and straightened back up. The guy nodded to her and turned back to his table.

Oh well. Maybe it wasn't the most hip way to say it. Anyway, she'd got the concept across. She shrugged and turned to sit back down again. This cigarette was a fairly primitive item, all right, but it tasted okay once you got used to it, and it was giving her that slight cigarette buzz to go along with her drink. She rested the back of her head on the show window and let her eyes begin to glaze over. On either side of her the conversations seemed to swell. *Gabble, gabble, gabble*, she better start understanding all this real quick. But right now she was too drowsy and comfortable to worry much about it . . . She sat back up straight when she saw that same guy coming back, the one that had given her the long look-over yesterday, the guy that looked a little like Prince. Her smile was all polished and ready for him, but he didn't even glance her way this time, just tramped right past her through the door. Mindy felt her head screwing around to follow his path like it was being pulled along on a string.

Well, what the *hell*. She'd be getting old soon if she let this go on. Time to show a little initiative, let her luck have a little more help. She got up and crushed out her butt in the ashtray, then picked up her drink and went into the bar. There was no sign of the guy anywhere at first, but then she spotted him coming back from the bathrooms, heading for the restaurant section. Mindy followed as far as the newsstand and stood idly turning one of the book racks, watching to see where he was going to sit down. For a minute he stood in front of the menu, looking down at it in a sort of wandering way, like maybe it confused him somehow. He was still real good looking when you got closer up. Also Mindy was getting a real strong suspicion that he was a foreigner around here himself.

It was strong dope, Clay had realized on his way back through the town, but it wasn't really helping his head all that much. He was just as unhappy as he had been before, only now it was harder for him to think why. His depression had become more of a weight than a thought. Also the dope was making him hungry. Just what he needed right now: a case of the munchies. He was walking down the restaurant strip and it seemed like every way he could point his nose it smelled a little more like food. When he couldn't stand it anymore, he dove into the first place that looked reasonably cheap.

The scrape on his hand was stinging him some, so he went to the bathroom to give it a rinse. The way things had been going, an infected cut might be enough to finish him off; he'd probably get hepatitis or gangrene or something. He washed the scrape carefully with plenty of soap, trying to avoid his face in the mirror, though his eyes kept floating back to the image. It was no longer the face of a lucky man. The suit didn't look *too* bad if you didn't look close, but the face was whipped looking all over now, and worst of all, he could see, the sea air was taking the treatment right out of his hair.

But it was mainly the hash, he told himself, so just don't get too hung up on it, now. He shook most of the water off his hands and walked back through the bar to the restaurant in back. All over the walls were these not-too-convincing pictures of food, and he swung in a slow half circle to look at them all. Couldn't think of the French for a single thing, though maybe that was just the dope working too. He stared at the chalkboard menu a while, trying to match the words to the pictures, then gave it up and crashed down on a chair. With one damp hand he juggled the change in his pocket. Something was worrying him about that too . . . Oh yeah, it was all the money he had. Might as well spend it all up quick, because it sure wasn't enough to bother with saving. A waitress had appeared by his chair, a droopy young woman with slightly popped eyes.

"*Vous désirez?*"

Clay leaned back in his chair and let his eyes close. His tongue rasped over his lips like a file.

"I would like . . ." he said. "Just let me have two hot dogs with mustard and onion. An order of fries and a big chocolate shake." Please, pretty please, he said to himself, but when he opened his eyes he was still there in France. The only difference was that this black-haired chick with purple-rimmed sunglasses had sat herself down at the table across from him.

"Like me to translate that for you?" she said. Clay heard

a slight click as his mouth dropped wide open. He couldn't figure out if this was somebody he was supposed to know or what. There was something vaguely familiar about her, and he couldn't tell if he was making it up or not. Anyway, she seemed friendly enough.

"You can jump right to it, darling," he said.

The babe switched herself around to look up at the waitress.

"*Monsieur aimerait le francfort et frites.*" She turned back to Clay. "You want the shake too?"

"Why not?" Clay said. "Anything you can get me." As long as this wasn't only the hash working too . . .

"*Une frappe au chocolat.*"

The waitress marked on her pad and took herself out. Clay tried a slow blink but the babe was still there, smiling at him across the rim of her drink. For a minute he couldn't quite think what to say. Then the waitress came back with the loaded plate and the sight of it seemed to unlock his tongue.

"Hey darling, I see you got it all figured out, making all this stuff appear just like magic . . ."

Mindy grinned at him and sipped from her glass. "Can't do a lot about the bun and the onions," she said. "But other than that, you should come out okay."

Clay sat back as the waitress clicked down the milk shake in front of him. "Got no complaint whatsoever, so far," he said. "So, you like to order anything for yourself?"

"Nah, not now," Mindy said, and Clay breathed easier. What was he thinking? He could never have paid for it.

"Wanna take it outside? It's cooler."

"I'd follow you anywhere," Clay said, and watched her get up, that white jim-jam outfit running all over her; he wondered if that thing was as cool as it looked.

Holding on to his plate and his glass, he followed her out to the front of the joint, eyes locked to the working of her hips. She didn't look bad, and she seemed real easy to get along with so far, though he had no idea yet where it was all going to go. She slid into a chair and he sat down beside her.

"Have a fry if you want one," he said. She lifted one from the plate and bit a quarter inch off the end of it while Clay went to work with his own knife and fork. It might not be Sabrett but he still wouldn't say no to it.

"Hungry," Mindy said, still smiling away.

"Uh . . . yeah, I was sorta," Clay said, wiping out his last fry. "You know how the day can get sometimes. You get so busy you forget to eat."

"Yeah, I'm the same way," Mindy said. "My parents are always on me about it." She coughed a little and covered her mouth.

"That right?" Clay said. "You here with your folks?"

"Kinda," she said. "But don't worry about it. I'm Mindy Ventura, so who're you?"

"Jones," Clay said without hardly thinking. He was starting to get an idea but he wasn't sure what kind.

"I think I would have guessed something a little more . . . unusual," Mindy said, sliding down farther in her chair.

"Oh well, you see Jones is just my first name." He took a quick glance at the street sign opposite. "My whole name is Jones Partouneaux, you see."

"Now that's kinda interesting." Mindy said. "Sounds kinda French, but you're American, aren'tcha?"

"Yeah," Clay said, and glanced over his shoulder. All the waitresses and things seemed to be way in the back. One giant step and he'd have had a free meal, but he thought this option might be worth sticking around for. "Well, you know, I come from New Orleans," he said. He hoped he'd be able to remember this stuff if he had to; when he got stoned he sometimes forgot things as quick as he said them. "I wonder how much you ever heard about the octoroons?"

An hour or so later he'd steered her all the way through the best octoroon fantasy he'd ever dreamed up in his life so far, with ribbons and gravy and anything else you could want. It had slave ships, plantations, alligators, whorehouses, duels and all, and it went from the Civil War all the way through

the Depression, to end up in the rough neighborhood of the
Theresa Hotel. By the time he got near the end he'd forgotten
the middle, but he wasn't worrying about that anymore because he'd already started to feel lucky again. Mindy, the
babe, was lapping it up, and she'd been throwing more and
more of her weight on his arm the farther they made it down
the beach. He'd had almost enough of walking that beat, but
he had a feeling he might have a real destination this time.
When he got through talking, they walked a way longer.
Nobody at all but them was down on the beach. The dark
was so solid a knife wouldn't have cut it, though if you looked
up you could see a few stars. They'd come most of the way
to Cap Martin, where not too much light leaked down from
street level.

"Hey, you got one terrific life story," Mindy said. "I don't
think anything like that ever happened to *us*. So, you wanna
sit down a minute?"

"Sure, no problem," Clay said to her. He'd clocked enough
miles on these rocks for the night.

"Hang on a sec while I put down the towel." Mindy was
rooting around in her bag. Clay could hardly see what she
was up to, it was so dark. After a minute her hand came up
from the spectral float of her sleeve and pulled him down to
land with a bump on the gravel.

"I see you travel with everything, huh?" Clay said.

"Everything you could possibly imagine," Mindy said, and
leaned into him. "Look what a beautiful night it is."

Clay glanced toward the water. What little he could see of
it was pretty enough, though the hash had worn off and left
him with a trace of a headache. He stroked one finger down
the back of her neck, and the next second she was stuck to
his mouth so hard he thought he was getting artificial res-
piration. Man, but these modern chicks were different; they
came at you fast and hit you hard. In fact, she'd toppled him
completely over, so he was lying laid all the way back with
his head propped up against a rock, with her straddling him

almost like a wrestler. He'd never known the fairy tale treatment to work quite so well; it was enough to make him wonder how old this girl could be. She was going over the inside of his mouth like a little kid licking out the cake-mixing bowl, with both hands clamped tight to the back of his head. Well, go ahead, sweetheart, chew face if you like it. His left hand went to work kneading the small of her back while his right crawled crabwise over some gravel and into the mouth of her bag. He couldn't find more than a little clutch purse, though, and when he got it open it held nothing but change. Was it a bill she'd used to pay his tab? It didn't disappoint him all that much; it was just curiosity, really, not the main attraction. He snapped the purse back shut one-handed and started to pay more attention to what she was doing. Didn't seem like she was wearing too much under those jimmy-jams, and it seemed like in about another minute she might rub them right off. He could feel warm skin plastering all over his front. If he didn't do something quick there'd be nothing left to do. He forced himself up onto one elbow, rolling her off onto the crook of his arm.

"I can tell you're a very passionate person, Mindy," he said. "You know, I really like that about you a lot. But maybe we better not go quite so fast."

"But sometimes I *like* to go fast," Mindy breathed at him. "Sometimes, you know, I just can't wait to get there."

"Uh, don't worry," Clay said. "We'll get there on time. But let's go the nicest, most comfortable way . . ."

"Yeah, these rocks do get a little rugged sometimes," Mindy said. "But I think we might have to do it at your place."

"My place?" Clay said. "I don't know about that."

"Why? You got a tough concierge or something?"

"That's exactly right," Clay said. "That old concierge is really a bear."

Mindy shrugged in the dark.

"Well, maybe you could sneak me in past her or something," she said. "Or I could go try to get a blanket out of our place, but you know, I might run into trouble getting back out."

"Oh," Clay said. "Is that kind of a problem?"

"Not always," Mindy said. "But sometimes, like if I stayed out all day."

"Really," Clay said. "You got any smokes?"

Mindy passed him the pack of Gauloise. "You'll have to come up with the matches, though," she said. "Light one for me too when you do."

"Hell, I don't have any either," Clay said, and handed her back the pack.

"Yeah," Mindy said. "I don't usually smoke."

"Me neither," Clay said. "I been cutting down recently. Hey, I forgot how old you told me you were."

"Well, I don't have all that many gray hairs yet," Mindy said. "I just turned twenty-one last month."

"You're keeping your figure too," Clay said, and began to pat all his pockets for matches, hoping he might have missed some on his last few hundred looks.

Twenty-one was not a conceivable age anymore; real people were twenty or twenty-four. This chick could maybe have passed for nineteen, but twenty-one was just out of the question. How old had she really looked in good light? Christ, he hoped she wasn't like *thirteen* or something. Her hot little teenage hand was sketching a spiral pattern on the inside of his thigh, making it harder and harder for him to think clearly. He wondered if they had anything like the Mann Act in France. Obviously it was time he put the plan in phase two.

"Mindy," he said. "You know, I'm really getting to like you a lot."

"Well, I like you too, Jones, or I wouldn't be here." Her hand was working a little higher, more or less on the path of his femoral artery. "Hey, I don't do stuff like this every day."

"I feel so close to you right now . . ." Clay said. "I don't want us to do anything that might spoil it. A feeling like this, it's like a little flower, you have to treat it very careful, know what I mean?"

"Oh, I'm all taken care of, if that's what you're thinking," Mindy said. "You don't have to worry, it's under control."

"No, baby, no no no," Clay said, hitching his leg a little way out of her reach. "Listen, darling, I don't think you're hearing me quite the right way. What I'm trying to tell you is, I got this definite feeling of *respect* for you too. I mean, we got this beautiful kind of a thing started up between us here. I don't want to ruin it getting all carried away."

"I don't get it," Mindy said, sitting up straight. "I mean, like, are you nervous or what?"

"*Nervous?*" Clay said. "What you talking *nervous*, girl? I don't think you hear what I'm saying at all. I'm saying like how we don't have to rush things. Like how I want to do it real slow and real proper and get to know you a lot better first. You know, like go meet your family and stuff."

Once the night had turned completely black, Ton-Ton Detroit walked down the beach to a dark place from which he could look up to see the stars. There was a triangular area between three large boulders that lay pushed up against the supporting wall of the promenade, and he settled himself into it and tipped his head back. Tonight the sky was resonantly deep, and though the darkness was equally profound he felt that he was seeing into it a very long way. The luminescent shimmer that streaked a part of the bowl of stars was not a cloud but the Milky Way. He felt hopeful that tomorrow would be clear.

Away from the shelter of his rocks, the beach was spattered here and there with stains of light spilling down from the street lights on the promenade above, though no light reached quite all the way to the water. Beyond a low lip of gravel the sea had pushed up during the day, a single wave repeated itself, swelling slowly to curve over in a precision-tooled arc

and worked its gradual way to the other side of it. Again the leash grew taut, and the little pickpocket swiveled and went after the dog, drifting farther away into the darkness beyond. Ton-Ton Detroit listened, straining his ears, until the last whisper of the child's footsteps was gone. Still, it was a very long time before he could rid himself of the sensation that he was being watched.

Martin could not have told just when it began to cost him an effort to preserve his calm, but certainly it was a good while after it had grown completely dark. All the visible changes in the landscape had stopped, except for the blinking of lights in Menton. At the far edge of the spangle of lights, the Saint-Michel bell tower was lit from below by a big orange flood. The tower was so distant and still it seemed to make a period to time, and Martin could almost forget time was passing at all, except when very occasionally a train shot out of the tunnel below him and rushed with a long sigh toward the town.

After three slow drinks he screwed the cap back on the bottle of pastis. He was not at all hungry, and Nadine was asleep; the antihistamines had knocked her cold like they usually did. It was getting a little too cool on the balcony, but he still didn't much feel like going inside. When finally he heard the key turn in the lock, he decided to stay where he was and not make a big scene of it. Only when he heard the second voice did he rise from the deck chair and go back indoors.

"Well, hi, Dad," Mindy said. She seemed a little ill at ease, the way she was jittering from one foot to the other. "This is my good friend, Jones Partouneaux."

Martin couldn't quite focus on the guy for a second; he seemed to swim strangely against that wild wallpaper. Maybe it was just the change of light. When the dazzle had passed he reached out for the handshake and took a good look at Jones Partouneaux from his head to his feet.

"Very pleased to meet you, Jones," he said, and then turned to Mindy with equal formality. "You'll have to excuse us a little while, sweetheart. Jones and I have a couple of things to discuss."

"What in the hell are you talking about?" Mindy said.

"Girl, is that any way to talk to your father?" Clay said. "Can't you see the man and I got to have our get-acquainted time?"

Mindy stared at Clay with raw amazement. "Am I sure I heard you right?" she said. "My ears have been a little stopped up since I got off the plane."

"I couldn't have put it any better myself," Martin said. Mindy swung her hair back over her shoulder with a cross movement like that of a horse switching flies.

"I mean, this is getting to be the *weirdest* night," she said. "Okay, you guys, I'm taking a bath."

Martin glanced at Clay, who was smiling vaguely down at the floor. "There's chairs out on the balcony," he said. "You can go on out, I'll be with you in a minute."

He turned and went into the kitchen to get two fresh glasses, then pushed open the door to the bedroom and entered. Nadine was sleeping on her side, her mouth slightly parted, dampening the pillow. Quietly Martin unzipped his carry-on and got out the bottle of Mirabelle, then left the room by the glass door to the balcony. Clay had sat down to face the opposite direction and he gave a satisfying start when Martin came up behind him.

"Gotcha," Martin said. "Feel like a drink?"

"If you're planning to have one," Clay said, his tone rather demure.

Martin poured a couple of fingers into each of the glasses and pulled up a deck chair next to Clay. The clear liquor bored into him like a blue flame. Behind him he could hear pipes straining in the bathroom.

Clay raised his glass, took a big drink and coughed.

"Better go careful," Martin advised.

"Right," Clay said. "I see what you mean."

"You like it?" Martin said.

"Hot stuff," Clay said. "What is it exactly?"

"Eau de vie," Martin said. "You know, like a brandy. I save it for special occasions like this."

"I mostly drink B and B myself," Clay said. "That's if I'm celebrating something, I mean. Hey, you people got a really nice view from up here."

"I've found it very relaxing so far," Martin said.

"I guess maybe you get tense in your regular job."

"Sometimes," Martin said. "That varies a lot."

"Sure," Clay said. "What is it you do?"

"I'm a lawyer," Martin said.

"Sounds like you're the kind of guy I most like to meet."

"You can't afford me," Martin said. "Not anymore."

"If you say so," Clay said. "I won't argue. But, you want to bet if I can guess what you're thinking?"

"How much?" Martin said.

"Oh, I guess just for fun when we start," Clay said. "You're thinking all you had to worry about was maybe some of those blond boys on the Vespas or something like that. Then what does she do but show up with a spade."

"Well, not exactly," Martin said. "We got relatives in L.A. a lot darker than you. But when I take a long look at the shape of that suit, I think romance is not likely to be the top thing on your mind."

"Well, yeah," Clay said. "I won't tell you you're wrong."

"Also, that name sounds really familiar," Martin said. "Like maybe I saw it on a map of the town."

"That part could always just be a coincidence," Clay said.

"Ah, well," Martin said. "It all just goes to prove what they tell you."

"What's that?" Clay said.

"Any time you go on a vacation, you can count on it costing you more than you think."

Clay slouched down deeper into his chair.

"I been noticing that a lot lately myself," he said. "So, what would you say to five thousand American?"

Martin started laughing in hard little barks.

"I didn't know she meant all that much to you, son," he said. "We can have the wedding whenever you say."

Mindy woke up in a cheerful mood, in the wake of good dreams she thought might come true. She wriggled around in the sheets for a while before she sat up. The bed she had slept in folded out toward the balcony and she could look over the foot of it through the glass sliding door. The room and balcony were still in the shade, but she saw sunshine warming the side of the mountains. She got up yawning and put on her blue polka-dot robe. The door to the balcony was open and she could hear the clinking of silverware outside. When she went out she found Nadine and Martin both there at the table. Martin was nursing a cup of coffee and Nadine was slicing into a little green melon. She had on a white blouse buttoned down to her wrists and there was a big blob of zinc oxide on her nose.

"Nice to see you around again, Mom," Mindy said. There was a place laid for her too, and she sat down in the chair. "So, you feeling a little better today?"

"A lot better," Nadine said. "Practically normal, as a matter of fact." She slid a melon half onto a plate and put it down at Mindy's place. Martin unfolded the *Herald Tribune*.

"What is this, some kinda midget cantaloupe?" Mindy said, digging at the melon's flesh with her spoon.

"You're the linguist," Martin said. "You could always scamper over to the fruit stand and ask. I just grunt and point, myself."

"Not bad, though, whatever it is," Mindy said, squinting at her warped reflection on the back of a spoon. "So you got us all this bread and jam and stuff too? Not bad, Dad, you musta got up early."

"Well, I had to go out, make a couple of phone calls,"

Martin said. "Besides which, a smile from the princess is a ray of sunshine in my heart."

"Get outa here," Mindy said. "So what were you and Jones talking about all that time? I tapped out waiting for you guys to get through."

"I noticed that," Martin said, tenting himself inside the newspaper. "Probably it's your jet lag catching up with you. Just blink your eyes and you're asleep and you have all these crazy dreams."

"Jones?" Nadine said. "Do I know any Jones?"

"He's just this new fellow Mindy dreamed up," Martin said. "Sort of a traveling man, I would say."

"Hey, it's great you guys had so much to talk about," Mindy said, and reached to pour herself some coffee. "I didn't think he was gonna be your type of guy."

"Well, I don't have to say he's exactly my *type*," Martin said. "But at some fundamental level I think we understand each other. He asked me to tell you goodbye, by the way."

"*Goodbye?*" Mindy put the coffee pot down with a clash. "Goodbye what, is he going somewhere?"

Though it was the first night in a couple he'd had a real bed and four walls to sleep in, Clay didn't have the most restful sleep; bad news kept weaseling into his dreams. So many things had been going wrong recently, he didn't quite trust his luck anymore, didn't fully believe the guy would make the call, though he'd cut such a tough deal he had no reason not to stick to it, if you looked at it that way. But once he woke up completely the next morning he felt a little better, and when he got to the travel agent everything was like it should be. On the way to the train station he stopped at a bar for a beer and some cigarettes. On impulse he also bought himself one fat cigar. He drank the first short glass of beer at the counter and carried the second out to a table. Two were enough to make a nice breakfast.

Outside it was bright and breezy, and cooler than it had

been for a couple of days. The lapels of his jacket ruffled back and subsided with the rising and falling of the wind. Clay sucked the last dribble of foam off the rim of his glass and walked the rest of the way up the street to the station. There was a bus that went straight to the airport from here, but he wasn't in all that much of a rush. Maybe there'd be a bar car on the train, and he could take a cab once he was in Nice. Even after the hotel and the train ticket, he had a little better than a thousand francs left. Although he was a quarter hour early, the train was already on the track, and he crossed through the underpass and went up to get on it. There were plenty of empty compartments. He picked out a good one and sat down to wait.

Of course the guy had to be a lawyer . . . but he'd done all right, considering that. If he'd had the nerve to make his call somewhere else, Clay could have been pulling some French jail right now, and he liked it better sitting on the train, even without all the money he had hoped for. A thousand francs ahead was not all that bad; he knew it wouldn't make enough dollars to go far in New York, but then he'd be back where his hustles would work. A fat lady shaped like a mushroom lurched into the compartment, boosting two lopsided suitcases ahead of her with her knees. Clay stood up, smiling and nodding, and helped her load them in the overhead rack. She was saying stuff the whole time he did it, to thank him, or tell him he was doing it wrong. But soon he'd be back to where people spoke English. The train started moving just as he got the bags jammed in, and he screwed around on one leg and fell back in his seat.

Through the warped glass of the window, the town seemed to melt. Clay wasn't sorry to see it slide back. Monte Carlo was the first stop on this line, man, and at least he was coming back through in a little more style than he'd left last time. Maybe he should get off and try to run up his thousand. His hand slipped absently to his inside pocket to squeeze the plump folder of the airplane ticket. There'd be some place in

Monaco where the thing could be sold. The cigar cellophane crackled, tucked next to the ticket. Never mind, fool, it's time to get out of here. He shucked the cigar out of its wrapper, bit the end off and lit up. When he'd barely let out the first roller of smoke, the fat lady began coughing in a significant way, looking at him sidelong with pointy eyes. Clay smiled and stood up and slid the compartment door open; he'd see if there was a bar car, there was plenty of time. Turning back in the doorway, he gave her a bow.

"You can go to hell if you want to, lady," he said. You could say whatever you wanted so long as you smiled. "I'm through with you people. I'm going home."

The jets of the shower were needle sharp and the head itself was as big as a sunflower. Inside the cubicle, the light was pearly gray. Ton-Ton Detroit stood with his face a foot from the shower head and let the rush of water plane down his features, turned hard and hot as it would go. When he couldn't stand it anymore he turned his back to the jet and scrubbed all over his body with a pyramid-shaped hunk of brown soap, hard and rough as a pumice stone, till he felt he'd rubbed off a layer of skin. The water burst off his back in four directions, slid down all the walls and went swirling into the dented brass ring of the drain between his two feet. He soaped his hair and rinsed till the water began to run clear.

Finished, he pulled the dashiki from the hook where he'd hung it and held it under the shower until it was soaked. Once it was drenched he rubbed the soap all over it, then began to scour the fabric with two stones from the beach. The cloth was still new enough to run a little dye, and the colors came brighter the wetter they got. He gave the robe a forceful twist to wring most of the water out and stuffed it into a plastic grocery bag he'd brought along for the purpose.

Damply dressed in his jeans and blue undershirt, Ton-Ton Detroit went down the steps to the hall where the attendant sat reading the paper and twisting the tuft of hair that grew from the dark mole on the side of her chin. Around her he could see a patch of the harbor, shining so keenly it made him squint. He put an extra fifty centimes in her saucer and smiled widely at her as he went out, though she didn't bother to look up.

Gooseflesh had begun to speckle from one arm to the other across his shoulders by the time he got to the outer sea wall. The tide was in and long iodine-blue swells ran in from the sea, striking the rocks with wild bursts of spray. Ton-Ton Detroit shook out the dashiki and spread it on the inside corner of one of the posts, where the spray could not reach it, stroking it flat to dry without wrinkles. It would take a half hour to dry in this sun.

He stood far out on the rocks and let the spray spatter him, tasting salt at the edge of his mouth with his tongue. The feel of his skin was still vibrant and clean. He went to the post and put together his flute and sat down, holding it on his lap with both hands curled around it. The haze of the last few days had lifted and the horizon was a sharp razor line which the waves ran back to in long roll after roll. He pictured his peace as a round white lifeboat, and it had been sucked out nearly that far, but now he could feel the tide bringing it back surely within his reach. Ton-Ton Detroit put on his fisherman's sunglasses. Under the fourth wave a dozen faintly silver fish hung flickering, all of them facing his way, letting the water lift them and lower them, lift them and lower them, as he brought the flute to his lips in a smooth round motion and began to play "Green Dolphin Street."

WITNESS

THE DAY HE HEARD that Paxton Morgan was released, Wilson had been planning to revise a will. It was a slack period for him and he didn't expect to be in court until late in the following week, but he'd come in early just the same. The door to his inner office was open on the lateral hallway, and he could hear the whisk of a letter opener as Mrs. Veech, behind the front desk, sliced into the morning mail. Mostly bills or offers of subscriptions, he'd glanced through it quickly on his way in.

There was a jingle as the front door opened and Wilson raised his head to listen, but it was a man he didn't want to see, and Mrs. Veech denied his presence. A grumble, sound of pacing, scrape of a match and a faint distant odor of tobacco. Mrs. Veech coughed. The voice grudgingly inquired if the smoke bothered her. Mrs. Veech said nothing but coughed again, more significantly. Her allergy to cigarettes was highly selective — Wilson, for instance, smoked himself. When the front door released a jangle of departure, he picked up his pencil and went back to the will. Mrs. Veech, he could hear, was dealing with the remains of the mail.

"Mr. Wilson, did you know they were letting Pax Morgan go?"

He heard her voice without immediately understanding it, registering only the anxiously rising note at the end. The task in his hand was complicated, though almost entirely frivolous: the testament of a women some forty years old who would probably live at least forty more, revising her bequests more or less semiannually. Still, it was an amusement she could afford if it pleased her, harmless enough, and he had use for the fee.

He drafted another line or two on the long yellow pad and broke the point of his pencil. Then the sense of Mrs. Veech's question reached him and he stood up, taking a cigarette from his shirt pocket as he stepped into the hall. Mrs. Veech sat bolt upright in her desk chair, clamping some sort of form in both her hands. Wilson took it from her and walked to the front window, setting the unlit cigarette in the corner of his mouth as he moved. It was a slick gray photocopy of a release form from Central State, with the name of Paxton Morgan typed along with other information and the illegibly scrawled signature of some doctor or official in the lower right-hand corner. He noted that the box for the date was not filled in.

"They might have already turned him out," Mrs. Veech said.

"Or they might just still be thinking about it." Wilson turned to face her. Round, plain and comfortable, she was a clean fifteen years older than he and normally unfazeable, though now she seemed perceptibly disturbed.

"I wonder who sent us this," he said.

"There wasn't any cover letter." Mrs. Veech frowned.

Wilson stepped across and picked up the slit envelope from the stack of circulars on the desk and paced back to the window, turning it over in his hands. It was letterhead stationery from the hospital, with his own address unremarkably typed and a postmark from two days before. Absently he folded it in three and peered out the window, around the hanging vines of the plants Mrs. Veech had insisted on stringing up there.

The office was on the ground floor at the corner of the square, and sighting through the letter O of his own reversed name on the glass, Wilson could see a couple of cars and one mud-splattered pickup truck revolving lazily around the concrete Confederate soldier on his high pedestal at the center. Opposite, the usual complement of idlers lounged around the courthouse steps. The office had a southern exposure, and he could feel a slight sunny warmth on the side of his face through the pane.

"Well, damn their eyes," he said, and then, as he noticed Mrs. Veech again, "Excuse me."

Back in his inner office, Wilson lit the cigarette and set it in an ashtray to burn itself out, then began dialing the phone with the butt end of his pencil. In some fifteen minutes he had variously heard that Pax Morgan had already been released, was not going to be released at all, or had never been admitted. He hadn't expected to discover who had sent the anonymous notification, and so was not surprised when he didn't. Although he did learn that a Dr. Meagrum was supposed to be presiding over the case, he could not get through to him. He left a message asking that his call be returned. The central spring of his revolving chair squealed slightly as he leaned back, away from the phone. On the rear wall of the room, behind the triangle of clients' chairs, bookshelves rose all the way to the high ceiling, bearing about half of Wilson's law library. Hands laced behind his head, he scanned the top row of heavy books as though looking for something, though he was not. After a moment he tightened his lips and leaned forward again and made the call he had been postponing.

He had the number by heart already because it had once been his own, the Nashville law firm where he'd formerly worked. In those days Sharon Morgan would likely have answered the phone herself, but they used her more as a researcher now, and had hired a different receptionist. She was good at the work, and with the two children there was no doubt the better pay made a difference. Still studying for her own law degree, part time; Pax had never liked that much. Wilson asked for her and waited till she came on the line, her voice brisk, as he remembered it. It had been some months since they had spoken and the first few exchanges passed in pleasantries, inquiries about each other's children and the like. Then, a pause.

"Well, you never called just to pass the time," Sharon said. "Not if I know you."

Wilson hesitated, thinking, What would she look like now? The same. Phone pinched between her chin and shoulder, a tail of her longish dark hair involved with the cord some way. Chances were she'd be doing something on her desk while she waited for him to continue, brown eyes sharp on some document, wasting no time.

"Right," he said. "Have you heard anything of Pax lately?"

"And don't care to," she said, her tone still easy. "Why would you ask?"

The chair spring squeaked as Wilson shifted position. The distant sound of a typewriter came to him over the line. He flicked his pencil with a fingernail and watched its bevels turning over the lines of the yellow pad. "And not the hospital either, I don't suppose."

"Oh-*ho*," Sharon said. He could hear her voice tightening down, homing in. She took the same grim satisfaction in any discovery, no matter its purport, which was part of what made her good at her job. "Is that what it is?"

"I'm afraid," Wilson said, "they're letting him out, if they haven't already."

"And never even let me know. There ought to be a law . . ."

". . . but there doesn't appear to be one," Wilson said. He picked up the hospital form and read off to her its most salient details. A stall, he thought, even before he was through with it. "The morning mail," he said. "No date, and I don't even know who sent it."

"Then what are you thinking to do?" she said.

"I've been calling the hospital," Wilson said. "If I ever get through to the right doctor, maybe I can convince them to hold him, if he's not already gone."

"*If*," Sharon said sharply. "All up to them, is it?"

"I would call it a case for persuasion," Wilson said. "So, did you have any plans for the weekend? I should be able to get in touch . . ."

"I'm taking the children out to the lake."

Wilson plucked another cigarette from his breast pocket and began to tamp it rhythmically on the old green desktop blotter. "I don't know," he said. "Why not go to your brother's, say? Instead."

"What would we want to do that for?"

"Look, Sharon," he said. "You know, it's to hell and gone from anywhere, that house on the lake. And nobody even out there this time of year."

"I will *not* run from that —" She interrupted herself, but he thought the calm of her voice was artificial when she went on. "The kids are packed for it. They're counting on it. I don't see any reason to change our plans."

"You don't, do you?" Wilson said without sarcasm, and put a match to his cigarette. He supposed he'd been expecting this, or something a whole lot like it.

"Why don't you get a peace bond on him?" Sharon said. "If he really is out, I mean. Something. Because it ought to be *his* problem. Not mine."

"I could do that," Wilson said. "Try to, anyway. You know what good it'll do, too. You know it better than I do."

There was silence in the receiver; the phantom typewriter had stopped. Pax Morgan had been under a restraining order that night back before the divorce decree when he'd appeared at the house in Nashville he and Sharon had shared and smashed out all the ground-floor windows with the butt end of his deer rifle; he'd made it all the way around the house before the police arrived.

"Well, devil take the hindmost," Wilson said. "I'll let you know what I can find out. And you take care."

"Thanks for letting me know."

"Take care, Sharon," Wilson said, but she had already hung up, so he did too.

Shifting the cigarette to his left hand, he picked up the pencil and began jotting a list at the foot of the pad with the blunted tip. Often he did his thinking with the pencil point; he'd discovered that sometimes a solution would appear in the interstices of what he wrote. There were only two items on the list.

—Judge Oldfield   injunction P.M.
—Dr. Meagrum   Central State

He added a third.

—call back S.M.

The pencil doodled away from the last initial. The list was obvious and complete, and after he acted on it nothing would be solved. A long ash was sprouting from his cigarette, but he didn't notice until the spark crawled far enough to burn his knuckle.

For the rest of the morning he worked abstractedly on the will with imperfect concentration. Every twenty minutes or so he interrupted himself to make some fruitless call. Dr. Meagrum was perpetually "on rounds" or "in consultation." Judge Oldfield was spending his morning on the bench. Wilson's own phone rang occasionally, but always over something trivial. When he called Oldfield's chambers again around noon, he found that the judge was gone to lunch. He tightened his tie, got his seersucker suit coat down from the hat rack and, with a word or two to Mrs. Veech, went out himself.

Circling the square counterclockwise, he passed the Standard Farm Store, the bank and the courthouse steps, where one man or another raised a broad flat palm to greet him. It was warm out, an Indian summer heat wave, though it was late October and the leaves had already turned. A new asphalt path on the southbound street felt tacky on his shoes as he crossed. A couple of blocks west of the square he was already verging on the edge of time; beyond the long low roof of Dotson's Restaurant there were woods, turned fired-clay red patched with sere yellow, with a few deep green cedars standing anomalously among the other trees.

The fans were on inside the restaurant, revolving on tall poles, fluttering the corners of the checked oilcloths on the small square tables. Judge Oldfield sat toward the rear—alone, for a wonder—behind a plate of fried catfish, hushpuppies and boiled greens. As Wilson approached he put down his newspaper and smiled. "What wind blows you here, young fellow my lad?"

"An ill one, I'd say." Wilson sat down on a ladder-back chair. "Do you remember Sharon Morgan? A Lawrence, she was, before she married."

"Married that crazy fellow, didn't she?"

"That's the one." Wilson ordered an iced tea from the waitress who'd appeared at his elbow, and turned back to the judge. "They're letting him out of Central State, at least that's what it looks like." He ran down the brief of the morning's activity while Oldfield grazed on his catfish and nodded.

"It worrying you personally?" the judge said when he was done. "For yourself, I mean?"

"Oh no," Wilson said. "Not hardly. It wasn't me he said he'd kill, was it? I doubt he'd remember much about me. I never knew him any too well. Even while the divorce was going on it was just her he was mad at."

"So it's the wife—ex-wife, I mean. She's the one with the worry."

"She's the one." Wilson frowned down at his hands. There was a small watery blister where the cigarette had burned him, surprisingly painful for its size. He turned the cold curve of the iced tea glass against it. "She asked me to get an injunction on him. That's why I came hunting you."

Oldfield took off his fragile rimless glasses, rubbed them with a handkerchief and put them back on. "That's tricky, old son," he said, "when you don't know for sure if he's loose or he's not."

"Hard to get good information out of that place, don't you know?" Wilson said. "Seems like a lot of them are crazy, doctors and patients alike."

"Must be that's why they call it a madhouse," Oldfield said with a faint smile. "Well. She does live in the county now? Full time?"

"She moved here right after the divorce," Wilson said.

"Just to oblige you, now," Oldfield said, "I could sign you a paper. You draw it up. It happens he *is* out, you let me know and we'll sign it and serve it right away. It won't be much of a help to her, though."

"Don't I know it," Wilson said. "But what else do you do?"

"Not a whole lot that you *can*," said Oldfield. "You really think she's got call to worry? Not just fretful, is she?"

"Not her," Wilson said. "I'm the one fretting. I'm wondering, how can I get a deputy to watch over them for a couple of days?"

"You know you can't set them on her," Oldfield said. "Not without she asks for it herself."

"She won't."

"She was a pretty thing, as I recall," Oldfield said irrelevantly. He took off his glasses and rubbed at the bridge of his nose. "And knew her own mind, or seemed to."

"You mean she's stubborn."

"Yes, that's right."

Wilson stood up. "I thank you," he said.

Oldfield smiled myopically up at him, his eyes a light watery blue. "You ought to stay and try the catfish."

"Well, I believe not," Wilson said. "Not much of an appetite today."

"A young man like you?" The judge shook his head. "Must be this heat."

"Your wife called," Mrs. Veech reported. "She'll call you back. And that man from Central State, he called. Dr. Meagrum."

"He would have, wouldn't he?" Wilson said, shrugging out of his jacket. "Wait till I was gone, I mean."

Mrs. Veech sniffed. "In a tearing-down hurry, too," she said. "He was right cross to find you not here."

"He'll get over it," Wilson said. "All right, then, would you make sure for me that Pax Morgan still has his house in Brentwood? We might want to serve a paper on him a little later in the day."

In the inner office it was a little too warm, though not quite oppressive. He put his coat on the hat rack, cracked the single window and paced for a moment at the far side of his desk. It was a shallow room and the high wall of dark bookbindings seemed uncomfortably close. With a sigh he went back to his seat, lit a cigarette, picked up the will, put it down, lifted a list of the other items on his immediate agenda and then let that drop too.

The urge to pick at the blister seemed irresistible. He tore loose an edge of it, reviewing, in spite of himself, what little he really knew about Pax Morgan. They'd gone to the same high school, but two years apart; Wilson was the younger. Pax had played football—he remembered that—indifferently, in the line. Later on he had inherited money and started dabbling in real estate, or insurance, neither making nor losing much at whatever it might have been. Grown, he was a loud bluff fellow with a ruddy face and crinkly, almost yellow hair. At the large parties where Wilson would occasionally run into him, he was known for drinking too much and becoming not just mush-mouthed but crazily incoherent. The drinking was said to be a factor in his later, more serious breakdowns.

Wilson had gone to Sharon's wedding but he couldn't think

if it was before or after it that he'd had the one brush with Pax he remembered with real clarity. Another party, undoubtedly some Christmas gathering, for Pax was wearing an incongruous Santa Claus tie and had managed to get quite drunk on eggnog. Shuffled together by the crowd, they somehow became embroiled in an argument over deer hunting. Wilson shot duck and dove, rabbit and squirrel, and on his father's farm he might shoot what he had to, to protect the livestock, but he had no taste for shooting deer, which now appeared to be Pax's ruling passion. Wilson was trying to get off the subject, but Pax wouldn't let it drop.

"You've never been blooded," he said thickly. "That's your trouble, you've never been *blooded*." He grasped Wilson's lapel and twisted it, drawing himself unpleasantly near, and Wilson was a little startled by what he himself did next, a trick someone had showed him in the Army. He took hold of Pax's thumb and squeezed the joints of it together, so that the sudden sharp pain made Pax flinch and let go. Reflexively, Wilson took a step backward, jostling someone behind him in the crowded room, but Pax's face went from surprise to a total blank, like a television switched to an empty channel, and so the whole episode was amputated.

Real craziness there, or an early sign of it. Wilson pulled the dead skin back from the blister, creating a small redrimmed sore. By the time of the divorce, there were many worse examples, enough to fill a dossier. Wilson had never cared for divorce work much, but Sharon was both a colleague and a sort of distant friend, and also it was in the first thin stage of his independent practice. But once it was over he swore off friends' divorces altogether, no matter how bad he might need the work. It had been an easy case in the sense that the outcome was not in real doubt, but it was angry and ugly on Pax's side, and there'd been some bitter squabbling over property. Sharon had held out for the house on the lake—impractically, as Wilson thought—surrendering the Nashville residence to Pax, who'd later sold it. Reaching for the phone to call the hospital one more time, he wished again she hadn't done that.

His game of telephone tag with Central State went on for a couple more hours, unpromisingly. When the phone finally rang back around two-thirty, it was his wife.

"Not interrupting, I hope," she said. "Is it busy?"

"Not so you'd notice," he said. "It's been pretty quiet."

"Well, we need a gallon of milk," she said, "and cornmeal. Would you stop on the way home?"

"I'll do it," Wilson said, scribbling on the pad. "Lisa driving you crazy today?" Their daughter was four years old, and frantic.

"How should I describe it?" she said, and laughed. "This time next year she'll be in school . . . I'll miss her, though."

"That's the spirit," Wilson said. The light on his phone began to flash and Mrs. Veech called down the hall, "It's that Dr. Meagrum!"

"I've got to take this call," Wilson said. "I'll be home on time, I think . . ." He pushed the button.

Dr. Meagrum seemed to be already *in medias res*. "—there's an issue of doctor-patient confidentiality here, Mr., uh, Wilson. I don't know who could have sent you that form but they did so without my authorization."

"Did they?" Wilson said, catching his breath. "As you may know, I represent Mr. Morgan's ex-wife, and given the circumstances of the case, it seems to me appropriate that *both* of us should have been informed."

"I can't agree with you there," Dr. Meagrum snapped.

"All due respect to your point of view," Wilson said, trying to collect himself. The conversation had taken an adversarial turn too soon. "I take it that Mr. Morgan *has*, in fact, been released from your, ah, custodial care."

"My records show that Mr. Morgan has been responding favorably to a course of medication and was transferred to outpatient status two days ago."

"I see," Wilson said. "What medication, may I ask?"

"I'm sorry, but that's confidential."

"And what assurance do we have that he will actually *take* this medication?"

"He's in our outpatient program now, and we'll be monitoring him on a biweekly basis."

"Biweekly, you say. That's *every two weeks?*" Wilson creaked back in his chair, gazing up at the join of his bookcase and the ceiling. "Dr. Meagrum, I would like you to consider" — he paused, thinking over the jargon as if fumbling for a key — "consider returning Mr. Morgan to *inpatient status*. Temporarily, shall we say. In the interests of the safety of his ex-wife and family."

"Our file shows that any such step would be contraindicated," the doctor said. "Not in the patient's best interests."

A white flash of light, something like heat lightning, burst over Wilson's mental horizon, obscuring his view of the bookcases. He found he was clenching the receiver in a strangle grip and talking much louder than before. "Sir, you are describing a *piece of paper* to me, and I am talking to you about a man who has threatened to kill his wife, not once but many times—"

Dr. Meagrum harrumphed. "Yes, someone with this type of pathology might make such a threat, but I wouldn't suggest that you take it too seriously . . ."

"He came to her house with a thirty-ought-six rifle," Wilson said. "A *loaded* rifle — I'm now referring to the police report. They found him and the gun and they found her barricaded in an upstairs bedroom. With her two children, I should say. The boy is six now, Dr. Meagrum, and the little girl is seven. Your *outpatient* has threatened to kill them too."

Dr. Meagrum resorted to the imperial "we": "We have no record that this patient is violent. We see no reason to alter the treatment program at this time."

With a mighty effort, Wilson established a greater degree of control over his voice. "Very well," he said frostily. "I do sincerely hope you'll see no reason to regret the course you've taken."

By dumb luck his next call caught Judge Oldfield in his chambers, between cases, on the fly.

"I'm asking the impossible now," Wilson said. "Let's have him picked up. An APB. Lock him up and have a look at him. Just for a day or so."

"You're right," Oldfield said. "That's impossible. I couldn't do it if I wanted to. This is Williamson County. We haven't got a police state here."

"It's a free country, isn't it," Wilson said. "Well, I had to ask."

"I wonder if you did, at that," Oldfield said. "You're acting mighty worked up about this, old son. Don't you think you might be making a little much of it all? He's been out two days already, so you say, and what happened? Nothing. The lady didn't even know until you called her. Simmer down some, think it over. Go home early. It's Friday, after all."

"All right," Wilson said. "Might give it a try."

"You get me that injunction and I'll pass it on to the sheriff direct," Oldfield said. "I can't do any more than that."

"I know," Wilson said. "Not until something happens. Well, I appreciate it."

He hung up and dialed Sharon Morgan at the office but she was gone, gone for the weekend, had left half an hour before to pick up the children from school. He plopped down the phone and tried, forcibly, to relax. Try it. Judge Oldfield was no fool, after all. Wilson picked up the pencil with a fleeting idea of listing off what he was thinking, feeling, but that was a ridiculous notion; probably that was how they spent their time at Central State. Possibly nothing would happen anyway. Possibly. He looked up Sharon's home number and dialed it, but there was no answer, though it rang twenty times.

In ten minutes he had scratched out the requisite injunction and handed it to Mrs. Veech with instructions to type it and walk it over to the courthouse when she was done. After she had gone out, he sat doing nothing but covering the phone, which didn't ring. The jingle of Mrs. Veech's return moved him to at least pretend to work. But he'd had it with the will for the day, though it still wasn't quite finished. He scraped his agenda toward him across the desk and ran his pencil point down item by item. There were two boundary disputes and a zoning complaint. A piece of frivolous litigation to do with somebody's unleashed dog. There was a murder case where the defendant would plead, draw two-to-ten and count himself lucky. A foregone conclusion, Wilson thought in his present skeptical mood, though matters had not yet reached that stage. At the foot of the list was a patent case that would make him and his client rich if he could win it. This one was the most remote, no court date even set for it yet, but at the same time the most intriguing, as much for its intricacy as its promise. He swiveled and dug in the cabinet for the file.

At four he called Sharon Morgan at the lake and got no answer. For another half hour he studied the patent case, though he was losing interest at an exponential rate. When he next called there was still no answer, and he was out of the chair and snatching his coat down from its peg before he even knew he meant to leave. On the highway bound for Keyhole Lake he began to feel a little foolish. He'd been presuming, counting the time from three o'clock, when school let out. It was not more than an hour from Nashville to the lake house, but he hadn't considered that she might have stopped to shop on the way, or taken the children to a movie or simply for a drive. Now it appeared to him that his every move that day had been an error. It was unlike him to have lost his temper with that doctor. Patience had always been his strength; he left it to his opponents to make mistakes in anger. Then too, that last call to Judge Oldfield was something he'd have to live down, and on top of all that he had wasted the day, and would need to come back in Saturday morning to recover the lost time.

All foolishness, and yet the thought did not comfort him. He drove carefully, a hair under the speed limit, sighting through the windshield across the burn mark on his knuckle. For no reason he could think of, he let the car roll past the Morgan mailbox and coast to a stop on the shoulder, where he got softly out. There was a little lip to climb before he could see down the driveway to the steeply pitched roof of the A-frame house and the blue lake distantly visible out past it. It was cooler here; the weather was turning, or else it was a chill coming off the water.

Below him, the drive was matted with fallen leaves. A staining fall of sunset light came slanting through the tree trunks on either side as the wind rose and combed the red leaves back, bringing a few more falling from the branches. Except for the wind it was utterly still; only across the lake the dogs in Jackson's kennel were barking, their voices echoing off the flat expanse of the water. But probably they were barking all the time. That was not the problem. What was wrong was that the passenger door of Sharon's orange Volkswagen had been left hanging open, sticking out stiffly like a broken arm. The car was pulled around parallel to the back porch, and over its roof he saw that the sliding glass door to the house had been left open too.

He walked to the dangling car door and stopped. Just past the edge of the drive, not more than three yards from him, there lay a child's blue tennis shoe, a Ked, with maple leaves spread around it like the prints of a large hand. Some twenty paces farther on he found the second shoe and then the little boy, barefoot, lying face down in a pile of sloppily raked leaves. Wilson thought that his name had been Billy, but he couldn't be quite certain of it, which bothered him unreasonably. The child had been shot in the base of the neck; the entry wound was rather small. Beyond the leaf pile a wide swath of dun lawn swept down to the lake shore where a canoe, tethered to a little dock, rocked softly on the water.

A strip of almost total darkness fit into the gap of the glass door. The porch floor moaned as Wilson crossed it, and glancing down he saw a brass shell casing caught in a crack between two boards. He bent to pick it up, then stopped himself and put both hands in his pockets. Through the door was a large living room with no ceiling, only the peaked roof and the rafters. At this time of day it was very dim within and it took Wilson's eyes a moment to adjust. The daughter (he was almost sure her name was Jill) was sprawled on a high-backed wicker chair as if flung there by some strong force. There was a single wound in her chest. Her mouth was open slightly and her eyes showed a little white. Wilson thought it more than likely that Pax had shot her from a standing position on the porch.

It took him only a quarter turn of his head to locate Sharon's body at the far end of the long room, lying across a wide flight of steps that rose to the kitchen and dining area. Pax might well have shot her from the doorway; he was a marksman, the proof was plain, and efficient with his shells. Wilson crossed the room to the steps and paused. He couldn't tell just where she'd been hit, though she'd bled very heavily. She lay crooked, twisted over at the waist, the fingers of one hand folded over the overhang of a step. Her hair had fallen full over her face, and Wilson was grateful for that, but her position looked so uncomfortable that he was tempted to turn and straighten her. His hands were still jammed in his pockets, however, and he left them there.

He went up the steps almost on tiptoe, careful to avoid bloodying his shoes, and made a turn to the left that brought him up against the metal kitchen cabinets. His breath was coming very short, each intake arrested as though by a punch in the midsection. He was aware of the tick of his wristwatch, and that was all. There was a telephone on the kitchen counter, and presently he detached a paper towel from a roll neatly suspended beneath the line of cabinets, wrapped it around the receiver and called the sheriff's office.

At the opposite end of the kitchen, a smaller set of sliding doors opened onto a deck overlooking the lawn and the lake. With the help of another paper towel, he slid back the door and went out and sat on a bench to wait. The lake's surface had a painful metallic glitter, with the sunset colors spreading across it like corrosion. He had left his sunglasses in the car, and being in no mood to retrieve them, he simply shut his eyes. In Korea, where the Army had sent him, he had *seen some action*, as they say, but afterward he had thought very little about what he had seen. In some quietly ticking corner of his mind a speculation was going forward as to how the bodies had come to be positioned as they were, and now it came to him that after they were all inside the house the boy must have missed his shoes and gone back to the car— He opened his eyes with a jerk and looked up. A solitary, premature firefly detached itself from the treetops on one side of the yard and floated dreamily across and into the treetops on the other.

It was twilight by the time he had parked his car behind the square, and for some reason he bypassed his office and walked on down Main Street as far as Saint Paul's Episcopal Church. More leaves had carpeted the white stone steps, and Wilson stood looking at them, one hand curved around a spear of the iron fence, and then turned back. The sidewalk was empty but for him, and he could hear the dry leaves crisping under his every footfall.

The street lights were coming on by the time he had returned to the square. The windows of his office were dark, but he could hear the telephone ringing as he came up the steps. Mrs. Veech had, of course, locked up before she left, and while he was searching out his key the phone stopped ringing. He went inside and pressed the light switch. Again the phone began to jangle, and he reached across Mrs. Veech's typewriter to pick it up.

"Mr. Wilson? It's Sam Trimble here. I had your paper to serve on Paxton Morgan?"

"Yes," Wilson said.

The deputy cleared his throat. "I thought you might like to know we picked him up. He'd gone straight back to his own house, you know, like they do."

"Yes," Wilson said again.

"We got him cold, if it's any comfort," Trimble said. "The gun still warm and blood on his shoes."

"That's all right," Wilson said. "He'll plead insanity."

He was not often here at night, and the overhead fixture was harsh and bright, bouncing blurred reflections from the flat black of the window panes, making his inner office look too much like a cell. But if he used only the desk lamp, the shadows reached toward him so. And yet he was still afraid to go home! He shouldn't have said what he had to Trimble, though at the moment he could hardly bring himself to feel regret for it. And he was late by now; he'd better call.

"Daddy, you're late," Lisa said.

"That's right, kiddo," Wilson said. "Where's your mother?"

"She's outside," Lisa said. "We were, both of us. I'll go call her."

"No, you don't need to," Wilson said. "Just tell her I'll be home shortly. Say I still have to stop by the store, though." Hanging up, he glanced at his watch. A fine evening like this, his wife would certainly spend outdoors, not bothering to watch the evening news.

Flushed with relief, he pictured their long curving yard, thick with fireflies, as it would be now, green pinpoints flashing and hovering in the dark. The lights of the house glowed warm behind the calm silhouettes of his wife and his daughter, and inside, the kitchen steamed with the scent of supper waiting. Upstairs, beside his bedside lamp, lay the copy of *War and Peace* he'd been rereading this fall; at a half hour or so a night, it would last him to Christmas or longer. He thought now of Prince Andrey lying wounded on the battlefield, looking up into the reaches of the sky, that radical change in his perspective.

Still, he was not quite ready to leave. He picked up his pencil and tapped the butt of the dried eraser on the pad. At home, tonight or tomorrow or whenever he finally had to tell the story there, then the murders would be absolutely realized and the alternative of their somehow not having happened would be permanently shut off. Above, the fluorescent fixture made a sort of whining sound; Wilson thought that he could feel it in his teeth.

He turned the pencil over in his hand and set the point on the pad, but there was nothing much to write. The yellow paper was down at the bottom of a long pale shaft, stroked with faint parallel lines which signified nothing. If he could note down all the ingredients of the episode, then they could be comprehended, wrapped in a parcel of law and so managed. Wilson was a believer in due process. Without meaning to, he had become a bystander in this case.

It was only dizziness because he had skipped lunch, undoubtedly, and when he remembered that, the pad came floating back up toward him and the desk flattened and held still. There were some scratch marks on the paper, as if during his vertigo he had been trying unsuccessfully to draw a picture. Now he wondered if he had *known* what would happen, and if he had *known,* what then? He had left no legitimate measure untried but still he could picture himself crossing the lip above the lake house with a gun in his own hand, seeing the Volkswagen door still closed, the glass door of the house pulled to and Pax Morgan outlined against the glimmer of the lake like a paper silhouette.

The pencil slipped from his fingers and hit the desk with a clacking report that broke the fantasy. Pax was alive and the others were dead. His freedom was better protected than their safety—that would be one way of putting it. Simple. It was time to go home. Wilson turned off the desk lamp, stood up and pulled his coat down from the hat rack. Safer and better to have no freedom maybe, but no, you wouldn't say that. The humming stopped when he flicked the light switch by the door. No, you wouldn't say that, would you? In the dark of the hall he could not see his way; he went toward the vague light of the front window with one hand on the wall. No, you wouldn't, but what would you say?

MOVE ON UP

HAL STOOD in the dawn haze, one hand resting lightly on the pebbled concrete balustrade, watching the iron-gray light filter out across Columbus Park. He shifted slightly from foot to foot, and every few minutes he twisted his torso to the rear, to stretch his lower back, which hurt a little. Down the double staircase from the long open concrete barn in which he'd spent the night, the park was empty, more or less. The ragged shrubbery rattled in a slicing March wind; an empty beer can gave out a hollow clacking sound, turning with the wind over the uneven cobbles. A couple of men had fit themselves through the hoops of a couple of benches to sleep, or maybe they were women. From where he stood they were nothing but bundles of rags and hair; he couldn't have recognized the difference. This notion reminded him exactly of what he had been trying not to think about.

Behind him, the growl of early Canal Street traffic was just audible, gnawing back and forth between the Holland Tunnel and the Manhattan Bridge. He turned and set the small of his back against the concrete and looked over at the slick gray rise of the Tombs wall. The wind picked up, swirling trash around his ankles, and automatically he thumbed his denim collar up. Under the short jacket he wore three different kinds of shirts and a piece of thermal underwear he'd found. His pants were thin and holey, though, and his fingers were waxy and stiff from the cold. But keep your chest warm and you won't get sick — someone had once told him that back when he was little. He sniffed and wiped his nose with a denim cuff.

The whole long rectangle under the roof was full of litter, paper and plastic and anything else that people might drag up there in the hope that it would keep them warm. Hal studied the currents and eddies the wind made in it all. At the far corner a big sheet of cardboard lifted, hovered, then blew back against the wall, and Loman sat up from underneath it, tightening his greasy overcoat around him. The wind dropped and the cardboard settled back onto him. He knocked it away with an elbow and peered uneasily around. When his eyes lit on Hal he smiled through his yellowish beard.

"Morning already?" he said. "You never woke me, did you?" They had a loose arrangement for each to watch while the other slept. It had been discovered that to fall below the status of victim was impossible for anyone nowadays.

"It's all right," Hal said. "I was thinking."

"Who, you?" Loman's joints popped like a string of fire-crackers as he stood up. "What about?"

"Nothing." Hal turned back to overlook the park. He could hear Loman coughing behind him.

Then Loman came over and spat something wet and brown across the rail and straightened up. "Mighty cold," he said. "Thought you told me spring was coming."

"It'll get here." Hal cut one eye Loman's way. There was a queer dry patch spreading from Loman's eye socket down over his cheekbone, purplish under the black skin. Hal had never asked if it was a birthmark or a scar.

"I tell you what," Loman said. He pulled out a cigarette stub and lit it shakily, tightening his lips inward so as not to burn them. "It keep up this way, Brother Henry, you might find me climbing on that van."

"Do what you want to," Hal said, and paused. "But just don't call me that."

"What's the matter, you don't like it?"

"My name is Hal," Hal said. "Just Hal, that's all." He pushed himself away from the balustrade and took a couple of steps down the stairway.

"You gone?" Loman said. "Hey, I didn't mean nothing."

"I just got something to look after," Hal said. "Catch up with you back here tonight."

A waist-high iron fence went from the corner of the building along the edge of the park, and he ran his fingers over the spear points of the vertical rails as he moved toward the opening onto the sidewalk. When he came to the loose one he stopped and lifted it an inch or so out of its socket, then let it drop back with a clank and went on. Most of the shop gates on Bayard Street were half raised, with Chinese men ducking under them, setting up for the day. The bakery was already open and busy, its windows steamed, and his stomach balled up briefly as he passed through the vaporing smell of the food. At the corner of Elizabeth he stooped over to peer in the window of Jeannie's Cocktail Lounge. The bar was set below the level of the street, and after his eyes adjusted he could see that both of the dragon ladies were already down there, moving along the length of the counter in the violet glow of the television set at its far end. He stayed bent over, hands braced on his knees, until one of them looked up and motioned him to wait.

He stood on the corner for five or ten minutes until the truck arrived, then spent the next half hour carrying liquor crates down through the narrow trap into the sub-basement. The work warmed him, though moving between the heat of the room and the outer cold started his cough. When he was done he closed the trap and waited while a dragon lady counted four one-dollar bills out to him with a long enameled fingernail. In the short entryway between the barroom and the street, he paused and added three of the bills to the roll tucked in the tear of his jacket's blanket lining. The fourth he shoved down in his front pocket, fingering its folded edges as he walked up to Canal Street.

From a clock on a bank he saw that it was seven. He threaded his way through the snarl and fume of Canal Street traffic and went up Mulberry, past Hester Street, past Grand. A delivery truck was already parked outside Catania, and Frank, the bartender, was leaning against the driver's door, going over a shipping list. Hal spent the next forty-five minutes or so jockeying another set of boxes down another rickety ladder. When he was done Frank gave him a five-dollar bill and he passed it back and asked for quarters. Going out, he pushed the bills and coins down in the same front pocket.

There was nothing to do, nothing, for hours. It was way too soon to go to the EAU, and the thought of the gray empty time made him break out in a clammy sweat, though it was still cold on the street. At the corner of Grand there was an Italian grocery where he went in and, under the suspicious eye of the cashier, selected a loaf of prosciutto bread, paid for it and went back out. The sun was all the way up now, centering a dot of faint warmth between his shoulder blades. Lower in his back, the pain had been rendered more precise by all the lifting. He tucked the long loaf in between two of his shirts and walked across toward West Broadway, turning his change over in his pocket, separating the quarters from the other coins, then letting them fall back among the rest.

On West Broadway almost all the stores were still shuttered down and there was hardly anyone around, only a few sets of feet poking out of doorways, none he recognized. The wind had faded and the warming light lay the length of the empty street. The bread slipped back and forth across his rib cage as he moved. At a corner grocery he bought a cup of black coffee and went on, sipping slowly and warming his hands on the cup, across Houston Street and up into Washington Square.

There was a little fugitive birdsong high in the trees. He made a circuit of the dead fountain, stroking his fingers along the basin's rim, then dropped the coffee cup in a bin and climbed the steps to the raised railed area the skateboarders used in summertime. Below, the park was nearly empty too. At one end a police car quietly hummed; at another, a few dealers' runners waited sullenly, hands in pockets, shuffling their feet. When Hal turned away from the railing, a crack vial spun away from his shoe, and the thought of Judith came to him again, whole and sharp. He touched the roll of money through the lining of his jacket: forty-one dollars, no, forty-four now. What was it for? And how did you know someone was dead for sure if they never let you see the body?

It was three days now. He left the park on the northwest diagonal, feeling the cops' eyes glide incuriously across him as he went past the car. A pile of rags on the circular benches in the corner of the park caught his attention, but there was no one inside it. After three days he more or less believed that she was dead, but he still wanted the tactile proof, though he no longer expected to get it. Benny had believed it the first day, probably without much question. He was unsentimental for an eight-year-old, even about his mother. Hal jangled the change in his pocket. He'd got the quarters to make more calls, but he didn't want to make them.

For a time he stopped the thoughts from coming by concentrating on the slap of his shoes against the pavement. On Sixth Avenue the chains of traffic rattled and jerked uptown and the sidewalks were segmented among the crack panhandlers, damming the pedestrian stream with outstretched hands and rote requests. Hal slipped through the crowd and walked up Greenwich Avenue, then turned on Perry Street, cutting toward the river. By habit he was cruising the cans, and when a bright flag of white cloth caught his eye he stopped.

A laundry bag. He unfurled it, held it at arm's length. It was reasonably clean and the hole at the bottom corner was insignificant. Wadding the bag, he went around the corner and stopped to examine it again. His pants were held to his waist by many turns of a knotted nylon cord, and after a little fumbling he undid a length of this and fixed it to the cloth bag in a sling, closing the tear at one end and making a drawstring around the mouth at the other. There was a smiling sun emblem printed on the bag, and it lay facing out from his hip when he slung it to his shoulder. He loosened the drawstring, slid in the bread, refastened it and moved on, flushed with optimism for the first time that day. This was a good area for scavenging; he'd found his shoes not far from here. Solid black brogans, whole and a perfect fit, the shoes were the best piece of luck that had come his way since he lost the roof; their discovery had freshened his belief in God.

At the end of the street he turned north and walked parallel to the West Side Highway. The rush hour traffic had abated and the cars came by at near top speed, with an enormous sheering sound. Beyond the highway the river turned the sunlight back as sharply as a mirror; past that, the low New Jersey skyline was hard-edged, as if cut into the horizon with a knife. The wind was much stronger along the river, sweeping away the sun's furtive warmth. He turned back east on Gansevoort Street.

Behind the windbreak of the warehouses it was definitely warm, the air still fresh but no longer bitter. In two or three weeks it would be real spring. Ahead of him, near Hudson Street, two spectral figures stooped in the shadow of a restaurant dumpster, piled over the rim with remains of T-bone steaks.

"Jackpot," one of them called to him. Coming closer, Hal saw that it was Dirty Will.

"There's more than enough," Will said.

Hal peered over Will's shoulder, but he didn't know the woman with him. She might have been young but you couldn't tell it through the dirt and meat grease on her face. Her eyes glazed over and her teeth worked at a steak rind.

Through the inner doorway behind the desk, Hal caught a glimpse of Benny, still wearing the same Masters of the Universe sweatshirt he'd had on the day before. "Hey, Benbro," he called.

The boy came out and stopped just back of the metal detector to rub one eye. His reddish hair was sticking up in five directions and the sweatshirt had ridden up to expose his bellybutton. The guard swiveled in his chair as if to stare him out of existence.

"Let's go," Hal said, patting the bag. "Lunchtime."

The guard turned back. "You're not authorized to take him out of here."

"Come on, now," Hal said. Benny walked through the metal detector, and Hal reached over and pulled the sweatshirt down.

"You know we don't even have to take him back," the guard said. "Not when you come along and take him out and you're not authorized."

"Yeah, I know that," Hal said. "It's what I get told just about every day." He turned the boy with a hand on his shoulder and piloted him out the door. A woman with a stroller crossed their path, headed for the processing area at the far end of the porch. Through that doorway, the shadows of functionaries floated behind a Plexiglas barrier, bristling with forms.

"All right," Hal said. "Should we go back to the park?"

"Yeah, okay," Benny said.

He stepped out from under Hal's hand and led the way around the corner of the building to a small concrete playground, where some benches, a toilet hutch and an unornamented jungle gym were grouped around a greenish bronze statue of various animals, all somehow balanced on the back of a small bear. At the south end of the square was a low fence and beyond it another area of the park reserved for use by winos. Benny climbed up onto a bench and straddled its back.

"You hungry?" Hal said.

"Sorta," Benny said. "Yeah."

"What was for breakfast?"

"Oatmeal. It's always oatmeal, remember?"

"You eat it?" Hal said, loosening the drawstring of his bag.

"Some of it," Benny said. "Hey, don't pick on me, Hal."

For an instant his voice became a juvenile simulacrum of Judith's. Hal blinked the comparison away and put one foot on the seat of the bench.

"New bag," Benny observed. "Where'd you get that?"

"Found it," Hal said. "You find things, if you look."

He tore half of the loaf down the middle and with a bent steel spoon scooped a crescent of butter and spread it on the inside, using his raised knee as a shelf. The butter had softened a little in the bag, but it was still awkward to spread it with the back of the spoon. He passed the butter sandwich to Benny, who raised it to his mouth in both hands and took a bite.

"This is all right," he said, chewing and squinting into the texture of the bread. "Hey, it's got meat in it."

"That's the idea," Hal said. He buttered a chunk of bread for himself and bit into it. The burst of saliva at the contact hurt his mouth.

"Aren't you gonna sit?" Benny said.

"Nah, don't think so."

"How come not?"

"Don't feel like it."

"You're strange, man."

Benny put down the nub of his bread on the bench's top plank, climbed down and strolled across to the jungle gym. He paused for a moment with one hand on the first rung, then climbed to the top and sat looking north, his legs gently swinging under him. Hal reached for the bread end and blew some grit off the bottom of it and put it back in the waxed paper sack. The wind was quiet for the moment, and the warmth of the sun was stronger.

"Weather's looking up a little, at least," Hal said. Benny didn't answer.

"They got better stuff at that playground up Oliver Street," Hal said. "They got a merry-go-round . . . You want to go up there and play?"

"I don't guess so."

Benny kept his face turned away. Hal put the bread sack into his cloth bag and went over to the animal statue, whose bronze was overlaid with white flourishes of graffiti. He looked over into the other half of the park, which was in deep shadow. A statue of a man in a three-piece suit made an expansive gesture toward the pile of litter at its base. Hal made out some half-pint bottles and a few more crack vials and a small dry heap of human dung. There was a thump behind him and he turned to see Benny crouched down in a three-point landing.

"Careful how you land on your hands around here," Hal said. "Too much glass around, cut you to ribbons."

Benny straightened up and briefly flashed his uncut palms. "Come on," he said. "Something I want to show you."

Hal followed him around the back side of the shelter to a storm-fenced playground facing South Street and the viaduct. At a corner of the fence Benny stopped and fastened his fingers to the wire.

"See it?" Inside the fence was a sculptured dolphin, its tail arcing up from a low pedestal.

"Big fish, huh?" Hal said.

"It's a porpoise, dumbhead," Benny said. "And you know what?"

"Yeah?" Hal said.

"Summertime, water gonna come out his nose right there." He stuck his forearm through the wire to point. "It's a fountain, see? It gets hot, we all run through that water and cool off."

"Slick," Hal said. He turned and propped his back against a sag of the wire. By summer Benny would be God knows where—in a foster home, with luck, or in some other institution without it. Now Judith was dead, they wouldn't keep him here much longer. Every day when Hal showed up for their meeting he expected to find the boy gone. He couldn't find out where they meant to send him either; not being a relative, he wasn't authorized to know.

"Benbro," he said. "Could you hide something? Hide it good?"

Benny shot him a curious look. "Maybe," he said. "Yeah. Something small, I could. What you got?"

Hal pulled the packet of bills from his jacket lining and unrolled it. Benny's eyes grew wide and warm.

"Yo, where'd you get that?"

"Saved it up," Hal said. "You hang on to your money tight enough, it gets bigger. I'm thinking of splitting this with you now, promise you'll keep it safe?"

Benny nodded.

"Don't tell anybody?"

A nod.

"Don't *show* anybody?"

"All right already," Benny said, and stuck out his hand. Hal counted off twenty-two of the grubby ones.

"There's your half," he said.

"Cool," Benny said, eyes riveted to the cash.

"Put it up, now, don't run around flapping it on the street."

Benny started and crammed the money down in a pants pocket.

"I want you to keep that for something you need," Hal said. "Not candy and comic books and stuff. And stay out of the video arcade . . . Get a jacket or a sweater, or shoes when you need them. Shoes are important. You hear me, boy?"

"I'm getting me a houseboat," Benny said, "cabin cruiser. I'll live on it and just drive around."

"It won't buy you that," Hal said. "Not enough there."

"Guess I'll get more."

"Okay, you do that." Hal could feel his smile shrinking and drying on his jaws. "Well, come on, I guess you better head back."

They paused on the porch, just out of line of the shelter's main doorway. Hal took out the bread sack and handed it over.

"Hide that under your sweatshirt," he said. "That's the way. Can't you fix your hair a little better? What happened to your comb?"

"Lost it," Benny said grumpily.

"Use your fingers, then."

Benny screwed up his face, then raked both hands along his head, slightly flattening the clumps of hair.

"All right, Benbro," Hal said. "You take it easy."

"See you tomorrow?" For the first time that day the boy seemed a little ill at ease.

"I'll be here," Hal said.

He shifted position slightly to watch the boy slip in the doorway and through the metal detector. If the guard remarked his passage, he gave no sign of it. Hal turned away and went back through the playground to Catherine Street and walked down to the river. On either side of him the Brooklyn and Manhattan bridges vectored off to different points on the opposite shore. The South Street traffic drowned whatever noise cars and trains on the bridges were making, and a pleasure boat churning upriver moved in the same queerly disconnected silence. Benny had been told that Judith was dead but Hal had no idea what the information meant to him. Sometimes he thought the boy didn't know the meaning of death, and at others he suspected that Benny might understand better than he did himself. But certainly he didn't seem to miss her much — maybe there wasn't much to miss. Judith was drunk a lot and she took drugs and even before they tore down the hotel she'd had the habit of dropping completely out of sight. She'd leave Benny alone for days on end, return to scream at him for no good reason or smother him in her equally irrational affection. In all ways she'd taught him not to trust her.

It was a tabled issue now. Hal turned under the Manhattan Bridge ramp and walked up to the mouth of Eldridge Street and on and on, uptown again. He was beginning to feel it a little in his legs, not an ache, not fatigue exactly, just a rather pleasant sense of strain responding to the forces of inertia that drove him interminably forward. At Forty-third Street he turned west and started for Grand Central Station. The afternoon sun was bringing out a clammy sweat across his chest, and he loosened his jacket and various shirts.

Sunny was sitting on her standpipe by the mouth of the Grand Central arcade, reading a coverless copy of *Princess Daisy* and smoking a long Newport. The sheet of cardboard that she and Thompson slept under at night was propped between the pipe and the wall.

"What's the word?" she said when she saw him coming.

"I don't know," Hal said. "No news is . . . no news. Where's Thompson?"

Sunny shrugged. "Out scrounging. He'll show back by sundown. You need him?"

"Not especially," Hal said. "Hey, do you know where Hart Island is?"

"That's the potter's field, everybody knows that."

"I know *what* it is," Hal said. "I'm talking about *where*."

Sunny swept her hand indefinitely north up Lexington, then slapped it back over her book before it toppled from her knee.

"Up the bay, somewhere, I wouldn't know exactly. It's a long way."

"Can somebody get over there?"

"Not while you're alive you can't." Sunny leaned back against the cardboard and stared at Hal with her flat black eyes. Her crinkly hair was cinched tight to the base of her head with a rubber band, bringing out the cat shape of her skull. "Still tracking Judy, aren't you?" she said. "Give it up, man, you won't find her there."

"Why won't I?" Hal said.

"'Cause they don't mark nothing up there, man." Sunny snorted. "That's where they bury people with a bulldozer, hadn't you ever heard of that?"

"I heard it," Hal said.

"Believe it, then." Sunny laughed and shook her head. "It's like what momma say about food, you know."

"Don't believe I know what momma say."

"All gets mixed up in the end just the same. In your belly. Or in the grave." She gave the same dry laugh again.

"Not an idea I really go for," Hal said.

"Give it up, then, give yourself a rest," she said. "Think about something else for a while. Here, you want a cigarette?" She took a pack of Newports from her pocket.

"That's all right," Hal said. "I quit."

"What, you worried about your health?"

"Don't like to have a thing I can't do without," Hal said. "Thanks the same, though. We'll see you later."

He hitched up the bag and went into the mouth of the tunnel and on toward the main waiting room of the station. Heavy streams of commuters parted around him; it was already the first little end of rush hour, though he couldn't think just where the time had gone. He walked across the booming floor and climbed the stairs at the west end and made a buttonhook to the right toward the high blank wall where the pay phones were.

In the breast pocket of his second shirt there was a piece of paper going black along its folds with numbers faintly penciled on it. He shook it loose and squinted at it, then lined up all his quarters on the pay phone shelf and began to punch up calls to different departments of the Human Resources Administration. As on the day before, he found himself forwarded from one number to the next, in circles and spirals that repeated one another. The least of the bored bureaucrats at the other end of the line had the knack of reflecting Hal's own questions back at him. When they began to inquire into the nature of his relationship with the deceased, he spoke haltingly, lied without conviction. He was put on hold. At eye level next to the phone booth was taped a poster of a monkey with its head sliced open and its wet brain wired to some apparatus. The monkey screamed below its wound and farther down, line after line of frantic small print claimed that there was no good reason for the monkey to suffer so.

In the phone's earpiece there was nothing now but an intermittent sprocketing sound. Hal looked dully into the monkey's inked eyes and considered the nature of his relationship to Judith, from its roots to its peculiar fruit . . . *I grew up in West Virginia, strip mine country. Moved over to Pennsylvania to work in steel and got laid off. Came up here to try and get in the merchant marine but they wouldn't have me. Worked in warehouses, here and around, worked on the docks a little, any kind of labor. I had a room in an SRO in Hell's Kitchen, go look for it now and a hole in the ground is what you'll find. Don't know what they're building there, don't want to know. That's how I got there, and Judith and Benny moved in across the hall those last few months before they came with the wrecking ball, I don't know where they'd been before. That was the nature of our relationship right there. Got along with the kid pretty well, looked after him some when she wasn't around. I called her Judith when everybody else said Judy, she got some kind of a kick out of that, though I couldn't say why. Maybe we slept together a time or two but if we did she treated me like a trick and I hated that. She had a nice way about her sometimes when she was straight but you never saw a whole lot of it at a stretch. I took her to detox more than one time. Don't know why I kept doing it. Most of the time you might say I downright disliked her. Still, she might be alive right now if they hadn't of invented crack. But if that didn't kill her, something else did, and I want to find out just what happened, because. Because. Because nobody else wants to.*

For some time the telephone had been exhorting him to please hang up and dial again if he would like to make a call. He put down the receiver and gathered up the couple of quarters that were left and went to the banister and stood there, shaking the coins in his hand and watching the people moiling below. There's your human resources, he thought, some of them at least, whatever's not piled up on Hart Island like a mineral deposit.

He left the station by Forty-second Street. Outside, the light was already dimming to gray; the sun had dropped behind the canyon walls. He went down Park as far as Union Square and then began to follow Broadway east. The wind had sprung up harshly again and he refastened his shirts and his jacket and ducked his head down into it. Below Canal he cut to the left and picked his way through the construction sites around the Tombs and so came again to Columbus Park.

Loman was sitting on one of the benches, eating noodle soup out of a cardboard canister from the little take-out up Chrystie Street. When Hal came up and halted, he offered the soup and the plastic spoon. Hal shook his head.

"Go on, take it," Loman said. "I can't finish it anyway, how much they give you for a dollar."

"Best deal in town," Hal said.

He ate standing, a hip propped on the back of the bench, revolving his head from side to side to work out a slight stiffness in his neck. During the day, the park had a veneer of civilized life; there would be women with strollers, children who played games, old people on the benches spreading themselves to the weak light of the sun. At dusk it emptied out very quickly. A Chinese man came wheezing through, supported by his wife on one side and a cane on the other. The woman's off arm was anchored by a heavy shopping bag stretched to within an inch of the pavement. They didn't stop. At the top of the park a lone crack dealer paced up and down inside the iron railing, making whip-stroke gestures to the people passing on Bayard Street. Two teenage Chinese gangsters in black leather jackets stopped and parlayed with him, then came to the steps of the park shelter and sat down to smoke.

"Would you look at those son of a bitches?" Loman muttered. "They blocking the way to my bedroom."

"They'll go," Hal said. "Give them a minute . . ." He

watched the boys fuss with the little glass pipe. They had long glossy black hair and beautiful tattoos, and in their near-identical getups they looked alike as twins.

"I just want to know one thing. What happened to the law enforcement around here?" Loman said. "Here we sit on the steps of the freaking jail and watch these kind of people come and go."

"They could be saying the same about us."

Hal tipped up the container and swallowed the last of the soup and dropped the spoon in the bottom of it. The Chinese gangsters pocketed their pipe and pranced out of the park; the dealer hailed them again as they passed but this time they didn't stop. All around the air was thickening with darkness and the cold was tightening back down. Hal watched the dealer pacing, silhouetted against the lit shop windows on the far side of the street. He was tall and lanky, basketball player–sized, with a smallish head at the end of a bony at-tenuated neck. The jerky set of moves he had made Hal think he'd been sampling his own supply.

"Got any use for this spoon?" Hal said, rattling it in the soup container.

"Nah, they're not good for much once the food's gone," Loman said.

Hal pushed himself away from the bench and walked to-ward the garbage can padlocked to the railing behind where the dealer stood and twitched. His legs had stiffened from standing still and they creaked as he began to move. The soup container went into the can with a slight whispering sound that seemed to make the dealer turn.

"Trash, get on away from here," he said. "Yo smell drive away my business."

"Stand where you are," Hal said as the dealer took a step toward him.

"Who you talking to, mofo?"

The dealer took another step and Hal turned his back and walked away at his normal pace, his right hand stroking the spearheads of the railing. Behind him, the dealer said something he didn't quite make out, and the touch he thought he felt on his shoulder might just have been imagined. The loose rail shifted under his hand and he snatched it out and came around swinging it in a high lateral plane. He didn't see just where it hit, but there was a bruising shock against the butt of his palms that ached all the way back to his shoulders.

"Sweet Jesus, what you do that for?" Loman was crouching over the dealer, lengthily outstretched parallel to the fence. "This man not giving out any sign of life at all . . ."

"He came in my place," Hal said.

He picked up the rail from where he had dropped it and fit it back into its slot. His hands had gone numb, whether from the blow or just the cold he wasn't sure.

"Place, what place?"

Loman's eyes tracked up and down the street. There were people passing on the sidewalk within a hand's reach of them, but it appeared that their invisibility had so far been preserved.

"Anywhere I'm standing." Hal rubbed his thumb along his jaw, considering. "It's like my house."

Loman stood up. "You don't got a house."

"No," Hal said. "But I got a place to be."

"That's good," Loman said. "'Cause what I'm telling you, you better not stay here."

He left the park by the east side and walked up Baxter Street and continued his way. He pounded his hands against his thighs until they warmed and then he sank them in his pockets. Dark ribbons of sidewalk fell away behind him; he told off the names and numbers of the passing streets like beads of some long rosary. Because he had no destination he didn't know how long it took to get there, but it was later, much, much later, when he turned on Forty-third Street and bore down on the west entrance to Grand Central. From the corner back toward him a long line of men and women of his kind stood shuffling and waiting to enter the vans that would take them away to the armory or elsewhere. Hal stopped on the upper side of the street and looked. From out of the black cavity of the nearest van a voice came booming, "Move on up." The line went staggering forward, then halted again. "Move on up," the voice cried, and Hal began to walk, turning the corner onto Vanderbilt Avenue, going up toward the wall at Forty-seventh Street.

He could still get off the street if he wanted, he thought, and flicked the hidden packet of bills. There was still enough left to buy him control of a set of walls for the night. Enough for booze or a hit of dope or three or four meat meals, but not enough to bury anybody, not as much as that. He had wanted to see Judith buried somewhere, would have put her, if he could, in the ancient cemetery below Chatham Square. But it would make little difference to her now. The city of the dead is older and more vast than the city of the living, and the dead possess the power and patience of infinity. Turning east, he saw the street open the long way across town. He watched his shoes striking down ahead of him on the mica glitter of the sidewalk, and believed that there was no stopping his progress. He had been on his feet the whole day long, but he was still not tired.

MR. POTATOHEAD
IN LOVE

. . . IT ISN'T REALLY *so* much like one, but—take the ears, for instance, they're more like cauliflower; still, they might be little embryonic potatoes that didn't quite manage to break free of the main lump: the mealy irregular oblong of his head. It's mostly bald, but sprouts of chill white rubbery hair rise up from unexpected patches of his cranium, twisting and writhing, following their own dark and secret tropisms . . . Eyebrows like cracked brown knuckles ground with dirt; the eyes pale protuberances tipped with black. The long bumpy jaw is topologically twisted out of line from his pate, and the whole of it's thrust forward and up at eighty-odd degrees on the permanently stiff neck. Doctors can't fix it, the neck *never moves*. Mr. Potatohead!

When his hands are busy you don't notice any of this. His hands are beautiful, Flemish; van der Weyden would have been proud of them. Mr. Potatohead never has to do head fakes; his hands are so lovely they distract you from themselves. He works with his head cocked up away from them on the inflexible neck, eyes always slightly averted. A bit of juggling, a few tricks from mime, but mostly prestidigitation.

A bright clear Friday in the park, plenty of people here. It's spring—no, summer—very warm. People wear shorts, some men are barechested. The fountain is set in a swivel pattern that now and then throws a little burst of spray on people at the back of Mr. Potatohead's crowd. He's always looking a little up and over them. Above the arch the sky is blue and through it Fifth Avenue goes away and away forever.

Things appear, things disappear, but Mr. Potatohead doesn't even seem to notice. People are consuming all sorts of strange things while they watch him; it's a good day for spending money. A good day for buskers: Tony the Fireman's here, Charlie Barnett's here, there's a new *a cappella* group doing Dion and the Belmonts. He hasn't seen the Dance Be-Jabbers, but then they're never quite reliable. A lot of animals are here and about, a good day for them too. Someone with a monkey, someone with a snake. Earlier the guy with three ferrets on leashes came through, all of them ferreting in three different directions.

Right in his own front row is this lovely tall woman, big-boned, big-fleshed, generously featured, who wears on one bare shoulder a parrot that matches the iridescent green ribbon wound through the strong black braid of her hair. Mr. Potatohead plays to her a little, sidling up, sidling back, rolling his eyes to the bottom of their sockets to draw her into the field of his sight. He pulls a bluebird's egg from her ear while keeping his fingers well clear of the parrot — they bite. When the show's over she flashes him a marvelous smile and strolls off without giving any money. Her mouth is red from kissing, not lipstick. Mr. Potatohead doesn't care.

His hat is a parti-colored thing with a long bill, which rides in his back pocket, never on his head. Extending the hollow crown of it, he quarters his circle, magicking the money as it falls. Coins walk across the back of his hands, great handfuls of them come corkscrewing in and out of the hat, twisted, involuted, spiraling like strands of DNA. There's some folding money, not a whole lot. When the crowd has thinned, he fades out with it, no matter if it's early. Got to knock off early today; it's imperative he be drunk before five o'clock.

He zigs across Greenwich Avenue on his long stilted legs,

then zags up Seventh, forever looking only up. He sees out of the concrete canyon. Behind the blue shroud of the daylit sky the stars are still secretly plotting his course. His hands revolve in front of him like dish antennae, testing the way ahead. He never bumps into anything.

At Fourteenth Street there's a bar, and who could remember the name of it? Nobody calls it anything but Mangan's. Fixed on his high stool, Mr. Potatohead counts his coins into paper tubes, a beer glass and a shot glass before him. He's got a couple pounds of quarters, eleven ones, and one lucky five that he folds away in the watch pocket of his breeches. The long dim interior is dried-blood red and brown-lung brown. At the rear, the swaybacked spavined booths buckle under the weight of drunks and derelicts, sleeping or comatose or maybe dead . . . If they *were* dead, how long before anyone noticed? Above the front window a TV set cackles. Mangan's ancient grizzled head grimly faces it down from the far end of the bar.

Mr. Potatohead buys Viola a drink when she comes in, changing his coin rolls for paper. Sixty-two fifty the quarters come to, not bad for only three afternoon shows. Viola takes a cigarette, they talk awhile. She's a brassy black lady, good looking too, excepting the one top tooth that's set in sideways there at the front. When her friends arrive she moves to their table. Mr. Potatohead buys a drink for himself, or maybe two, beer and a shot, beer and a shot —

"Hey Mangan," he cries. "Where's the freaks?"

Two doors down is a school where the *handicapped* people are brought to overcome their *deficits;* they become cobblers, things like that. They are respectable. But now and again they'll come in here, to wear a little of the new sheen off their good repute, come tapping with canes or rolling in wheelchairs, some walking in on their tongues, just about. Always a mob and no room for the merely ugly among them.

"Not their night," Mangan grunts. "They come in Thursdays now."

Catching a sight of his own image in the mirror, eyes

turning aside from themselves, Mr. Potatohead ducks and loses it behind the rows of bottles. He goes on drinking busily, speedily, chain smoking and watching the sunlight lower on the street outside.

"Might cut you off," Mangan allows.

"Never," says Mr. Potatohead. His cigarette laces amongst his five digits, the hot head of it dipping and stitching and never burning or grazing the skin. A snap of his fingers sends it end over end back into the prehensile clasp of his lips. He blows out a tidy smoke ring.

"All right, then," Mangan says, tilting the bottle to the glass. Some feckless stranger sits down and claps a hand on Mr. Potatohead's shoulder.

"Hey there, Mr. Potatohead," he begins.

"*Dontcallmethatdontevercallmethat!*" Mr. Potatohead says, viciously slicing around on his stool.

The stranger's moon face is deeply perplexed. "But you *told* me that was your *name*," he says. "Yesterday, right here, you know, you bought me a drink, I bought you one, come on, Mr. Potatohead, don't tell me you don't remembaarghaarghgllhhggllhhhh—" as Mr. Potatohead's arms strike out like twin anacondas, wrapping around the stranger's throat and thorax. One sharp elbow bats the stranger about the eyes and nose, not doing any serious damage but hurting plenty, yes. Mr. Potatohead is surprisingly quick and strong, but Mangan can surprise you even more—

. . . flying out the door, Mr. Potatohead collides with all five of the Dance Be-Jabbers, who seem to have gotten off a stop too soon, possibly meaning to shoplift a late lunch or early supper at Balducci's on their way down to the park. Mangan snarls from the doorway and brandishes his big square fist, his face coronary red. It's a familiar scene. The Dance Be-Jabbers dance Mr. Potatohead back onto his feet. Each wears a T-shirt with a number. Switching around from the door to face them, Mr. Potatohead observes that Dance

Be-Jabber number 5 is rotating around on his coccyx, arms and legs tucked in, somewhat resembling a potato. Dance Be-Jabber number 4 is making power slides that take him back and back again to the selfsame place, his arms winding through air in reptilian loops, his head snapping from one queer angle to another. Dance Be-Jabber number 3, his arms and legs tucked in, is rotating around on the top of his head, looking like, well, *another* potato. Dance Be-Jabber number 2 does stationary power slides, his eyes googling down at invisible workings of magic mimed between his long pale palms. Dance Be-Jabber Numero Uno keeps up an easy four-step shuffle, chanting as the others continuously bone and unbone themselves: "Mista Potatohead, he *lean* and *mean*. He fake to the *leff*. He fake to the *right*. And wham! boppo! lunchmeataphobia! *Watch out fo' Mista Potatohead!*"

"Gentlemen, I thank you," Mr. Potatohead says, his hat appearing expressively in his hands. "You make my poor life into poetry." Dance Be-Jabbers 2 through 5 have just become a subway train. Numero Uno slaps him a handful, then flings himself into the last car. Mr. Potatohead gathers his legs up under him, and as the Dance Be-Jabber train bumps and grinds downtown, he goes spindling off in his own directions . . .

. . . before the little mirror in the Magic and Costume Shop, not too far from the Flatiron Building, Mr. Potatohead is accessorizing himself with wigs, hats, rubber ears, rubber noses, Groucho glasses, a pipe and a trick bow tie . . . But no, but no, nothing is right. He shucks it all off and tries the boar's-head mask again, bending from the waist to see the effect: he's all wild boar from crown to gullet.

"All right, Vic, I'll take this one . . ." Mr. Potatohead thumbs a couple of bills up onto the counter. The mask is expensive, thirty bucks.

"How's the rats?" Victor inquires, smoothing his cue-ball hair with one hand and making change with the other.

"Beautiful, perfect," says Mr. Potatohead. "I couldn't imagine better rats. Oh, and I need the black tux too, swallowtails, dress shirt, studs, the works."

"Hundred dollar deposit on that."

"Come on, can't you front it to me?" Butterflies flutter in Mr. Potatohead's stomach, he's *counting* on that tux.

"F'what," Victor says. "You got a funeral?"

"Birthday party," says Mr. Potatohead, prestidigitating the notion from air. "Rich kid, you know. Upper East Side."

"Some lucky kid," Victor says moodily, peering into the boar's rubber eye sockets. "Nightmares till his *next* birthday, probably. I don't know, Mr. P., you smell a lot like a brewery tonight. I'm wondering are you really in a responsible frame of mind?"

"Come on, Victor," Mr. Potatohead says. "I'll let you hold the rest of my gear. Didn't I always come back before? You *know* I couldn't go too far without you . . ."

. . . slightly flattened by the rush-hour subway, Mr. Potatohead re-expands himself, flowing along with the commuter stream toward the Grand Central Station main waiting room. He plucks the white handkerchief from the tux's breast pocket — with a flourish it becomes a gardenia, a bold boutonnière fixed to his lapel. Adjusting the boar's lusty throat to his high collar, he strides out under the great concrete vault, where all the light bulb stars are gleaming down on him from the ceiling's gilt heaven. Already he sees her near the information booth, dressed in a deep blue one-piece garment that shimmers with some constellated pattern, and she's already begun to sing, that -O-, the one note so profound and powerful it makes the whole huge hall her instrument.

The cops have already cut through to her; they never let her get any further than that. No buskers in Grand Central Station, not allowed. Before, he's seen them treat her with a kind of grudging courtesy, but tonight it looks like they might take her in — as Mr. Potatohead draws nigh, two mechanical rats descend on spider-web filaments from his palms, to scuttle and chitter across the shining shoes of all the good citizens bound for Larchmont. Screaming and scrambling ensue, and all of a sudden the cops have quite a bit to think about. Mr. Potatohead tweaks the fish lines; the rats yoyo back into his pockets; he moves on.

She's moving out ahead of him, maybe four or five people away. She's in good shape except for a slight hunchback and one hip set higher than the other. It appears that her hands have been broken off at the wrists and reattached at right angles to her arms. She goes up the western stairway like a crab, and turns along the heavy balustrade into a large square space that no one requires for anything except to overlook the echoing floor below. Here he catches up with her.

"Hey, lady—"

She turns to him. Close-cropped hair, little mouse ears, sweet and tranquil face of a dark madonna.

"Hey lady, you know? You got a nice voice."

"Thank you," she says. "Thank you so much."

The lucky five appears in his hand, turns into an origami crane and flies to her—where it disappears, for everybody has to know a little rough magic nowadays. She smiles at him, her teeth small, perfect, brilliantly white, her brown eyes bright as she looks for him down in the boar's floppy eye holes.

"Hey mister? You're something yourself." With a helical movement she takes his hand, and -O-, that grace note thrills down through him, searching out his loneliness, his longing, his exaltation . . .

". . . he's blowing beets."

His head cranked high, Mr. Potatohead watches the Staten Island Ferry's ramp hydraulically lower onto the dock. Not far from him some abandoned soul is puking pale pink waves, stinking of Boone's Farm and stomach bile. "He's blowing beets," the witness remarks once more. Mr. Potatohead does not see or hear or smell a bit of it. When the crowd surges forward, he surges too.

It's a bit cold and a bit windy out on the bay, so Mr. Potatohead has the prow of the boat all to himself. The sky has dropped its disguise by this time. His head is naturally in position, so as soon as he pulls off the boar's-head mask he can see all of his stars to perfection, here for him again and always, exactly as he knew they would be. Swan and Dragon, Eagle and Dolphin, Great Bear, Hercules, Asclepius, the Scorpion . . . monsters and heroes intermingled, how strangely, how wonderfully they move.

FOR THE BEST IN PAPERBACKS, LOOK FOR THE 🐧

In every corner of the world, on every subject under the sun, Penguin represents quality and variety—the very best in publishing today.

For complete information about books available from Penguin—including Pelicans, Puffins, Peregrines, and Penguin Classics—and how to order them, write to us at the appropriate address below. Please note that for copyright reasons the selection of books varies from country to country.

In the United Kingdom: For a complete list of books available from Penguin in the U.K., please write to *Dept E.P., Penguin Books Ltd, Harmondsworth, Middlesex, UB7 0DA.*

In the United States: For a complete list of books available from Penguin in the U.S., please write to *Dept BA, Penguin*, Box 120, Bergenfield, New Jersey 07621-0120.

In Canada: For a complete list of books available from Penguin in Canada, please write to *Penguin Books Ltd, 2801 John Street, Markham, Ontario L3R 1B4.*

In Australia: For a complete list of books available from Penguin in Australia, please write to the *Marketing Department, Penguin Books Ltd, P.O. Box 257, Ringwood, Victoria 3134.*

In New Zealand: For a complete list of books available from Penguin in New Zealand, please write to the *Marketing Department, Penguin Books (NZ) Ltd, Private Bag, Takapuna, Auckland 9.*

In India: For a complete list of books available from Penguin, please write to *Penguin Overseas Ltd, 706 Eros Apartments, 56 Nehru Place, New Delhi, 110019.*

In Holland: For a complete list of books available from Penguin in Holland, please write to *Penguin Books Nederland B.V., Postbus 195, NL-1380AD Weesp, Netherlands.*

In Germany: For a complete list of books available from Penguin, please write to *Penguin Books Ltd, Friedrichstrasse 10-12, D-6000 Frankfurt Main I, Federal Republic of Germany.*

In Spain: For a complete list of books available from Penguin in Spain, please write to *Longman, Penguin España, Calle San Nicolas 15, E-28013 Madrid, Spain.*

In Japan: For a complete list of books available from Penguin in Japan, please write to *Longman Penguin Japan Co Ltd, Yamaguchi Building, 2-12-9 Kanda Jimbocho, Chiyoda-Ku, Tokyo 101, Japan.*